RIVER OF SHADOWS

Valerio Varesi

RIVER OF SHADOWS

Translated from the Italian by
Joseph Farrell

MACLEHOSE PRESS
QUERCUS · LONDON

First published in Great Britain in 2010 by

MacLehose Press
an imprint of Quercus
21 Bloomsbury Square
London WC1A 2NS

First published in the Italian language as *Il fiume delle nebbie*
by Edizioni Frassinelli
Copyright © 2003 by Edizioni Frassinelli

English Translation Copyright © 2010 by Joseph Farrell

Map by Emily Faccini, from original drawings by Anna Varesi

A CIP catalogue reference for this book is
available from the British Library

ISBN (HB) 978 1 906694 27 2
ISBN (TPB) 978 1 906694 28 9

1 3 5 7 9 8 6 4 2

Printed and bound in England by Clays Ltd, St Ives plc

For Raffaele and Luca Crovi

Author's Note

There are two different police forces in Italy: the CARABINIERI are a military unit belonging to the Ministry of Defence; the POLIZIA are a state police force belonging to the Ministry of the Interior.

The maresciallo (carabinieri) and Commissario Soneri (polizia) can only be coordinated by the questura, otherwise they report to different ministries. As to the different hierarchies, the maresciallo is a rank below the commissario.

TO CREMONA

STAGNO

GUSSOLA

THE SUBMERGED VILLAGE OF
SAN QUIRICO

CASALMAGGIORE

SEE
INSET

TORRICELLA

RIVER TARO

RIVER ENZA

RIVER PO

PARTISANS'
MEMORIAL

SAN
MATTEO
ORATORY

EMBANKMENT

STONE-
CRUSHING
PLANT

BOATMAN'S
CLUBHOUSE
AND JETTY

EMBANKMENT

CARABINIERI

BAR ITALIA

OSTERIA DEL SORDO

BAR PORTICI

TORRICELLA

THE
PO VALLEY

✓ TO PARMA
✓ TO CASONI

10km

I

A STEADY DOWNPOUR descended from the skies. The big lamp over the boatman's clubhouse, put there as a beacon for the dredgers which navigate by memory, in the dark, could hardly be made out through the raindrops bouncing off the main embankment alongside the river.

"Foul weather," Vernizzi said.

"And no sign of a let-up," Torelli said, without raising his head.

The two had been sitting facing each other over a game of *briscola* which showed no sign of reaching a conclusion.

"How high has it risen?" Vernizzi said.

"Twenty centimetres in three hours," said the other, keeping his eyes on the cards.

"By morning the waters will have covered the sandbank."

"And the current will be tugging at the moorings."

There were games at all four tables, but play was more desultory than usual since the rain and the rising river were distracting the boatmen. At intervals they could hear the groan of the capstan at the nearby jetty as someone laboured to haul the hulls of the boats out of the river. The continuous dripping of the rain, splashing gently, sounding like a man peeing against a wall, was an undertone. It was the fourth day of rain, falling at first with the fury of a summer storm and then with greater persistence. Now a kind of mist was descending and a breeze was gently ruffling the surface of the pools of water outside the clubhouse. Old Barigazzi appeared at the doorway, his hat and oilskin running with water. A draft of cold air swept across the room, and behind the bar Gianna shivered.

"Did you put your stakes in?" Vernizzi asked him.

Barigazzi nodded, hanging up his dripping outer garments.

"It's up another three centimetres," he announced as he moved over to the bar where Gianna had already filled a glass for him. "If it carries on at this rate, it'll be on the first of the floodplains during the night," he said in the tone of a man thinking aloud. No-one said a word. No-one ever took issue with Barigazzi, who knew the river like the back of his hand.

From outside there came the dull thud of a wooden object crashing into something. Everyone jumped to their feet. It felt as though the river had reached the wall of the clubhouse and carried away the bicycles from the shelter next door. It was then that they noticed the massive outline of Tonna's barge, square enough to resemble a sluice gate raised up on the surface of the water.

No-one had noticed its arrival, except for Barigazzi. "He's come from Martignana," he said. "With a cargo of wheat for the mill."

Tonna was more than eighty years old, most of them spent working the river. Not long before, against the day when he would have to tie up for good, they had persuaded him to take on his grandson, but the boy soon got bored. Weary of the solitude, he had abandoned his grandfather, leaving him to spend his nights alone on the river.

"Water above and water below," Torelli said, pointing to the barge.

"He must have blue mould on his jacket. He's more at home in wet weather than Noah," Vernizzi said.

"Have they finished pulling up the boats?"

"They've winched up four of them," Barigazzi said, peering through the window, from where he could just make out Tonna's barge. "They want to keep them close to the houses because they're sure the water's going to come right up to the main embankment."

Barigazzi sat down, collapsing heavily on to a seat, and the others went back to shuffling the cards. It was around eleven o'clock, and in the club there was not a sound to be heard apart from the constant drip from the rafters. From time to time, the light swayed about. The barge was still moored to the jetty, its cables strong enough to withstand the swollen current. Dark objects passed by on the surface of the river. From their tables, the men could see the doorway of the look-out post, where a radio crackled. A volunteer from the club was doing the emergency shift. In such weather, the men would take turns all through the night. Every so often, someone would pick up the microphone to speak to the others on watch along both banks of the river. They exchanged information and forecasts about the flooding.

"Is it rising fast up there? What's that you said? Already into the poplar wood?"

Barigazzi went back outside to check the stakes: an hour had passed. When he returned, a dark light from the jetty filtered in under the door.

"Is Tonna setting off now?"

"Wouldn't put it past him," Vernizzi said. "He knows the river well."

They all turned to look at the barge. The only light came from the cabin, but there was no way of knowing if there was anyone moving about inside.

"He can't be going," Vernizzi broke in. "He'd have put on his navigation lights fore and aft."

The light went out and Barigazzi closed the door slowly on the incessant rain.

"What's going on?" Gianna said.

"It's coming up like coffee percolating, eight centimetres," the old man said.

There was no reaction at all. Everyone's thoughts seemed fixed on the light in Tonna's cabin. The only one who appeared uninterested was Gianna, who continued to move among the tables in her working jacket, her upper body looking as though perched awkwardly on her thighs. "If we went down to take a look, he might well lose his rag," she warned.

"He's left the gangway down. Could he be expecting someone?" Torelli said.

"It's always left down because of his grandson," Barigazzi said. "He sometimes comes back at the strangest times."

"Eight centimetres, repeat eight centimetres," the shift worker shouted into the microphone. "And still rising there? That's some flood. And it's still raining. You what?... Have you sent word to the prefettura?... Did you say that we should get in touch with them as well?"

A car was coming along the embankment road and turned towards the clubhouse. For a few seconds, its headlights shone through the window, swinging round the walls one after the other. Moments later the door was opened and at the same time the light in the cabin of the barge came back on. Two men in uniform, evidently soaked to the skin, walked to the bar. They looked around nervously, feeling themselves under observation, until Gianna – with what sounded like an order – said: "Take a seat."

They did as they were told. They took out a Flood Warning notice with instructions on the procedure to be followed in the event of the water coming up to the main embankment. "You might put this up somewhere," one of them said.

Old Barigazzi jerked his head back. "You've been sent here to teach the fish how to swim?"

The men looked at each other uncomprehendingly: they were numb with cold and ill at ease.

"We'll put it here, O.K.?" Gianna resolved the problem by sticking the notice to a board where the fishing calendar was normally fixed. She gave the adhesive a firm slap.

"Do you think we don't know what to do?" Barigazzi said.

The two men sipped their grappa, but no-one in the room paid them any more attention. They were all watching the light in the barge, even though there was no sign of life in the cabin. A faint light was now falling across the prow, where TONNA in large letters could be made out.

The officers got to their feet.

"You do know the water is rising at eight centimetres an hour?"

"The emergency squad will attend to it."

They seemed to be quite unaccustomed to the appalling weather and gave every impression of wanting to be on their way. Their trousers were drenched at the turn-ups, their light shoes were sodden and their overcoats were dotted with so many raindrops that they looked to be covered in frost.

Barigazzi scrutinized them, smiling complacently: "Well, you may as well know that nothing like this has happened for ten years, and the last time things didn't go too smoothly."

"The prefetto is ready to sign an evacuation order."

"He can sign what he likes. We're not evacuating. We're not scared of the water. It's better than the roads around here..."

Shortly after, the officers set off, going gingerly in second gear in the direction of the main road. Their headlights picked out the tumbling sheets of rain. Thousands of litres per second, reducing the land to a marshy waste, and under that slow curse the light in the barge cabin came on again.

"Either he's having bad dreams or else he can't get to sleep," Vernizzi said.

"It's that grandson of his," Torelli said. "Maybe he's just got back and the old man is bawling him out."

"I doubt it." It was Gianna who interrupted. "They hardly talk, they communicate through sign language. With this weather, I have an idea that the boy'll be keeping well away from the river."

"Well then, the old bugger's got muddled. He's setting off."

"At this time? That means navigating all night in the fog."

"And staying awake, like on guard duty," Gianna muttered.

Barigazzi stared at her reprovingly. "The water's high and that keeps you away from the sandbanks. There's no traffic on a night like this. And Tonna knows what he's up to."

More than half an hour had gone by, so he went out again to check the stakes.

Meantime the radio continued broadcasting messages from up and down the river. "The tributaries are like torrents. It's overflowing at some points. They've started evacuating? Where?"

In the room, they followed the radio, interrupting the game when some fresh item of news came through. A lamp flickered on the yard outside, before fading out. It was Ghezzi, leaving his bicycle in the shelter. "The lorry with the sandbags has arrived," he came in to tell them. "The mayor has sent the officers around the houses to tell the families to prepare for evacuation."

"He's off his head," Torelli spluttered. "Nobody's going to move before the water is lapping around their front doors."

"Well, Tonna's cast off," Vernizzi told them, looking out in the direction of the quay.

The barge looked even more imposing. At that moment, it gave the impression of light buoyancy, pitching slightly as it manoeuvred out into midstream, slipping slowly away from its mooring, straddling the current briefly as it hesitantly left the quay before getting on its way, carried effortlessly off by the flow.

"Still no navigation lights," Torelli said, pointing to the cabin light, just visible in the seconds before the barge reached the middle of the river.

"Tonna's getting on a bit," Vernizzi cut him off sharply. "Did you not see the manoeuvre he's just done? He wanted to rely on the wind to get him out and he nearly crashed his prow into the sandbank. He was saved by the flood."

Nobody added anything and in the silence all that could be heard was the radio giving out more data on the water levels. "It's coming over the floodplains... They're going to have to open the channels to reduce pressure... They're filling the sandbags..."

Everything alongside the river was in a ferment, while it itself seemed to be flowing peacefully in the night. There was no other movement apart from the incessant downpour. Barigazzi remained silent, his eyes fixed on the middle of the Po where the barge had moved off into the distance. Now he could see only its three-quarter outline and the light still shining in the cabin. The old man made a gesture of bewilderment or disbelief with his hand. The only sound was the unending crackling of the radio.

"He went off like a piece of wood tossed into the current," Torelli said.

"It looked as though it was the current that carried him off," Ghezzi said.

"A coypu burrow? Whereabouts? Letting water through? Is anyone working on it? You'll need to place the sandbags where the embankment is lowest…" The radio dialogue went on, interrupted only by an electrostatic crackle.

"Tell him that Tonna has set off," Vernizzi shouted to the boy who was operating the radio.

The boy picked up the microphone to let all the stations down the valley know that the barge would be passing. At that moment they became aware that Barigazzi was not there. Gianna made a gesture with her chin indicating the jetty. "He went out," she said. "He's away again to check his stakes."

Torelli looked at the clock. "Is he checking them every quarter of an hour now?"

The sudden brightness of headlights told them that a car pulling a trailer with a boat hoisted on to it was passing along the muddy road under the main embankment, proceeding slowly, lighting up the raindrops as it went.

"Taking it home," Ghezzi said.

"In weather like this, it'll be more use in the back-yard than at the jetty," Vernizzi said.

"He's taking his time," Torelli said, referring to Barigazzi.

"If he keeps going out to check and cut notches in them, all he'll do is cause confusion," Gianna said. "Another round?" She raised the bottle.

The Fortana was held aloft for a few seconds like San Rocco in a procession, but no-one replied. It was as if they had become aware only then of the oddness of Barigazzi's absence.

"It's a long time till dawn," Torelli said, staring out at the impenetrable darkness. He was trying to imagine how far Tonna would have got on his journey down the river. He might already be at Casalmaggiore, and perhaps could see the lights of the dredgers swaying as they were buffeted by the relentless rainfall.

Barigazzi came back in without a word. He sat down and turned to look at the jetty where until a little while ago the barge had been.

"Any higher?" Vernizzi said.

The old boatman made no reply. He raised himself to his feet, supporting himself with both hands on the table, and then went over to the boy working the radio.

"Can you give the alarm with that, or is it better to use the telephone?"

The boy gave Barigazzi a puzzled look, deeply unsure of what to do next.

"Do you mean Tonna?" Torelli said.

Barigazzi nodded. "He set off as though he had hot coals up his arse. He threw off the gangplank sideways, and left a rope on the quay. I've never seen him do that before."

"What did I tell you?" Vernizzi said. "That was not a manoeuvre, whatever else it was."

"Nobody saw if he was working down there on the quay."

Torelli stared out with the look of a man taking aim at bowls. "We couldn't see him from here," he said. "Not in this dark..."

"The rope looks to have been sliced through, cleanly, with a knife."

"Keep a look-out for barge, already subject of warning," the boy said into his microphone. "Danger to shipping: more than two hundred tons afloat... The way he cast off aroused suspicion... Tonna knows his business, but this time... Repeat, no navigation lights, only a cabin light, and in this weather... He set off without engine... Problem steering by helm alone..."

"If he bangs into the column of a bridge, he could bring the whole thing down," Vernizzi said.

"If he gets stuck and the barge turns into a dam, the current will capsize him," Barigazzi said. "The river's really high now, and you need your wits about you."

Vernizzi was on the telephone to the carabinieri, but the conversation sounded unduly laborious. "Maresciallo, I'm telling you I have no idea whether Tonna was actually on the barge. Certainly, you need someone who knows what he's about, or else... We saw the light going on and off twice, then the barge moved into midstream... Was he there? Obviously someone had to be there... That's right, the ropes were thrown ashore any old way..." He hung up almost in a sweat. "The maresciallo says there are only two of them on duty," he informed the company. "They all go home for All Souls. He'll alert the stations along the way."

Ghezzi looked out at the enormous sheet of water and felt almost afraid. "Where will he be by now?"

"Maybe at the mouth of the Enza," Barigazzi said. "If my boat were in decent shape, I'd go after him. Maybe I'd manage to draw alongside..."

"I don't think we'd find anything good," Barigazzi murmured.

No-one spoke. The black waters of the swollen river were flowing ever more rapidly, and the sandbank in the middle of the river was all but submerged. It was hard to see far beyond the moorings, but in the liquid darkness the impression was that the great basin, altogether visible in the days of low water, was already overflowing. The water level was just below their line of vision. It was possible to observe the current from above only from the main embankment itself, and the town alongside the river, with a vast mass of water looming threateningly over the houses, gave every appearance of being already inundated.

Several cars arrived and a dozen or so young men came in to ask what had happened to Tonna. They listened, then made their way back out, letting in a gust of damp air. They would follow the boat from the embankment in their cars, they said they could go faster than the current. By now the barge had made the flood a matter of secondary interest.

"Yes, I'm here… Are you sure? He hit the railway bridge? A quarter of an hour ago?"

Silence fell. There was no need for the boy to repeat what he was being told. Everyone instinctively grasped the situation.

"It's what I was saying. He hasn't even got as far as Reggio," Barigazzi spluttered. "The riverbed widens there and the water is more sluggish."

"The way things are going, they must have sounded the alarm all the way downstream to Mantua," Vernizzi said.

A couple of car doors slammed shut, and the vehicles set off at speed up the embankment. In the beam of the headlights, the rain looked to be heavier still.

"If there's a hole in the hull…" Ghezzi said hesitantly, "Tonna's done for. He's food for the pike."

"With all the wheat he has in the hold, they'll be flocking down all the way from Piedmont."

"It was only a bump," Barigazzi said. "It's a tough old craft. If it goes into a spin, he's in big trouble. It all depends on the rudder. And on the grip of whoever's on the tiller."

"If it starts spinning, the game's up. The first bridge he hits side on, he's going to get jammed, and he'll be pulled under," Torelli said.

"With some bridges, you only need to nudge the prow against them. With all the weight that's aboard, he'll bring the columns down on top of him," the old boatman said.

"He's passing in front of the mouth of the Enza," the radio operator informed them.

"Let's hope the extra current doesn't push him over to the

Lombard side," Barigazzi said, as he peered into the emptiness by the jetty.

The conversation drifted on, one guess after another, each man in his mind's eye going over that stretch of water which Tonna would have reached by then. Beneath it all lay one more troubling thought, as insistent as the rain which continued to fall or as the current which dragged everything in its wake. Finally it was Vernizzi who gave voice to a doubt which seemed dictated by a will not his own: "But he set off in such a great rush, and with that crazy manoeuvre…"

There followed a long silence, broken only by the sound of water dripping from the roof beams, until Gianna said: "Maybe it wasn't Tonna at the helm."

"It's most certainly not like Tonna to collide with bridges…" Barigazzi said, his voice trailing off.

No-one drew any conclusions. Everything was so confused. The telephone rang: it was one of the youths who had gone off in a car. "Every town is on the look-out and a lot of people have climbed the embankment to watch the barge careering past," he whispered into Vernizzi's ear.

"You saw it?"

"Yeah, a short while ago. It seemed out of control, swinging about crazily, sometimes listing to one side, but the current's keeping it on course. You can see where the paint came off on the side where it hit the bridge."

"Is the cabin light still on?"

"Yes, still on. When the barge comes close to the bank, you can see in, but it's hard to make anything out. Somebody said they had seen a man at the helm, but I don't think there's anyone there."

Barigazzi sat calmly, absorbed in his own thoughts, resting his head on his left hand, going over the course of the river as though he could see it from Tonna's bow. He imagined where it was at that moment, he saw the bridges looming out of the night, dark skeletons afloat on the immensity of the current. The conversation on the radio broadly confirmed his hypotheses.

"The carabinieri have what?... Closed all the bridges as far as Revere? The only one open is the railway bridge? They're ready to suspend all shipping?"

"He won't knock into anything," Barigazzi murmured, who seemed to be elsewhere.

"He'll crash into the iron arches at Pontelagoscuro," Vernizzi said. "But in that case it'll be tomorrow around mid-day before we get to hear about it."

Silence fell again in the room. And they became aware of the rain falling even more heavily on the tiles.

Barigazzi was shaking his head, in the manner of the horses in the Po valley. "He'll never get near Ferrara. Tonna will avoid the delta in these conditions. He'll stop before then."

Meantime, the telephone had rung again and Gianna was in conversation with the young men who were tracking the barge. "When?... One or more than one?"

Ghezzi had moved over beside her and seemed on the point of grabbing the telephone from her hand.

"They say that in the light from the cabin they've seen some shadows moving about. Maybe more than one, but it seems they haven't been able to identify Tonna," Gianna told the room.

Barigazzi's imagination was still fixed on the river, so wide midstream that the banks were out of sight, on the craft tossed about on the surface of the water as carelessly as a leaf, on the unending groan of the hull, on the blind drift of the barge as it was battered from all sides, on the darkness. He imagined crowds of locals standing like sentinels along the banks in the rain, greeting the little light on the river even if it was no more visible than a bicycle lamp slowly passing along the embankment road on a foggy night. He felt the sideways jerk of the barge every time it ran into a tree trunk or into a stretch of swirling waters, and felt too the list it took on for a time before righting itself and straightening in the fast-flowing current.

He would not be able to see a thing because there was zero visibility. The Luzzara curve is wide and bent like the *bondiola* sausage. That was the most hazardous point, especially if the barge were indeed in the hands of some novice who had taken over from Tonna. There the current and the deep waters could throw anyone off course. Sluggish on the surface, the water, following the channels in the sands, flows faster below and pushes against the embankment. Without an engine, it would be impossible to avoid running aground, except by making a pre-emptive manoeuvre 300 metres upstream, hugging close to the bank on the Lombard side and holding tight. With anyone lacking the expertise, the barge would crash into the embankment like a stake being driven into the ground.

"Tell them to go and wait for it at Luzzara," Barigazzi muttered. "It'll be there by three in the morning."

But he spoke so softly that no-one picked up his words. A gust of wind and rain shook the windows. "The *libeccio*, from the south-west," Vernizzi said. "Always a bad sign."

The rain was getting heavier still, and now the beams were reverberating.

"Have you seen it go by?" the radio operator wanted to know. "What? It's passing right now? Look and see if you can make out anyone in the cabin. No? The light is on, but the cabin is empty? Just a while ago, someone on the embankment told us there were signs of movement inside. Yes, yes. I agree. If Tonna were in charge, it would not be sailing this way. And would not have touched the railway bridge either. Tonna? Who can tell? Perhaps he's on board or maybe it's his grandson who has taken over… What do you mean, have we thought of that? Of course we have, but in this weather who could have seen him run away?… Yes, I know, he's an old fox, but the whole business still looks funny to me…"

Everyone in the room at the boat club was listening in, but no-one spoke. It was as though they were listening to a dispatch from a war zone. After glancing at the clock, Barigazzi got up and went out. It was past his time for checking the stakes. From the doorway, he looked back and grimaced. For him everything was clear.

Ghezzi went over to the window to stare out. It was as though black ink was dropping from the sky. All that could be seen was the leaden water in motion with a cargo of flotsam and jetsam on the surface. Further on stood the poplar wood, a shadowy mass against the horizon, the only relief in a flat countryside.

"The water's on the floodplain," he said. He could not see it and was only guessing.

"Has been for the last half an hour," Barigazzi said.

"We can only hope it flows slowly," Torelli said.

"It's rising constantly, so it'll be gradual," Barigazzi assured them. "It's already knee deep in the poplars. The ponds will be overflowing."

Each one of them imagined the water gushing out over the floodplain, like water bubbling over from a pot cooking *cotechino* at New Year.

"By now," Vernizzi said, "it will have drenched the monument to the partisans below the embankment."

"It's just giving it a blessing."

The radio croaked back into life. At Casalmaggiore, the river had reached the "alert" level, and the houses on the floodplain were being evacuated by the military. The elderly had been carried off, sometimes forcibly, in the firemen's dinghies.

People who had barricaded themselves on the top floor were putting up some resistance. It was not so unusual for the river to come calling every so often to wet the feet of those who lived along its banks.

The jeep driven by the carabinieri made its way along the road on top of the embankment and then turned down towards the boat club. The maresciallo came in, his overcoat dripping. "I've received the evacuation order for everything in the main embankment zone," he announced. Including the club, it was clearly understood. No-one said anything, and the maresciallo took the silence as a challenge.

"Do you think that after seventy years on the Po, I don't know when it's time to jump over the embankment?" Barigazzi said at last.

The maresciallo looked along the row of bottles behind Gianna and realized what kind of people he was dealing with. If the river had not managed to scare them off, what chance had he?

"Go and see the people who bought the poplar wood. They might need advice from the prefetto. All you've got here are experts, or fishermen's huts."

The maresciallo's frown expressed his annoyance, and he changed tack. He pointed at the radio. "Where is he now?"

Barigazzi glanced at the clock, then said, "He'll be near Guastalla. But don't worry. He's not going to collide with the bridge, because the current there'll carry him into the middle of the stream, just right for navigation."

"My colleagues will shut it anyway."

"They can do what they like. It's only a matter of hours. Sooner or later you'd have to close it off because of the flooding."

The man uttered a curse, but against a different target, the feast of All Souls, when everybody wanted a holiday, leaving him with an empty office. And then against the flood which gave him extra work when there were only two of them left on duty.

"Every year around All Souls the river swells up," Barigazzi told him. "It too wants to remember its dead, and goes to pay them a visit in the cemeteries. It caresses the tombstones for a few days, shows the funeral chapels their reflections in the waters it has brought up from the riverbed. It stops off inside the graveyard walls, before settling back, leaving everything clean and sparkling."

The maresciallo listened in silence to that unpolished elder, who could turn poetical when he was talking about his own world. He observed for a moment those hard-headed men whose lives had been spent on the banks of the Po and decided it would be a waste of his time talking to them or attempting to lay down the law. They reminded him of the fishermen in his own land, in Sicily. He set off in his jeep.

The clock above the bar struck midnight and Barigazzi continued travelling in his mind along the route taken by the barge. The current would flow more slowly where the river spreads out into the floodplain. Tractors and lorries had begun to move along the embankment road. There were carts loaded with furniture covered roughly with tarpaulin to protect them from the wind and rain. The leafless poplar trees were blowing about wildly at the wide curve in the embankment, behind the stone-crushing plant, where once the stables for the cart horses had stood.

"The partisans' monument will be well and truly underwater by now," Vernizzi said.

"Like a sea-wall at high tide."

"The time will come when no-one will remember it any more and the river will carry it all away. Then the stone-crusher will crush it as well," Torelli said bitterly.

"Tonna's being carried off by the current right now," Barigazzi said, as though talking to himself. He reckoned that, with the current as strong as it was, he would be just about at the mouth of the Crostolo.

Meantime the radio provided an accompaniment to their talk. "It went under the arches at Boretto quite smoothly?... As though Tonna were himself at the helm?"

"It's done that so often it could manage by itself," Ghezzi murmured.

The telephone rang, and Gianna repeated aloud what she was hearing.

"There's not a soul to be seen in the cabin... The light is still on. It's much weaker now?... The barge has swung round and started listing. It ran into a whirlpool?... And now has righted itself."

"A marvel of a hull, that one," Barigazzi said. "It can hold the current without anyone working the helm."

"Once you clear the Becca bridge, you can go to sleep until Porto Tolle," Vernizzi said.

Another silence, heads nodding in wonderment. Then Barigazzi said: "I don't believe Tonna's piloting that boat."

He got to his feet and went out to check the midnight level on the stakes.

On the road on top of the embankment, there was more traffic than on a Sunday. The carabinieri, blue light flashing, drove up and down several times, escorting lorries and tractors. Inside the misted-up vehicles, there seemed to be mothers holding in their arms babies wrapped in brightly coloured blankets, and men with bags over their shoulders. Voices on the radio were recommending that some kind of surveillance of the empty houses in the villages should be organized.

"Another eight centimetres," Barigazzi told them as he came back.

The radio operator asked for a line and communicated immediately the news that the river was a good three metres above low-water level.

"Did they say anything about Tonna?" Barigazzi said.

"He's still midstream."

"If that's the case, by three he'll run into the bend at Luz-zara. Once he's passed the bridge at Viadana, there's no way he can move towards the Mantua bank without rudder and engine."

"If he's dead, it'd be better if he went down with the barge. It's what he would have wanted," Gianna said.

It was the first time anyone had voiced the notion of Tonna perhaps being dead, but the thought had come into each one's mind.

"No barge can navigate four bridges on its own," Ghezzi said, cutting short the discussion.

Once again it was the radio which broke the silence. The order had been given to pile the newly filled sandbags near the embankments and alongside old coypu burrows.

Barigazzi once again left the clubhouse, crossed the yard under the driving rain and climbed the embankment. The river had risen considerably in a few hours. The sandbank which separated the quay from midstream had been swallowed up, and the boats which were still tied up looked as restless as stallions. The town was afloat in a lake of lights oxidized by the wet weather. A few hours more and the fish would be swimming higher than the magpie nests. An immense pressure was build-ing up against the embankment, stubbornly searching for some cavity. Barigazzi was making his way back to the club through sheets of driving rain, but first went back down to take another look at the stakes. The midnight marks were already deep under-water. The light from the club, battered by the driving rain, seemed like wisps of smoke or steam in the yard.

The old man shook himself in the doorway before going in, relishing the warmth within. The radio was talking about Tonna. "They've lost sight of it... The light is out?... You think it's the battery?... Ah! It flickered out... And now there is nothing to be seen?... The carabinieri have switched on floodlights near the Guastalla bridge. At other spots they've turned the headlights of their jeeps on to the river?"

"The final curtain," Vernizzi said.

"Now they'll turn their attention to the flooding."

The telephone rang again.

"Yes, yes, we know that the light has gone out," Gianna said. "You're coming back? Barigazzi," she said, looking over at him, "Barigazzi says it'll run aground at the Luzzara bend... He says about three o'clock."

When she had hung up, she explained: "They're going to the Guastalla bridge to watch it pass under the floodlights, then they'll wait for it at Luzzara."

Barigazzi shrugged. "Now that the light's gone off, they'll leave him to his fate."

The radio repeated the news several times with maddening insistence. "Tonna's barge is making its way downstream. It's holding to the middle, but it seems the hand on the tiller is not exactly up to it... Yes, yes, I am telling you, the engine's not running."

"Who believes it's navigating normally in this weather?" Torelli was growing impatient.

"With no engine, the battery will run flat."

"In just a few hours?"

"Tonna's as mean as the drought in '61. He uses batteries lorry drivers have thrown away."

"He always lives in the dark or he uses the candles you put round coffins. As soon as it gets dark, he moors at the first place, gets off to have something to eat and then goes to bed."

"What a cheery life! You can see why his grandson…"

"So the light kept burning all that time, down at the mooring…" Barigazzi said. He spun his hand round, all five fingers pointing upwards in a gesture suggesting some piece of machinery searching in vain for a plug.

"It's not that difficult to work out," Vernizzi said.

"No," Barigazzi murmured, looking up at the clock. "In less than two hours we'll know everything."

They all looked up. The hands on the club clock were almost at 1.00.

The carabinieri returned. "I'll say I haven't seen you," the maresciallo mumbled, as damp and swollen as a *savoiardo* biscuit dipped in Marsala. He was an unhealthy colour, whether from the onset of influenza or from suppressed rage.

"You're just not used to this rain," Barigazzi told the maresciallo, who gave him an evil look in return.

"Another nine centimetres. It's coming up like Fortanina wine when you pull the cork," the old man went on.

The radio operator passed on this news, and received equally alarming data in reply.

"At this rate, you're going to have to sound the retreat in the carabinieri headquarters as well," Barigazzi said. "But it won't take much evacuating," he said, staring at the only carabiniere, a shy young man accompanying his superior officer.

The maresciallo swallowed the grappa which Gianna had poured for him without waiting to be asked.

Barigazzi joined him at the bar. "It suits you fine to let your colleagues in Luzzara attend to this other business," he said gravely.

"What other business?" came the surly response from somewhere under the officer's helmet.

"This business of the barge."

The officer's face brightened. He was evidently relieved. "Why Luzzara?"

"It will get as far as that," Barigazzi assured him. "Tell them at the station, if anyone's still there."

Vernizzi went out for a pee. "It brings good luck if you piss in the river," he said. He lived in the town but he had never got used to peeing in a closed W.C. As he drew near the riverbank, he became aware of just how high the water had risen. There was someone at work with the winch at the moorings, trying to pull ashore a boat still riding at anchor. The clammy *libeccio* wind ensured that the rain drove into the side of his body.

"You've pissed yourself," Torelli teased him when he saw Vernizzi come in with his trousers wet.

"Not at all. I've salted the sea."

The radio announced that the barge was close to the Guastalla bridge.

"Call them and ask if they can actually see it," Ghezzi instructed Gianna.

In seconds the woman was on the line. "Moving slowly ... And the lights are still off, right? Ah, difficult to see. The cars have pointed their headlights where it sails in and out of view."

Barigazzi imagined himself on the embankment, standing behind the vehicles whose headlights were resting on the surface of the water, picking out glimpses of the hull in the bobbing confusion of barrels, logs, dead animals, tree trunks.

"It's going past?" Gianna was shouting into the receiver. "Are you sure? Too dark? In midstream ... This bit has gone smoothly as well."

Barigazzi looked up at the clock. "It's all over now."

The others looked at him, not sure if he was referring to the river or to Tonna. Probably both. Vernizzi remembered hearing his pee gurgle on the surface of the water scarcely a metre from where he had been standing.

"Gianna, start packing up," Barigazzi told her.

The operator unplugged the radio in preparation for moving out. Everything that could be carried to safety was swiftly put into large boxes, making the club look in no time like temporary premises. Torelli manoeuvred the lorry into place in the yard and for a moment the lights played on the surface of the river without reaching the far shore. Then they started loading. In all the coming and going, the radios on both sides of the river continued broadcasting a litany which became a sort of rosary for all the wrecks dragged away by the current.

"What about the clock?" Vernizzi said.

"The water'll never get that high," Barigazzi said firmly, noting that it was a few minutes before three. "This is the epilogue," he reminded everyone.

Then, in the almost bare room, silence fell. One bottle of white wine remained on a table. Gianna found some paper cups and shared the wine out among the company until it was all gone. A few more minutes of waiting passed, leaving them to listen to the rain hammering on the roof and to the incessant drip drip from the beams. At 3.10, the telephone rang. At the first tone, Gianna got quickly to her feet, but Barigazzi stopped her with a sign and made for the telephone himself. Without waiting for whoever it was on the other end to speak, and without even a "hello", he said: "Has he run aground?"

The others watched him only nod. Then, slowly, as though in a trance, he put the telephone down. "There was no-one on the barge."

2

COMMISSARIO SONERI DELICATELY raised the white sheet while two volunteers from the Red Cross sheltered the body with their umbrellas. What he saw was a broken body which looked as though its bones had been removed. He looked up at the window from which a male nurse was staring down at the scene below. One of the volunteers pointed to the canopy over the entrance to the courtyard. On the cement, which had been softened by the rain, there was a mark from the impact.

"He fell on that first," he said.

Soneri climbed the stairs and pushed open the door of ward 3, where he was met by a clammy heat which felt like a kitchen with several pots coming to the boil at the same time. The window was the main source of light for a recess along the corridor where the nurses stored the drip-feeds and broken chairs. There was an old metal cabinet on one side. The corridor led to the consulting rooms in one direction and in the other to the nurses' off-duty room.

Soneri stuck his head out. "Quite a jump."

"But you saw the state he's in?"

The commissario nodded before stopping to study the broken glass from the bay window. Shards were scattered among the fittings. He looked out again. The two volunteers were putting down the umbrellas and others were busying themselves with the body. He recognized the profile of Alemanni, the magistrate assigned to the case, a tedious individual who was forever talking about taking early retirement without ever actually taking it. Alemanni was just in the act of authorizing the removal of the corpse.

The cabinet was open and inside there were detergents, cloths and dusters. At the bottom, near the vent, there was a dent which looked recent. He studied the steel door from inside. The paint had come away where something had knocked against it. There were flakes of the paint on the floor.

As he went back along the corridor, he bumped into Juvara, the only ispettore he could bear having near him and who for that reason he had taken for his personal assistant.

"You might have warned me sooner."

"Your mobile is turned off."

The commissario checked. He had switched it off after the umpteenth call, or maybe had never had it on. "Any idea who it could be?"

"Certainly – I know who it is."

Soneri raised his eyes heavenwards.

"Well, get on with it!" He was in a highly excitable state of mind. Whenever he embarked on a case which promised from the outset to be murky, he felt like an addict suffering withdrawal symptoms.

"Tonna, Decimo Tonna."

The name meant nothing to Soneri.

"Age?"

"Seventy-six."

He stood there with his cigar in his mouth, staring at a diagram of the digestive system on the wall behind Juvara. His own digestive system had been feeling the pinch for about an hour, but this promised to be another day when he was going to have to go without lunch.

"Any ideas?"

"Suicide, most likely." He had a mania for statistics.

"Have you called forensics?"

"Yes, Nanetti will be along any minute."

"Close off that cubbyhole, will you? No-one is to be allowed in before they complete their inquiries."

Soneri set off towards the consulting rooms, but halfway along he stopped in his tracks, turned back and went in the opposite direction towards the nurses' room. He looked like a man unsure of the way out.

The ward sister glowered at the cigar until she was certain it was not lit. The commissario stood facing her for a few seconds without speaking, his head spinning. It was she who began: "We heard a thump and the sound of glass shattering, and when we got here we saw the window wide open. I didn't think much of it. Then I heard people in the courtyard shouting, I looked out and..." Her voice trailed off. She shrugged in a fatalistic gesture.

"You all ran immediately to the window?"

"Actually, no. I was on the phone to Casualty and my colleagues were busy elsewhere on the ward."

"How long between your hearing the noise and your getting here?"

The telephone started ringing again, but the woman ignored it.

"A couple of minutes at the most. We thought it was the wind rattling the windows. Those shutters are always kept half-closed."

"But you didn't see anyone?"

The sister pursed her lips and gave a look over her shoulder.

"No, no-one comes that way except when the doctors are doing their rounds."

"Will they do their rounds today?"

"Until 11.00. Then some patients hang around, but never more than a quarter of an hour."

"Does the name Tonna mean anything to you? Decimo Tonna."

"Tonna? Was it Tonna who threw himself out the window?"

"Do you know him?"

"Who doesn't know him? A strange creature. He used to turn up in the waiting room for the pleasure of chatting to the patients. He would come here the same way other men go to a bar."

"How often?"

"Once or twice a week. I believe he used to go to other departments as well."

"So you all knew him well?"

"No, not well. For us he was a bit of an oddball, we passed the time of day with him, but we knew nothing about him. He spoke only about illnesses, even if he himself seemed in good health."

Soneri nodded in assent. Odd facts and traits were always invaluable sources of information for him.

"Did he seem to you…" and he tapped his index finger against the side of his head.

"What do you think?" The sister laughed. "Someone like that seems normal to you?"

Soneri nodded several more times as though to apologize. His mind had now soared off into distant realms, causing him to take a few steps back and give a cursory greeting to a group of curious nurses who had gathered round.

In the corridor, he found Nanetti, the head of the forensic squad, who came straight to the point: "Not one of those who land on their feet, was he?"

"Have you seen the corpse?"

"I had a quick look in the hearse before it was taken off to the mortuary."

"What do you make of those broken panes of glass?"

"I'd say it was not usual for a suicide. And then there is that dent…"

The two looked at each other, instantly on the same wavelength.

"I reckon that everything will be cleared up by the post-mortem."

"So do I," Soneri said, "even if…" But suddenly he fell silent. It was never easy for him to find the right words to articulate his concerns.

He called Juvara over. "Find out everything you can in this unit, and collect all the information you can get about this Tonna. He used to spend whole mornings here." His voice tailed off in what seemed strangely like an apology.

He left the hospital and walked towards the city centre. He felt the need to walk and smoke half a cigar to calm himself. That collection of odd facts had upset him and curiosity had the same impact on him as caffeine. What was there to talk about while waiting to consult a doctor? And what on earth did Tonna find so interesting there? Cutting through the narrow streets of the *Oltretorrente* quarter, he almost walked into a newspaper billboard across his path: TRANSPORT BARGE ADRIFT ON FLOODED PO. Seconds later his mobile rang with the triumphal march from "Aida". Ever since they had saddled him with that telephone, he had been trying and failing to alter the ring tone.

"Have you seen that story about the barge?" Angela asked him, synchronizing perfectly with his thoughts.

"I've just seen the billboard but haven't had a chance to look at the paper."

"There could be a headline saying you had robbed a bank, and still you wouldn't notice," she said, laughing.

"There's a wodge of notes in the office…"

"Anyway, you had better know that the barge did about forty kilometres and went aground on the embankment at Luzzara, and there was no-one on board."

"Somebody didn't take enough trouble with the mooring cables," Soneri said carelessly. He was not much interested.

"In point of fact, one of the cables was cut clean through," Angela told him. "They were talking about nothing else today in court."

"They'll all be busting themselves to land the insurance case."

"Nonsense. They say that the owner, a man called Tonna, loved that barge more than anything else in the world."

"What did you say his name was?"

"Tonna! Apparently he's famous on the river. That's what my colleagues are saying. A transporter. There can't be many of them."

The commissario's head began buzzing like a beehive in May. Angela was almost shouting down the line but the swirl of thoughts had made him nearly deaf.

"Are you listening to me or have you fallen down a man-hole?"

"The man who committed suicide today was also a Tonna," he murmured, as if in a dream, talking more to himself than to Angela.

"O.K., I'm in court in a while. I'm the duty lawyer and have to defend some poor soul or other. Call me later," she said, cutting him off.

Soneri stuck the mobile in his pocket and made for his

office. He pulled the string off the bundle of newspapers and took out the local daily. The headline in the provincial news section read: MYSTERY OF THE BARGE. He read about the sudden departure, about the rope that had seemingly been slashed, the light which had been switched on and off and the shock of the empty cabin. And then that surname: Tonna. The owner of the barge was Anteo and he was two years older than Decimo, the suicide victim.

He rang Juvara. "Drop everything at the hospital and get over here. There's something more interesting to attend to."

Then he called the control room: "Would you investigate two names for me? Anteo Tonna and Decimo Tonna."

Immediately, his telephone rang again. Alemanni struck his invariable funereal tone. "That man found dead today. The shattered body? The business at the hospital?"

"Of course, sir."

"I've arranged the post-mortem for tomorrow. Even if personally I do not believe that…"

"One never knows, sir."

With the erratic grace of a billiard ball on cobbled paving, Nanetti crossed the yard which separated the special force from the forensic unit.

"Right on time for a *digestivo*," he said keeping his eye on Soneri, who was busy polishing off his Parma ham sandwich.

"As punctual as a cheque," the commissario said, reaching into the cupboard for a bottle of port. "This little number was left to mature for a full fifteen years before it was allowed out of the barrel."

"You understand why I prefer coming to you rather than the other way round."

"Found anything?"

Nanetti smoothed his moustache. He looked like a dog straining at the leash.

"Incongruities rather than proof, but my experience teaches me that—"

"There are many, many odd facts," the commissario interrupted him, raising his glass for a toast. "For instance, the dead man used to spend hours in the surgery talking to the patients."

"Plus there's the broken glass. And that indentation…"

"That looked suspicious to me as well."

"Not to put too fine a point on it,' Nanetti said decisively, "a man who's going to commit suicide is hardly going to break the glass opening the window."

"The more so if the window was always half open."

"And yet more so if we found blood on one of the shards. Blood not belonging to the dead man."

Soneri put his glass down and looked his colleague squarely in the eye. He now had everything clear his mind, but he gestured with his cigar, inviting Nanetti to go on.

"The indentation, the mark on the cabinet, is new and it's on the outside of the door, indicating, presumably, where somebody kicked out, and there are traces of rubber. We checked and the rubber is from the shoes the dead man was wearing. You get it, right? There's been a scuffle, at the end of which one of the two people involved went through the third-floor window."

"No question about it," Soneri said.

The telephone rang. It was the officer from the control room.

"Anteo Tonna, born 1921, bargeman by profession, collaborated with Mussolini's Republic of Salò after being a Fascist official in the lower Cremona district, unmarried, no previous convictions."

The commissario chewed on his cigar under the watchful gaze of Nanetti, who was observing his agitation.

"Decimo Tonna, born 1923, formerly a self-employed craftsman, he too was a one-time Fascist activist, fled to South America in the '50s, came back in '62, detained in a mental hospital five years ago, clean record to date."

Soneri was about to hang up, taking the pause in the delivery for a sign that the report was at an end.

"Hello? Commissario?"

"I'm still here."

"The two Tonnas are brothers."

This time Soneri let the receiver drop on to the cradle as though it had slipped out of his hand.

"Judging from your expression, the case has turned interesting," Nanetti said, his own expression mischievous.

The commissario thought for a moment. Two brothers involved in separate cases a few kilometres apart. One who had somehow gone through a window, the other who had disappeared while his barge was navigating the river in spate. Thinking of the Po reminded him that it had been raining non-stop for five days.

Nanetti got up with difficulty. The humidity made the pains in his joints more acute.

"See you tomorrow for the results of the post-mortem."

Soneri nodded, but he was deep in consideration of the port, almost hypnotized by the liquid in the glass in his hand. In the whirl of that vintage red, he seemed to see the bargeman Tonna carried along by the current until he was swallowed up by the waters. He drank the port in one gulp and reached for the list of the carabinieri quarters in the province.

In Torricella, the telephone was left ringing for some time before the officer on duty decided to answer it. The maresciallo listened to Soneri's account in silence, leaving the commissario with the impression that he was listening with some considerable impatience.

"One is dead, the other one has disappeared..." Soneri told him.

The maresciallo then explained in detail how he divided responsibility for everything with his colleagues at Luzzara, and that for the time being the flood was as much as he could handle. "I've got to evacuate all the families at risk, and the resources at my disposal are limited," he said, and cut the commissario off.

It was the same story at Luzzara, where the barge had been towed into the river dock, moored and sealed off. Soneri's inclination was to go there straightaway, but he would have to have authorization from a magistrate. And besides, were the cases linked or was it a coincidence?

Alemanni was nowhere to be found. There was nothing for it but to wait until the results of the post-mortem were available.

At that moment Juvara arrived. He had obviously come some distance on foot and was breathing heavily. The commissario gave him an amused look. "Middle distance is not your speciality."

"Nor are the squad cars the force's strong point. My battery gave out on me."

"Did you find anything of interest at the hospital?"

"They told me of one patient who knew Tonna well, but right at that moment you called."

"Who is the patient?"

"He's called Sartori, he has a kidney problem and has to go for dialysis every other day."

"In the nephrology unit?"

"Right. He goes on Tuesdays, Thursdays and Saturdays at around four."

It was half past three and Soneri was undecided. He tried Alemanni again, but his telephone rang out and his mobile was switched off. Soneri's nerves would not allow him to sit, so he got up, walked to the window and looked out over the station yard with its bustle of umbrellas and cars. He put on his duffel coat, not before telling Juvara to telephone the carabinieri at Torricella and Luzzara to check if there were any developments relating to Tonna the bargeman.

Sartori must once have been a robust man, but now with wrinkled skin the colour of a chicken's claw, he looked to be no more than surviving.

"You can ask me all the questions you like. It's not as if I'm short of time," he said with an ironic smile, taking his nurse by the arm.

"I'm here to talk about Tonna."

"Poor soul. He didn't know much happiness."

"I have reason to believe..." Soneri was on the brink of revealing conclusions which it would have been premature to share. "I mean to say, by speaking to people who knew him... we might perhaps be able to explain why..." He stammered to a halt.

The man smiled again as he stretched out on the bed. "Yes, well, he was a bit odd, but he was also a decent man."

"Did he ever tell you why he would come here to see the patients?"

"He never did, but I believe I worked it out. He had a deep need to make himself useful, and he was very lonely. His family weren't interested in him. His brother spent all his life on the Po."

"We have reason to think he may be dead."

Sartori's expression grew dark.

"What did you talk about?"

"Oh, many things. He seemed to feel a need to communicate and could find no better way than coming here, being among people in pain. Out of a missionary spirit, I believe."

In view of the advanced age of the man, Soneri asked him: "Did you speak about the past?"

"No, never. If the conversation ever tended in that direction, he was off. He preferred the present. He said that the past was a series of years of misery which he had no wish to revisit. Which said, it was not so easy to avoid these subjects altogether. You can see that nearly everyone here is elderly, and old people talk about their own younger times, the days when they were happier."

"Ah, indeed," the commissario said. Instinctively he thought back to his own days at university, of his first meeting with his wife, of the happy years they had spent before she died and he found himself struggling with a wave of painful memory.

"He came here regularly, but sometimes he seemed to keep himself to himself," Sartori was saying. "There were days when he appeared not even to breathe, and was content simply to listen to others. It's not that the conversation here was particularly deep. Most of the time people here just go on about their medical problems."

Soneri fell silent and must have assumed a strange, self-absorbed expression because when he looked up again, he saw the man staring pointedly at him, with just the suggestion of a grin. "Who knows why he came here instead of going to the park to play *bocce*? Or to the bar? There are so many clubs…"

"I have wondered that myself," Sartori said. "What I think is that he was not at ease with himself. I mean, some people are like that. Here, on the other hand, he would meet suffering people to whom he could bring a measure of comfort and even, sometimes, practical help. Or maybe he just came for the pleasure of being in company. He used to sit in that seat," he said, pointing to a chair in the corner. "He would watch the patients coming in and out. Whenever someone he recognized came in, he would raise his hand shyly to greet them, but he never took the lead in conversation."

"Did he stay for long?"

"He did. Until the last person had left. The nurses would find him alone in the waiting room and had to more or less throw him out."

"This was not the only unit he came to, I gather."

"No. He would turn up at other consulting rooms and surgeries. It depended on who was doing the consultancy and on their shifts. He would arrive in the morning, and still be here in the evening. Ten hours without a break. For meals, well, he had become friendly with the nurses, and they would put a tray aside for him at lunchtime and for supper."

"Did he tell you which departments he went to?"

"This one and the surgical wards, of which there are four, all in the same building. There might have been other places too…"

The dialysis machine buzzed in the background, purifying Sartori's blood drop by drop. Other patients gathered round to listen in to the discussion with the commissario, just as Tonna had done.

"Little by little," the man said, "we had become friends, those of us who come here three times a week. We've known each other for years now. The difference was" – he paused – "that Tonna was not ill, anything but."

"So that was what you talked about, only your health?"

Sartori raised the arm which was free of needles and waved it as though displeased. "When the conversation moved to other topics, Tonna would fall silent. It was not obvious how to get him involved. Sometimes he would pretend not to hear, or he would get up and go to the toilet."

"Some years back, he was ill himself. A mental illness, I mean," Soneri said.

"We knew that. We didn't know each other then. Somebody told me something about a depressive fit and the risk of self-harming. Perhaps," Sartori said, alluding to the fall from the window, "it was all down to a return of that illness."

"Possibly," the commissario said.

"Had anyone seen the two of us together, they would certainly have said that I was the one nearer to death. But instead…"

"Death walks side by side with all of us and sometimes assumes the most innocent of guises," Soneri said, rising to his feet. "Who could know that better than I do, I whose job it is to deal with crime?"

Sartori smiled. "Who indeed, commissario?"

In the hospital yard, it was turning dark and the only sound was the incessant rain falling on the withered leaves. One large drop made a direct hit on the tip of Soneri's cigar, extinguishing it with a hiss. Only at that point did he decide to put up his umbrella. As he walked, he wondered why Tonna had thought to spend his time in a hospital. What did he find there that he could not have found elsewhere? Alternatively, what did he not find there?

His mobile rang. He had, as always, to rummage in his pockets. He never had any memory of where he had put the thing.

"My sense is that our friends the carabinieri are not unduly concerned about the disappearance of the bargeman," Juvara said. "At Torricella, they sounded exasperated even being asked. I thought at one point they were going to invite me to get lost."

"Forgive them, for they know not what they do."

"Commissario, are you going to launch into a sermon?"

"Not at all, I just think that this business is turning ugly and that our good friends the carabinieri don't seem to be getting it."

He turned a corner into the old town. The houses had lost the pale, straw-coloured joy of their sun-lit days and seemed drenched in a sticky sweat, as though they were newly beached from the swollen torrent that flowed nearby. The streets seemed to him to have taken on the appearance of a soaked sponge.

Back in the police station he found the administrators scurrying about preparing for a meeting on the river emergency. No-one stopped to ask about Tonna, and Alemanni could still not be found.

"It won't be long before the carabinieri turn up here to evacuate us too," Soneri thought, as he looked at the river, now almost over the columns of the city's bridges. And then the mangled snippet of Verdi's opera rang out once more.

"You were supposed to call me, remember?"

"That opening was not quite tuneful. You came in at least three notes too high."

"One of these days you're going to be in big trouble! You haven't forgotten about this evening?"

"Certainly not. It's all fixed, isn't it?"

"Has no-one ever told you that appointments should be confirmed?"

"I'm sure that's the way it is with lawyers, but in the police everything is always subject to…" He got no further before the connection was abruptly terminated.

He hated scenes, but he was only telling the truth. He

never could plan his days, and when he tried he invariably found his plans come crashing down around him. Who would have guessed that the Tonna case, for instance, would turn into a murder inquiry? He thought of the call he had taken that morning: a suicide at the hospital, could they send along a police officer, routine investigation. And now...

He had just decided that it would be a waste of time to call Angela back when she was in a rage – she would switch off all the telephones – when he bumped into Juvara at the door.

"Two dyed-in-the-wool Fascists, real fanatics," his assistant said with no preamble.

The commissario picked up the reference, but he made no comment. He felt very much alone in the face of a mystery which instinctively attracted him but which at the same time appeared to carry the threat and promise of deeper trouble. "Did you come up with anything else?"

"They lived completely isolated lives, cocooned away from everybody else."

"I knew that already."

"I did an internet search to see if in those years..."

The commissario felt a surge of irritation. He seriously disliked Juvara's weakness for technology, even if he perfectly knew that the younger generation of policeman had to spend more time confronting a computer screen than confronting criminals.

"Do you really think you're going to get anything worthwhile out of that gadget?"

Juvara watched silently while Soneri once again dialled Alemanni's number, once again to no avail. He had at all costs to get authorization to extend his inquiries to the banks of the Po. When he looked up, the ispettore had gone. Their personalities fitted impeccably. Juvara knew at once when it was time to leave Soneri alone.

He was thinking of the Po, of the flooding, of Tonna the bargeman who had left his barge in the care of an unskilled accomplice so as to slip off into the city to murder his brother for who knows what motive. Could it have gone that way? Or had the two men both been murdered a short time apart by a single assassin? Or then again, was it pure chance, mere coincidence? He ran over a catalogue of possibilities in his mind, that catalogue which every time confronted him with the anxiety of choice and changed the routine of his days. He had an instant illustration of this very point when Angela appeared menacingly before him.

"Get your things together, commissario, and follow me."

"Am I under arrest?"

"You should be so lucky… It's much worse."

In the courtyard, Angela put up her umbrella and Soneri took her by the elbow to keep himself dry. She made a show of pushing him away. "What an uncommon display of affection! That it should take a downpour to persuade you to get so close to me."

Soneri made to turn back, but Angela took hold of the hem of his duffel coat. He tried to tug himself free under the startled gaze of a returning patrol, but gave up. Any such skirmishing, more playful than angry, would have made him look ridiculous.

"I'm not letting go, don't imagine that I will…"

Soneri grinned in his turn. "A pity, I had so deluded myself."

She took his arm, elbowing him in the ribs as she did so. "You're going to see stars, even in this weather."

When they reached the *Milord*, Angela glowered at Alceste, as she always did. He returned the look when he received her usual order for grilled vegetables and a bottle of mineral water.

Soneri, however, had noticed a pencilled-in addition to the menu. "Fried *polenta* with wild boar sauce," he said, as he heard his mobile ring.

It was Alemanni, in his customary strained tones. "I have been tied up all afternoon in meetings about rivers. I understand you've been looking for me."

"I have, and to say that I no longer think we are dealing with a case of suicide. I think our inquiries will have to be extended."

"Could you spell that out a bit more clearly?" Alemanni said, after a lengthy pause.

"In the first place – and my colleagues in the forensic unit agree – we have identified some factors which lead us to believe that there were two people involved and that there was some kind of struggle before the victim fell from the window. Furthermore, there is a second Tonna who has disappeared while his barge went zig-zagging down the Po, the brother of the dead man."

This second fact seemed to make a deeper impression on the magistrate than the first. "So you are requesting that we join up the investigation into the barge with the inquiry relating to the death at the hospital?"

"You know better than me that it is highly probable there's a connection."

There followed a long pause covered by noises which resembled those produced by a slack set of dentures.

"Very well," Alemanni said at last. "You understand that if you are wrong about these conjectures, we will have to abandon the investigation, and I will retire leaving behind me the memory of this failure? However, permit me to await the results of the post-mortem which will be made known to us tomorrow morning before proceeding to issue the authorization now requested."

That final statement troubled the commissario. Twenty years' experience had made him bitterly aware of the difficulties of dealing with an elderly magistrate. He hung up in a foul mood, and out of pique switched off his mobile altogether.

"Do I have to remind you, commissario, that you ought to be reachable at all times?" was Angela's ironic observation.

He threw her a hostile look. "You always know where to find me, and you always come in person."

"Would you prefer a telephone call from a magistrate?" she teased him.

"When you set your mind to it, you can be a lot worse than any magistrate," he said, moving his legs to one side in case she aimed a kick at his shins under the table.

In fact nothing happened, and she looked at him contentedly. "Don't get upset. Zealots never get along with the complacent." But soon she turned rancorous once more as she thought back to that near kidnap in his office. "It's a dismal state of affairs that the only thing that really gets your attention is your work."

3

HIS AGITATION HAD him awake well before the alarm clock did. He sat up in bed to the sound of the relentless rain on the roof. It was still dark and the weight of the clouds seemed to be pressing down on the air below. The volume of water now flowing along the gutters had washed all colour from the city, and left it as pale as a body recovering from a haemorrhage. He groped about for the coffee pot without switching on the light. The blue flame of the gas hypnotized him, setting his thoughts racing once again. The prospect of visiting the barge held greater appeal for him than did the post-mortem scheduled for that morning. Perhaps it was all that rain.

He took delight in the semi-darkness which preceded the first play of the ash-coloured, morning light on the roof tops. He left the house and started out towards the mortuary, even if he was much too early. The rain continued without relief. The clouds hanging low over the city seemed to fray at the edges in a way which somehow reminded him of the woolly interiors of mattresses pulled apart by the narcotics squad during a house search. The only dry spot was the glow of his cigar. Even his bones, as he walked in the early morning light, had grown soft, like the handles of shovels left out in the rain.

Nanetti was already there, sitting beside the radiator, but Alemanni and the police doctor had yet to arrive.

"The only way to get dry would be to stick your head in a bread oven," Soneri said.

"If this rain doesn't let up, I'll have to go off sick. Even my toenails are hurting."

The commissario changed the subject. "So what do you think now?"

Nanetti made a face. "Do you want a bet?"

"On what?"

"You know very well. Don't act the simpleton. In my opinion, Tonna was dead when he went through that window. At the very least, he had lost consciousness."

"Did you see anything on the body?"

"Yes, I saw one or two things that seemed out of place, but there's another point," Nanetti said, interrupting himself for a moment to reflect. "Is it really possible to throw a man out of a window from a narrow space if he puts up any resistance?"

"I wondered about that myself, but I've learned that real life makes possible things which in theory seem absurd. Suppose the killer was young and powerfully built. Tonna, on the other hand, was seventy-six and on the short side."

"He would still have screamed his head off. There would have been signs of a fight, much more than a kick on a cabinet and a few bits of broken glass."

At that moment the door opened and Alemanni made his entrance together with the police doctor. Soneri greeted the doctor and nodded coldly to the magistrate. Their exchange of the previous evening still rankled.

"If you wish to come along, you are welcome to be present," the doctor invited them.

The commissario looked knowingly at Nanetti, who rose

reluctantly to his feet. When he drew alongside him, Soneri whispered: "You've done the warm-up. Now it's time to face them."

"If I win the bet, you owe me lunch at the *Milord*," Nanetti said.

The commissario had never had any doubt about the stakes. He got up, went over to the door and looked up at the rain still falling as though it was monsoon season and at the frozen doves sheltering under the eaves. He thought of the Po, where everything converged and where sooner or later he too would end up, he thought, like the water perpetually flowing downstream. He was on the point of picking up the telephone on the wall when he remembered he had a mobile of his own and that the local authority paid the bill. Juvara replied instantly, leading Soneri to imagine him seated in front of a screen surfing the net.

"Anything new, boss?"

"It's too soon. They've only just gone in. Is there any news at your end?"

"Nothing new. I'm being told that the patrols are all out."

"How high is the river now?"

"A state of emergency, category two, has been declared. That's for everyone living in the proximity of the embankment."

The situation was becoming more serious by the minute. The meteorologists were saying the only hope lay in a cold east wind bringing on a cold snap in the mountains and causing some of the water to freeze over. Soneri peered at the raindrops blown about in the air. A strong wind had indeed got up, but it seemed not to know where to turn. It snatched puffs of smoke from the chimneys, tossing them wildly hither and thither. Fierce gusts came hurtling along the avenues around the hospital, forming whirlwinds at the points where they clashed. A maelstrom of hypotheses was producing the same effect inside his head.

Just as the glow of his short cigar was snuffed out by contact with the damp air, the door of the operating theatre opened. The first out was the police doctor, who on seeing the commissario laid his leather bag on the coffee table in the waiting room and hitched his trousers up. "Regrettably, I do not think I have been of much use to you. He has numerous, serious wounds, all compatible with a fall from a third floor." After a pause, he added: "But also with other things."

Alemanni and Nanetti, deep in discussion, joined them. When they found themselves face to face with Soneri, they stopped talking, each waiting for the other to begin. It was the magistrate who broke the ice: "We have not managed to come up with definitive answers," he said. "If it were not for the indications found by the forensic squad on the window from which he threw himself, I would have no hesitation in filing the case as suicide. However, your colleague was telling me…" he went on, implying Nanetti with a vague, sceptical gesture.

The commissario had difficulty in suppressing his rage towards that man who, with advancing years, had developed a sourness which had hardened into pig-headed resentfulness. For a moment, a tense look was exchanged, interrupted only by the doctor saying good-bye. As the door thudded shut, Soneri said: "So what do you intend to do?"

Alemanni stared at him in bewilderment and only then did the commissario grasp what was concealed behind that attitude of cold conceit: he had before him a man made fearful by a career in decline. For that reason, he paused a little before adding with the maximum of studied arrogance: "Sir, I think it would be an idea if you were to turn your mind to the other Tonna as well. I think there may be a link."

Alemanni bent even lower, bowing his head: "If there is

some scruple still niggling at you… I will sign the authorization today."

When he had gone, Nanetti breathed a sigh of relief: "You've succeeded with the most difficult part of the post-mortem."

Soneri said nothing. With an authorization so grudgingly conceded, he would feel under intense scrutiny for the duration of the investigation.

"Don't worry," Nanetti consoled him. "He kicks up the same fuss every time. He suffers from chronic insecurity, so he wants to minimize his part and thereby be always in the clear, come what may."

"I was hoping that…" Soneri stuttered, before his words trailed off.

As he was leaving, Nanetti held him by the sleeve. "You haven't forgotten our bet?"

"You haven't won."

"But Alemanni did agree to sign."

"I'll concede only because of that stain of blood on the windowpane…"

"We'll discuss it over lunch."

They were seated in a side room which Alceste kept exclusively for his best customers.

"When are you setting off?"

"I'll go this afternoon. It only takes twenty minutes."

A wager was celebrated like a rite and a fixed menu was prescribed. *Culatello* as a starter, followed by *anolini in brodo* and then wild boar with *polenta*. Gutturnio was the non-negotiable wine.

"So nothing at all came from the post-mortem?"

Nanetti said, "An elderly man who falls from that height is going to smash into thousands of pieces, like a ceramic dish.

And then to complicate matters, there was that bounce off the canopy over the entrance … that apart, I would be almost certain that the blow to the head was not caused by the fall."

"There is a blow to the head that does not seem to you compatible?"

"We're talking about a fracture of the skull with a deep depression. This rarely happens to people who throw themselves from a height. Normally the injuries are wide and flat, similar to someone who's been crushed. In his case, however … but it could just be due to an impact with a protruding piece of concrete on the canopy."

Soneri remembered the stretcher bearer pointing out to him the place where the body had bounced before it fell on to the courtyard.

When they left the restaurant, the air was cooler and the commissario remembered the forecast. Gusts of wind and rain continued the work of cleansing the city, but the sky had taken on the shade of pewter. By the time he accompanied Nanetti back to the police station, there were only two hours of light remaining. While his colleague got out of his Alfa Romeo, cursing sports cars for being built so low, he hesitated for a few minutes before deciding what to do. He then sped off under the watchful eye of the guard who had come out to see what was afoot.

The road ended alongside the embankment which was as high as a city wall. A couple of kilometres back he had been stopped in the rain and checked with maximum distrust by two very youthful carabinieri. After examining his identity card at length, they moved wordlessly aside to let him continue his journey. The commissario, relieved not to have the officers' machine guns any longer trained on him, drove on among the low houses fronted by porches, weaving his way between puddles on a tarmac surface softened by the deluge.

He parked in front of the *Italia* bar, some twenty metres short of the embankment, the only relief in an otherwise flat plain and the real border in that wholly level landscape.

As he got out of the car, three elderly men kept him under observation from behind a misted-up window. Soneri disappointed them by turning away towards the embankment and clambering up the incline to the elevated road where several people were milling about and tractors were continually passing to and fro. The water was not far off. Facing him, battered by the current, a pennant was still waving in defiance of the elements, albeit with the desperation of a survivor of a shipwreck. Further on, the flag and the jetty of the riverside port were submerged under the yellowing water. The shack housing the boat club appeared almost to be toppling. Centimetre by centimetre, shallow, dark waves were taking over the yard which ran down to the main embankment, while some men, wellington boots up to their knees, moved around furtively, like ants, carting all manner of objects to safety. Soneri saw two uniformed carabinieri with gun belts over their dark coats step out of the club. A maresciallo was in animated conversation with an old man who was evidently refusing to give way while around him a group of boatmen were listening intently.

"Close down this shack and get out," the officer was saying.

"We will go as and when. We know what we're doing," the man replied.

"You are under my jurisdiction."

"Maresciallo, we know more about the river than you do, so let us get on with it and you go and help the people who need your help."

The two men stared at each other, furiously. The maresciallo turned to the others beside the old man, but seeing they were equally unimpressed, he turned away with an angry movement that shook the water off his overcoat and climbed back into his vehicle. From halfway up the incline, Soneri signalled to the driver to stop.

"I am Commissario Soneri from the police," he said, extending his hand.

The maresciallo, still highly irritated, held out his wet hand with ill grace. "The prefetto will need to come himself and give orders to this lot," he muttered threateningly from under his helmet. "Get in. We'll talk back at the station."

It was not far from the *Italia*, and through the window the solid mass of the great embankment stood out clearly.

"Let's hope it holds," Soneri said to break the silence.

The maresciallo paid no heed to the commissario's words and limited himself to glancing over to satisfy himself that there was no sign of any leaks. "So you're here because of Tonna?" he said. From the nameplate in imitation silver on his desk, Soneri deduced he was called Aricò.

"Yes," he said. Having detected a note of disdain in the officer's voice, he added: "He had a brother who died yesterday and we may well be dealing with a case of murder."

For the first time, Aricò showed a spark of interest. "How did he die?"

"He fell from the third floor of the hospital. It looked like suicide."

The maresciallo seemed deep in thought for a moment or two, then he looked down again at the papers in front of him. When the telephone rang, he gave some peremptory orders in a raised voice. Even before the officer turned back to face him, Soneri was persuaded that he was dealing with a difficult individual. "My dear commissario, what can I tell you? The Tonna from here has disappeared. The barge set off without warning, and was found unmanned by my colleagues at Luzzara. I put out a call for information on Tonna's whereabouts, but so far no-one has come forward. You can see for yourself how badly understaffed we are here." He launched into a fresh tirade against time off and holidays, but it was pretty clear that, given the opportunity, he would have been off himself. "And then this river!" He cursed in the vague direction of the embankment. "Meantime, the prefetto's going off his head," he said, picking up a bundle of transcripts as though he were lifting a burglar by the collar.

"Does Tonna have any relations here?"

"A niece. She has a bar on the piazza."

"Does she know anything?"

"Nothing at all. She only ever saw him, maybe once a week, when he got off his boat to bring her his things to wash."

The telephone rang once more. Aricò was attentive, this time with an attitude of resignation. It was no doubt a superior. All the while, he was looking outside at the grey sky covered with what looked like bruise marks, and Soneri had the impression he was dreaming of the orange groves of Sicily on hills sloping down to the sea. He, on the other hand, was as happy in the rain as an earthworm. Shortly afterwards, he was back on the embankment, *en route* to the boat club. He had learned that the old man who had been debating with the maresciallo was called Barigazzi.

He went in search of him and found him bent over his stakes. "Is it rising fast?"

"It's rising constantly, which is worse."

"You don't see eye to eye with the maresciallo?"

"No, he's sticking his nose into matters he doesn't understand. Are you from round here?"

"I'm a commissario from the police headquarters. My name is Soneri. I'm here about Tonna."

Barigazzi stared at him. "A funny business, that."

"Oh, I agree. Otherwise I wouldn't be here."

They went into the boat club. The radio was frenetically churning out bulletins as though it were wartime. It had been freed from its fittings and was the only object left in the bar.

"You've got six hours before the water gets here, so be prepared," Barigazzi said.

"All we've got to do is pull out the cable and unscrew the control panel," replied the man standing next to the radio.

"I see you haven't altogether ignored the maresciallo's advice," Soneri said.

There was annoyance in Barigazzi's look. "If it had been up to him, we'd have been on the other side of the embankment two days ago. There are some people as would give orders without having even seen the river. They go on like someone who's just invented the wheel."

"When it comes to navigation, perhaps Tonna thought of himself in those terms."

"Perhaps. Nobody knew the river like him."

"When was the last time you saw him?"

"Leaving aside the night he moored here and disappeared, it was four days ago,' Barigazzi said. "He tied up to go to his niece's. He stopped off here at the club, but only for an hour or so, time to down a couple of glasses of grappa, the kind that's distilled locally and he was so keen on."

"Was there anything unusual about how he was that night?"

"Tonna was always the same. Quiet. He only spoke about the Po, or about fishing and boats. But he wasn't much of a talker even on those topics."

"Did he have friends at the club?"

Barigazzi looked at him, rolled his eyes and then shrugged his shoulders so that they seemed to touch his ears. "I doubt if he had many friends anywhere. Only other boatmen who worked the river like him. He communicated by gestures both on land and on the water."

The radio was broadcasting alarming news. A leak had opened up in the San Daniele embankment, on the Lombard side facing Zibello.

"This is something new," said the man who was working the radio. "It's caught them all on the hop."

"Are there still many who make their living sailing up and down the river?" the commissario said.

"Agh!" Barigazzi exclaimed, with a gesture that indicated deep anger. "Two men and a dog. Nobody invests in boats nowadays and you've seen the state of the moorings."

"But Tonna apparently wouldn't give up, in spite of his age."

"It was his life," the old man said, a bit irritated by the question. "Do you expect a man to change his vices at eighty?"

"Many men opt for a quiet life at that age."

"Not Tonna. He never entertained the notion of leaving his barge and digging a garden. And anyway, he always wanted to stay away from people and their empty chatter."

"Any unfinished business?"

Barigazzi made a vague gesture. "He liked his own company…" he said in a tone which seemed to the commissario intended to convey some deeper meaning.

"Even when he was sailing?"

"Sometimes he took his nephew along, but he didn't manage to make a riverman of him. The young nowadays like their comforts, and the river makes its demands."

Soneri thought of Tonna and his solitary life, dedicated to commuting endlessly between Pavia and the mouth of the river, his two termini. A riverman who had no liking for company or for dry land. So caught up was he in these thoughts, he failed to notice that it had stopped raining.

Barigazzi lifted his head as a sign of gratitude. "Don Firmino got it right for once. San Donino has bestowed his grace on us," he sniggered.

At that very moment, the lamp over the boat club, three metres above the roof, was switched on. The water, in gently rippling waves, continued to rise over the yard and was now scarcely two metres from the entrance.

"You arrive when everyone else is getting out," Barigazzi said.

"It's my job."

The man gave a slight nod to show he understood. "Anyway, there is no danger. Every so often the river comes along to take back what is his, and we let him get on with it. He doesn't keep it long. The Po always restores everything."

"Including the dead?"

Barigazzi looked him over attentively. "Even the dead," he agreed. "If you are referring to what I think you are, you can be sure he'll turn up. But are you really sure the Po has taken him?"

The commissario thought it over for a while before replying. "No," he said with resignation, telling himself that the investigation was still to get under way. "Can I offer you a drink?" he proposed to the old man.

"I'd be very grateful, in a little while," Barigazzi said. "First we have to shift the radio. We'll take it to the Town Hall. That way the mayor will be able to listen for himself."

"Where's the best place for a drink?"

"Depends on your tastes," the old man said. "I prefer *Il Sordo*, run by the deaf barman, under the colonnades, but they've got good wine in the *Italia*, where you'll have been already."

Soneri was astonished that the man knew where he had left his car, but then he remembered that from the embankment it was easy to see down to the road in front of the bar.

It was growing dark as he went down towards the town. He was aware of a level of feverish agitation among the houses and he understood why when he noticed a group of people gathered around a carabiniere patrol car parked nearby. The maresciallo was issuing evacuation orders, but the people were unwilling to move. As he passed by, the commissario caught sight of the officer's face, with beads of sweat caused by the excitement mingling with drops of rain. Only a few families loading goods on to the van were paying him any heed. The others seemed on the point of mutiny. On the piazza, on the other hand, everything was quiet, as though the river were receding. A yellow sign concealed behind a large chestnut tree whose last leaves were hanging listlessly on the branches pointed to the *Portici* bar. Inside there were a few tables and several video games occupied by some young people.

"You must be Tonna's niece," Soneri said to the woman behind the bar.

A woman of around forty, not especially well preserved, looked at him with obvious distrust. "Yes," she said, in a forced, vaguely threatening tone.

"I am Commissario Soneri, from the police."

The woman grew even more rigid. She put down the glass she was drying to give him her full attention. "If it's about my uncle, I have already told all I know to the carabinieri," she said. "But they don't exactly seem to be going out of their way to find him."

"Do you think there's been an accident?"

"Do you have a better explanation?"

"At the moment, no," Soneri said. "But the idea that he would have fallen into the water does seem strange."

The woman stared at him, with open hostility. She was wearing no make-up, and gave the impression of systematic self-neglect.

"You haven't told me your name."

"Claretta," she said. That name, more suitable for a doll, was at odds with the brazen set of her face.

By a kind of conditioned reflex, Soneri thought of Claretta Petacci, Mussolini's mistress. Perhaps because the woman was dressed in black.

"I imagine you've dismissed the possibility that your uncle might have decided to end it all."

She dismissed the idea with a sweep of her hand. "He was too fond of the life he was leading, of the river and of his barge. I wouldn't have been surprised if they had found his body in the cabin, but this way—"

"When did you see him last?"

"Four days ago. He came with his clothes to wash, as he did every week. Each time I asked him when he planned to give it all up, but he wouldn't discuss it."

"Did he have enemies?"

"Ancient history, from before the war," Claretta stated, her voice hardening. "Politics."

With Claretta Petacci still in his mind, Soneri asked instinctively: "Because of his Fascist past?"

The woman nodded. Anteo sought solitude on the river, spending his days as a wandering hermit on the water, avoiding contact with hostile towns and people. Perhaps his brother had had the same problem, and that was why he spoke only of illnesses, fleeing from his own past and hiding away whenever anyone wanted to pry into his youth.

"But here, in this town, did he ever receive threats?"

"Perhaps he did right after the war, but not nowadays. It's really a question for the older generation, and many of them are dead now. Young people simply ignored him. They're nearly all Reds here."

Claretta made as if to move off towards the cappuccino machine, but the commissario raised his hand to hold her back.

"I came to tell you about something else."

She stopped in her tracks, as though she were under threat.

"Your other uncle, Decimo, has gone as well," Soneri told her in a voice that had dropped two tones below its normal register. "He jumped out of a third-floor window in the hospital in Parma," he said, not referring to the possibility of murder.

The woman remained briefly silent. "Two at one time," she murmured. Then, folding her arms to support her flaccid, heavy breasts, she whispered: "Poor Decimo."

The commissario observed her closely, but before he could speak, she got in first. "Where is he now?"

"In the mortuary."

She seemed dumbstruck. She kept her eyes on the floor while the theme tunes from the video games made a mockery of all the tumult inside her.

Soneri attempted to take advantage of the fact that she had dropped her guard. "Could you tell me if you have any suspicions, if anyone had got in touch with your uncle, or perhaps he dropped some hints... it was your son who sometimes sailed with him, is that not so?"

"Anteo didn't talk, not even to me. For my son, the problem was not sailing on the river. It was his silences that got to him."

Soneri was about to let the matter drop. He let his arms fall to his side and gave a deep sigh. It was then that the woman raised her eyes from the floor and stared straight at him. The commissario was on the point of striking a match but stopped and waited expectantly.

"There was something strange, but I don't know if it has anything to do with it." Soneri did not move a muscle. "A week ago, someone phoned here looking for him."

"Had that ever happened before?"

"Never."

"Did they say who they were?"

"No. A man. From the voice it seemed he was an older person."

"Did he seem to you to belong to these parts?"

Claretta stood thinking, as though she were unsure of the precise answer to give. "He spoke dialect perfectly, but he didn't speak good Italian."

"That can happen with people who hadn't been to school all that much."

"No, I mean he spoke Italian with a foreign accent."

"What do you mean, foreign?"

"I'm not sure. Spanish, perhaps."

"And what did he say?"

"That he was looking for my uncle." After a pause, Claretta was more precise. "But he didn't say straightaway that he was looking for Anteo Tonna. He said he was looking for 'Barbisin'."

"And who is 'Barbisin'?"

"It was a nickname they used to give my uncle in the past."

Someone opened a window, allowing in a gust of wet wind. The woman shivered as though she had been struck a blow, and went behind the bar to serve a customer who had just come in. The commissario's mobile rang. He left the bar, saying good-bye with a wave, and waited until he was in the middle of the street before pressing the answer button. Juvara shouted out "Hello!" a couple of times without hearing anything in reply. Soneri cursed the machine and had to move to another corner of the piazza to get a signal.

"Boss, I haven't really got much to report. Decimo Tonna really and truly did live on his own. His neighbours saw him come and go, but he only ever exchanged the time of day with them. He did his shopping at the supermarket and never went to the local bar. I've also heard that some social workers went to see him a couple of times, but he chased them away."

"Does the parish priest know anything about him?" the commissario said. More and more frequently the priests were the only ones you could turn to. And more and more frequently, they knew nothing either. "Check the files on the two Tonnas. They were once Fascists…"

"That's nearly fifty years ago," Juvara said.

Soneri thought this over for a few moments until he heard the ispettore repeat again: "Hello, hello?"

"Maybe you're right," he said, closing his mobile without saying good-bye.

He walked a little way with myriad thoughts churning in his head, and only after a minute did he realize that what he was experiencing was the overture to a thoroughly bad mood. He felt he was caught up in twin cases but was incapable of disentangling from either any workable lead or even the outline of a hypothesis to work on. Meantime, he found himself confronting the silent faces of the Tonna brothers whom he had never seen alive. The only one he had seen was Decimo under the special white sheet used for corpses, with only the white of his eyes visible and blood trickling from his mouth in the graceless grin of death.

In one of the narrow streets, the mobile rang again.

"So you're not drowned." It was Angela.

"Not yet, but don't lose hope. The river's still rising."

"Why not throw yourself in, seeing you're so keen to be there."

"I'm afraid of drowning in the dark. Anyway, I've just eaten."

"That's the one thing you'll never forget to do."

"Christ, Angela, I've only just got here. And I can't make head nor tail of the business."

"O.K., Commissario, you do your investigating. And when you come back, bring me a little something."

"It's so much easier for you lawyers: you play about with words, you pull down and build on the facts other people have dug up for you."

"Don't play the victim," Angela said. "I'd like to see you plunge every day into that tank of alligators called a courtroom. I have colleagues who would sell their mothers for a handful of coins."

"Could anyone be worse than a murderer?"

"Have you any idea what happened to the barge?" she said, her mood becoming more cheerful.

"No, but I have persuaded Alemanni to unite the inquiries into the two brothers."

"You can pat yourself on the back, then. In all my dealings with that one, I've never once got anything out of him. He rejects every application I make, even the most straightforward ones."

"He's nothing but a gloomy old bugger who can't get it into his head that it's time for him to move on."

"I hope to see you before you go drifting off somewhere. Maybe there'll be an opportunity in a couple of days. If you have any memory left, you'll understand..."

He heard the mobile being closed with a snap which seemed to him like the sound of something being broken, but at that moment, walking under the colonnade, he chanced on the *osteria* called *Il Sordo*. Inside, under hanging chandeliers with a few candles in each, there were eight beechwood tables. The light was faint but sufficient for games of *briscola*. He recognized Barigazzi and three other men he had seen at the boat club standing at the bar.

"Did you get out in time?"

"Nando, the boy operating the radio, is still there dismantling it. He'll be here shortly."

"Did it come up sooner than you expected?"

"No. It will reach the shack about three o'clock. We know the river, so we know it's pointless hanging about waiting for it." It was Barigazzi who did the talking.

"Can I get you something?"

"We never say no. It's an offer that might cost you dear around here," they all replied, making for an empty table.

The deaf barman, whose misfortune gave its name to the *Il Sordo* bar, kept his eye on them until they sat down. When he came over, no words were spoken, but Barigazzi held up four fingers and his thumb and the man nodded. Soneri was about to ask him about something else, but he stopped when he felt a hand on his elbow. "No point. He's taken out his hearing aid this evening, so he wouldn't hear a thing."

It was only then that the commissario became aware that small amplifiers the size of cotton wool balls were protruding from both of the landlord's ears.

Barigazzi introduced Vernizzi, Ghezzi and Torelli. "In fact," he said, "you've met the whole committee of the boat club all at once."

Then he pointed to the owner of the bar. "He does that when he's in a bad temper. He pulls the apparatus out of his ears and listens only to his own silence."

"What a bit of luck," Soneri said, thinking of certain calls from Angela. He looked around at the walls covered with photographs of great opera singers, all in parts from Verdi. His eyes fell on a Rigoletto while, in the background, the notes from one of the more romantic numbers swelled up.

"Aureliano Pertile," Ghezzi said, without a moment's hesitation.

The deaf landlord himself wanted to live in silence, but he provided music for his guests. He reappeared with a dark, thick glass bottle and four majolica bowls foaming at the brim. Soneri recognized it as a Fortanina, a wine low in alcohol but high in tannin, sparkling like lemonade.

"I thought it had vanished from circulation," he said.

"It was declared illegal because it didn't reach the required grade of alcohol, but the landlord makes it in his cellar," Vernizzi informed him. "You're not here as a spy, are you?"

"No, not if he'll bring me some *spalla cotta*," the commissario said. "I'm concerned with a different kind of crime."

"Of course," Barigazzi said, intercepting Soneri's thought.

He looked at them one after the other, as though issuing a challenge. "Have you any idea what could have happened?"

Vernizzi and Torelli leaned back in their chairs, raising their eyes upwards to imply they had no idea. Ghezzi kept his counsel and the commissario had the impression that he had no intention of speaking, leaving this to Barigazzi, a ritual that reminded him of meetings in the prefettura where people spoke in order of seniority.

"It's no good asking us. You know as much as we do about how it all might have gone," said the recognized senior.

"I haven't formed a precise idea. I'm not a riverman."

"Tonna would never have abandoned his barge. It was the only place he could live in peace."

"In that case, either he had a stroke and fell into the river, or else someone bumped him off and cut the mooring. Some irresponsible idiot, even if it all turned out alright for him in the end."

In reply, all four busied themselves with the food in front of them.

The *spalla cotta* was quite exceptional, pinkish with just the right level of streaky fat. Soneri made a sandwich with the bread and as the music grew louder and louder, some people at the tables behind joined in with an improvised version of "Rigoletto or The Duke of Mantua".

The commissario knew when to bide his time. The main

thing was to allow thoughts to mature, give them time to take form and organize themselves into speech. The wine played its part. When he had finished chewing, Barigazzi took up the subject.

"Look, Commissario, there's one thing I don't get about the last voyage of the barge. Do you believe it's possible for a forty-metre vessel to pass under four bridges without smashing into the columns, with no-one at the helm and, to crown it all, with the engine switched off?"

Soneri's expression told them that he had no idea.

"Four, uh!" the old man repeated, raising his hand and holding up the same number of bent fingers with the thick, broken nails typical of a man who had laboured on the docks. "Three road bridges and one railway bridge: Viadana, Boretto and Guastalla."

"So, then, there was someone on the barge. But if it was Tonna, what happened to him?"

"You're the investigator," Ghezzi said.

"We've just agreed that Tonna would not have abandoned his barge. He might have fallen into the river if something or someone struck him, and then the current might have carried the boat downstream. So perhaps it sneaked under the bridges by itself by pure chance."

"There is one way of finding out if that's what happened..." Barigazzi was sitting sideways on the seat, his arm against the back of the chair in a theatrical pose which seemed in keeping with the music.

Soneri, respecting the pause, raised his bowl to his lips and drank a deep draft of the Fortanina. It was like a young wine, halfway between a fresh must and the heavy, black Lambrusco from the lands around the Po.

"You'd have to find out if he's still on the dinghy."

"The dinghy?"

"Something like that," Barigazzi said. "It's something you need when you have to get ashore and the mooring is out of reach. Maybe because of a sandbank or shallows."

The dinghy. Soneri looked at his watch with the idea of contacting the carabinieri in Luzzara, but then he thought it might be more fruitful to go there in person and perhaps even get on board. Meantime, the music had changed. "Aida" echoed off the walls of the *osteria*, tripping along the beams of the ceiling and bouncing back into the ears of the listeners. The wall facing the commissario was bare brick, the plain, red brick prevalent in the lower Po valley, while the other walls were partially covered with plaster. In a low corner, near the bar, there was a gauge with a series of notches indicating the dates of various floods. The highest was '51.

"An insult, so much water in a drinking den like this," Soneri said to Barigazzi.

"We put up with it occasionally, but give it half a chance and it'd be all over us."

"We've taken more water in through our ears swimming in the Po than through our mouths drinking the stuff," Vernizzi said. "Like the owner of this place, who can't hear a thing now."

"There's some people I could mention that have taken in water through the holes in their arses," Ghezzi sniggered.

The commissario smiled while his eyes continued to run over the walls where various Falstaffs and Othellos stood out against a background of heavy clay streaked with white lime, the colours of a good Felino *salame*. His eyes fell on a life-size, medium-quality fresco of a Christ executed by some mad artist. The face seemed to express not so much pain as the anger of a man cursing and swearing, while his sturdy, oarsman's arms seemed capable of tearing the nails from the cross. When the commissario looked lower, he saw that the artist had painted the legs folded over, crossed slightly beneath the pelvis.

"You've noticed it too," Barigazzi said sarcastically. "Jesus Christ did not die of cold feet."

Guffaws rang out around the table and created ripples in the Fortanina in the bowls.

"It wasn't always like that," he said, turning more serious. "It happened in '51, with the flood."

The commissario looked around all the tables. The chances were that not one of them was a church-goer.

"You don't hold back with your jokes," he said.

"It's not a joke," Torelli protested. "Even the priest agrees, and he made the old women believe it was a miracle."

"The thing is he might be right."

Soneri shook his head to say it was time to stop. He felt himself trapped in the middle. He had come to pose questions, and now he found himself in a bizarre situation. The wine was inducing a mood of euphoria in him, while the talk spun round him like a gauze bandage immobilizing him layer by layer.

"I don't believe in miracles," Barigazzi said, turning serious. "But nobody can say who redid Christ's legs, not even the bar owner himself. He found them like that when he got back to his *osteria* after the flood water receded. They say it was some street artist who did the painting standing up to his knees in water."

Soneri looked back at the Christ. He looked like an Indian holy man, but there was nothing blasphemous or mocking about him. "It's strange to see an image like that here, where no-one goes to church," he almost said.

"We don't go to church and we can't stand priests, but he," Barigazzi said, pointing at the painting with deep respect, "he was a man who underwent suffering, like us."

"He taught us not to kill," Soneri said.

The three, suddenly suspicious, looked up for a moment and stared at him: "You don't really think that we..."

"No, I don't. But they did kill Tonna's brother."

"Decimo?"

"Yes."

The conversation halted and even the music paused. The din of the *osteria* took over. None of the four asked any questions. Their mood was now serious and only Vernizzi murmured, "That's certainly strange," and he seemed to be speaking for the others.

There was a silence for a few minutes, which Soneri passed listening to the somewhat acerbic Verdi of "I Lombardi alla prima Crociata" before Barigazzi found the courage to venture: "So in your view, Anteo too was..."

The commissario first stretched out his arms then moved his face closer to Barigazzi's square, high-cheekboned face. He was not wearing a beret, and this showed off his still thick but whitening hair. "I'm not sure, but as we set aside other hypotheses, I'm almost beginning to grow convinced."

The other drew back and seemed lost in thought. From the expression on his face, the commissario deduced that he had been very convincing.

"Until this moment, I had been under the impression that the current could have carried the barge downstream and through the arches of a bridge, but you've undermined this conviction and with it any real possibility that we're dealing with an accident. You have simplified the hypotheses, but complicated the story."

Vernizzi and Torelli nodded in the style of a priest hearing confession.

"So then," Soneri started up again, "There must have been someone on the barge. Someone who knew what he was doing, who knew the river well enough to be able to navigate at night-time, in the dark, using only the tiller. Someone who started off from the boat club, casting off the moorings, giving the impression that the rising water of the Po had made the barge break free, or else that Tonna himself had decided to sail without engine or lights. After all, that was strange, was it not? But to make this last hypothesis credible, there needs to be some indication that there was a boatman on board."

"The light," Barigazzi said. "The light on the barge was switched on a couple of times while it was on the river."

Soneri smiled at this confirmation, while the music rose in a crescendo at a crucial point in the opera, even if he couldn't recall exactly which. It was the first supposition which stood up, but it was followed immediately by the realization that it was worthless, no more than a straightforward deduction from facts which he had not yet sifted.

Barigazzi looked at him. "Commissario, do you see the Po? The river is always smooth and placid, but deep down it's turbulent. No-one ever thinks about life down there, fish struggling for survival in an unending duel in the murky depths. And everything is endlessly changing, according to the whim of the water. None of us can imagine those depths unless and until we end up scraping against them. Dredging is always provisional work. Like everything in this world, wouldn't you say?"

4

ANGELA KEPT HIM awake during the return journey to
the city, twenty minutes winding through the mist which
followed the rain, her voice cutting into his brain and setting
off electric shocks each time the Fortanina threatened to carry
out its digestive and somniferous duties. He had failed to call
her at the agreed hour and this had been taken as a sign of
indifference. She was not as yet entirely accustomed to his
lapses of memory, and if she were, he would have viewed that
as a matter for concern. When he came off the telephone, he
tried to call Juvara, but had insufficient battery on his mobile,
as he was advised by a slightly mocking, double bleep. He
tossed the implement on to the seat beside him, but before he
had time to get worked up about it, he was turning into his
own driveway.

He collapsed into the armchair in the living room, lit
a cigar and surveyed the apartment. This was his favourite
moment of the day: slippers, pyjamas, dressing gown and his
own home, always the same. The house where he had grown
up, the house complete with furniture his parents had left him,
all unaltered after so many years. When the day was done,
he had the impression of escaping to a place whose map was
known to him alone, and where he could think freely, leaving everything outside in a street which he saw as grey and

featureless, as though through a windowpane with trickles of water running down it.

Angela had asked him if he would be coming back to the city or staying by the banks of the Po. He did not know. He could have decided there and then, but he felt he could pull either end of that particular ball of wool and arrive at the same point. However, the banks of the river seemed to offer the least demanding of the alternatives, and anyway, the barge aground at Luzzara, sealed off by the carabinieri, needed to be inspected.

He grabbed the telephone and placed it on his knees, just at the moment when it began to squeal like an animal in pain. He recognized Juvara's voice. "What is it? Can't you get to sleep?" he asked, glancing at his watch.

"I didn't expect to find you at home. Your mobile is switched off."

"The battery's dead."

"Tomorrow, will you be in your office or down at the Po?"

"I've got to look over Tonna's barge."

"Do you need a hand?"

"No, you carry on delving into Decimo and I'll attend to Anteo. I guess that working on two fronts we might make more headway."

"Tomorrow Nanetti hopes to get the results of the tests on the blood from the broken windows in the ward."

"Good, let me know."

"I will, and don't forget to recharge your battery."

Once again he awoke very early and found himself seated at the edge of the bed before his eyes were properly open. By the time he got to the coffee-maker, he decided he should have his blood pressure checked. Whenever he was on a case, it invariably shot up, and this time, to make matters worse, he had to cope with Alemanni and his scepticism. If he were to fail, every single one of them in the H.Q. would hold him responsible for the fiasco and for giving the old magistrate the chance to bring his career to a glorious end by humiliating a commissario of the *squadra mobile*.

The mist had settled on the roofs as he journeyed along the deserted, early-morning streets. Once out of the city, he observed the swamps in the flat countryside from which it appeared impossible to take off for the skies, since the skies with their vapours had descended to kiss the earth. He had yet again to present his identity card before he was allowed to pass the security barrier and drive on to the embankment. On the road, he met lorries, vans and tractors loaded with household goods coming in the opposite direction, all fleeing the threat of the barely contained flood waters several metres above the vulnerable plain.

From the elevated road, the river seemed boundless, like a mud-coloured sea confined inside a system of dykes. The current was flowing approximately two metres below the summit of the main embankment, and on top of it rows of sandbags had been lined up to provide extra protection. The barge appeared before the commissario between leafless branches tossed this way and that by the current, an enormous, squat, rusting monster on which there was only one thing that could be called new – the word TONNA in big letters on the bow. At first sight, it looked like a catfish, with a cover over it as flat as the plain and only the wheelhouse sticking up at the stern. For the rest, all that stood out were the topsides of the hull surrounding the deck and a few small vents to allow air into the hold.

Soneri parked amidst the puddles below the embankment, within sight of the barge, now circled with mist. From time to time, it rose and fell in the current, but this movement, far from being a sign of life, seemed the death throes of a moribund beast.

He had moved only a few paces forward when he noticed the carabiniere car. A youthful officer, plainly suffering from the cold, got out. He showed him his identity card, and the man pointed to the gangplank and helped him hoist it on to the deck. The commissario noted the solid marine hawsers holding the craft in place, while the young officer, with fussy deference, removed the seals from the cabin and, after a lengthy struggle with the spring handle, opened it for him. Soneri advised him to keep his gloves on and not to touch anything until the forensic squad had been able to examine the interior of the barge. The officer remained at the entrance, stock-still.

The cabin was somewhat cramped. The helm, only slightly larger than a car's driving wheel, held pride of place. Through the windscreen, the deck and stempost were clearly visible. The instrument panel, with its fuel, oil-pressure and engine-temperature gauges and an array of light switches stood to one side. Alongside the steering column, there was a conduit for the cable that activated the combustion-chamber pre-heat plugs, as with old-style diesel engines. Behind the column, there was just space for a seat and a trapdoor leading down below.

He climbed down a companionway, short and steep as a ladder. He pressed with his knuckles the switches in the small corridor which led to the two berths, but no light came on. He was forced to pull out his torch to shine some light on the stale, dusty environment which suggested to him an old, abandoned family tomb.

The first berth he saw was almost bare. Apart from the unmade bed, there were some comic strips on a shelf, a crumpled-up windcheater and some old newspapers. There was neither a window nor a porthole for observing the river or for letting in light. Everything added to the feeling of asphyxiation: the gloom, the ceiling which scarcely allowed you to stand upright, the claustrophobia and the general air of neglect which hung over the barge, starting with the rust which was now so ingrained as to have become the dominant colour.

The other berth was plainly the one where Tonna himself slept. It too was bare, but it seemed to have been abandoned only recently. Apart from a few other things, it contained one little item of wooden furniture of such style that it stood out like a jewel in a pile of junk. Four tiny drawers opened in front, each with handles as minute as buttons. Soneri took out his handkerchief and opened the top drawer, where he found nothing but bills for the supply of diesel oil. In the second, there was a register in which Tonna had recorded the details of each voyage and of the cargoes he had carried up and down the river. The third contained yellowing postcards and photographs of the barge, together with a user's guide to the vessel. Finally Soneri bent down to open the bottom drawer, where he found bobbins, needles and threads of various colours. Hidden among them, he found a note in an unaddressed, unsealed envelope. He read a few words, as mysterious as the life which had been lived on the barge. *The Kite has nothing to do with it: the decision was taken higher up.*

He stood there for some time, scrutinizing the somewhat laboured handwriting which clung to the page like a creeper to a wall. He then replaced the note, written on cardboard which might have been torn from a shoe box, and put the envelope back in the drawer.

It occurred to him that putting a face to the Kite and placing those arcane words in some meaningful context would give a new momentum to the inquiry, but around him there was nothing but darkness. He came out of the cubicle and climbed the steps two at a time until he regained the deck. In the thick fog, he made out the figure of the carabiniere alongside the gangplank, guarding a vessel no-one wished to claim.

He went back down to Tonna's quarters. He pulled open the drawer containing the register of the times he had sailed the river and the record of the cargoes loaded and unloaded, and examined it once more. It looked as though Tonna had done a great deal of work, shuffling up and down between Cremona and the mouth of the river. He took the register with him and went out on to the deck, moving over towards the hatches from where it would be possible to check the cargoes. He went over to a round flap and had to use all the strength in his back, both feet placed wide apart, before he could get the lever to budge. After a while the cover came away with a sudden jerk, permitting him to peer into the darkness of the hold.

With his torch, he examined the cavernous space. There was not a trace of the cargoes of wheat he had been told about in the boat club. Before him lay the deep, wide, rusty emptiness of the belly of the barge, a cave between the sky and the water on which nothing floated. He pulled the hatch shut, and flicked through the register. There was an entry for three days before which stated that a cargo of grain had been loaded at Casalmaggiore and at the port of Cremona, destined for the mills of Polesella. Soneri looked over the side at the immense river which coursed by, treacherous and heedless. It carried with it a small boat with no oars, dragged away from its mooring by the river in spate. At that moment Soneri remembered the dinghy.

Briefly he reconnoitred the perimeter of the barge, looking over the low bulwarks. There was no sign of the dinghy. As he made his way back to the cabin, he noticed a couple of rings soldered on to the hatch covers and some ropes worn by the passing years. The rust had been rubbed away at one point, leaving the metal shining. The dinghy had been removed only recently from where its keel, swaying from side to side in the slow movement of the barge, had for so many years left in its wake a track as clear as the trail of a snail. Someone had taken the helm of the barge, and when he could no longer maintain control or when he had decided it was time to make off, had escaped by dinghy. Perhaps Tonna? But why? Or perhaps someone who had considered the riverbank at Luzzara the best place to make an escape? Barigazzi had been right: a barge could not navigate four bridges by itself.

He clambered again along the gangway. The force of the water beneath him, causing the barge to shift, was terrifying. From that position, Soneri looked out over the plain where the grass was at a lower level than the shoals of fish around him. The carabiniere replaced the seals over the entrance to the cabin.

"I am sorry to have to ask you to keep constant watch," the commissario said.

The police officer looked at him untroubled. "We'd have to do it in any case."

"Why?"

"The prefetto wants us to keep an eye on the riverbanks to see that nothing's happening. It wouldn't be the first time someone attempts an act of sabotage."

"Sabotage of what?"

"Of the embankments," the carabiniere said. "There are some people who, when the water rises, do not leave the river to decide where to overflow. They make an opening for the water, on the opposite side from where they live, obviously. They flood their neighbours to save themselves. A sort of blood-letting to ease the pressure on the river, and to hell with everyone else."

The commissario looked along the extra metre of embankment made up of sandbags and reflected that it would be child's play to cut an opening in it when the water had risen to that level. The current would do the rest. He said good-bye to the carabiniere who got back into his car, but his thoughts returned to the opening which he would like to be able to make in the inquiry. The note had been written recently. The piece of cardboard and the envelope it was in were still quite white, unlike everything else aboard the barge, which had the feel of neglect and age. The register he had handled had yellowing pages and curled-up edges, as well as blots and dark marks. The Kite had only recently come on the scene to trouble the thoughts of Tonna the boatman. But to whom did that nickname belong?

Nanetti called him as he made his way back from Luzzara. "The blood on the windowpane does not belong to Decimo Tonna," he said without preliminaries.

"Have you reported that to the magistrate?"

"Certainly, but he didn't attach great importance to it, not as much as you were hoping. He says it doesn't add anything much, even if it is a step forward."

"What do you mean – not add anything much!" the commissario exploded, swerving violently, his mind elsewhere. "The glass was broken before Decimo jumped and the blood is not his. It means there was someone else there."

"I did point this out to him," Nanetti said calmly. "He said that in these cases you always find someone getting himself injured and careering about, or some nosey fool getting cut and... I have to say he's got something there. It does happen all the time."

Soneri had to stop himself taking it out on the mobile.

Whenever his temper got the better of him, he always felt the desire to dash it against something. He tried to calm down by letting a few seconds pass before Nanetti brought him back to himself with a deafening "Hello!"

"Alright. I'll tell Juvara to do a check on the staff in the ward and on everyone who had any business there," he roared.

"Good idea. Reply to sceptics with actions. It's always good to see them twisting in their seats when you demonstrate to them that they've got it all wrong."

Soneri drove into the town, following the bends of the embankment. Volunteers hard at work glowered at him resentfully as he went by. In his Alfa sports, he must have looked like someone out on a jaunt while others sweated under the menace of Armageddon. He found Barigazzi observing the boat club shack, now one quarter filled with water. The river was lapping around the window of the front door.

"I have no more need of stakes. All I have to do is take a look at our premises. I know the measurements."

They were both looking in the same direction, at the water caressing the riverbanks and the walls of the shack. It was disconcerting to think that concealed beneath such gentleness lay the capacity to inflict terrible destruction.

"Is it still rising as fast?"

"No, fortunately. A couple of centimetres an hour, but soon it will stop and then it will begin to drop. Look, see how it's stopped raining on the mountains and started freezing."

"So how will it all end?"

"Nothing will happen if the fog persists. All this rushing about…" Barigazzi wailed, pointing at tractors and lorries which were taking away people and their furniture. "If only they would listen to people who know. It's as if their arses were on fire."

"I have to ask you something," Soneri said.

Barigazzi turned quickly towards him with a piercing glance, as though to make sure he was still at his side. "O.K., but let's go over to the bar," he replied, indicating *Il Sordo* with a jerk of his head.

The landlord still had his hearing aid switched off. This time Barigazzi kept his two fingers raised until he received a silent assent.

The commissario watched him move into the kitchen, and so failed to note the arrival of Torelli, Vernizzi and Ghezzi. He felt himself surrounded, one of the undesirable situations they used to harp on about during training. The men took their seats around the table as silently as they had entered. It was as if they were keeping an eye on each other, as though a password had been exchanged between them. In that position, Soneri felt the unease of a man in the dock. The embarrassment was broken by the deaf landlord, to whom Barigazzi, after a wave which plainly indicated an addition to the order, made a sign with three fingers. Then, looking at the Christ with the drawn-up feet, the old man announced: "Another three days of flooding."

No-one made any comment until the drinks arrived and the slow notes of Verdi's "Requiem", coming from some mysterious emptiness, reached them. They raised their glasses of the foaming Fortanina in a wordless toast. The wine gave its own mute pleasure, but the tension became unbearable after the first sip.

Soneri decided to break the silence: "So, who was 'the Kite'?"

It seemed as though all four men had swallowed a glass of dregs. Their ashen, impassive faces were masks of hostile indifference, as though carved in marble. His eyes circled from one to the other, ending with Barigazzi, like a roulette ball finding its slot.

"Why do you ask?"

"It's to do with Tonna."

"There are no kites around here. At most, there might be some hawks, but…" Barigazzi was attempting to extricate himself.

"There was one. I have Tonna's word for it," the commissario insisted.

"All sorts of things go on along the Po. You see some of them, you hear about others. The first are obvious, the second are a matter of faith."

"You don't believe what Tonna said?"

"I don't know. There's so much chatter… there was one guy who saw sturgeons leap over the Viadana bridge, another one whose chickens were devoured by a catfish… in Ferrara, they still talk about the magician Chiozzini who one day at Pontelagoscuro sailed up into the skies in a horse-drawn carriage…"

"We even have a village which appears and disappears…" Torelli said.

"No," said Soneri decisively. "'The Kite' is a nickname. A nickname of someone from around here."

"Are you sure of that?" Ghezzi said with a voice in which the commissario detected the faintest trace of alarm.

"Yes," he said, dissembling as skilfully as he could.

The four men exchanged rapid glances. They had spent years together and must have understood each other in a matter of seconds, in a wager between Verdi and the Fortanina.

"A partisan," Soneri said, doubling the wager. His mind raced to Tonna and his Fascist past.

"So many have passed along this way…" Barigazzi said, now sure of himself.

The commissario immediately realized he had made a false move. He should have fostered the tension he noticed growing among the four men, but instead he had quite suddenly given it release, affording them an easy way out. However, as he had been about to play his hand, Alemanni, with his scepticism and his invitation to stick to facts and steer clear of conjecture, had swum back into view. And everything had collapsed.

"This was frontier land. There were some on the run, some who crossed the river to join up with others. Fascists disguised as partisans. Partisans dressed in black shirts, double agents, spies. There were all sorts."

"There were also real partisans," Soneri said, trying to find his feet again.

"Yes, members of the group called – what was it? – G.A.P., Gruppo di azione pattriotica, the armed partisan group. For the others, this plain was too dangerous. A brigade of Germans could sweep across it in half a day."

"And no-one who went by that name?"

"Listen." Barigazzi came in quietly. "I am seventy-five and at the time I was not much more than a boy. This lot" – he indicated the others – "were children. How could we remember?"

"You don't only remember the things you have lived through yourself."

"Here the partisans were all communists. The man you are talking about might have been loyal to General Badoglio, cut off from his unit… There were a lot like that in Lombardy."

"Would no-one in the party know him? Among the older members, I mean."

"The party," Barigazzi snorted, with a theatrical wave which seemed in harmony with the music as it rose in a crescendo towards a closing climax. "What's left of the party? Just what you can see outside here," he said, pointing down to the Po. "A fleeing rabble trying to carry with them as much as they can, knowing full well that they'll not be able to save much and that the best part of their things will be taken by the river.

That's what the party is." His words tailed off, leaving him to stare grimly ahead, angrily gulping at the wine left in the bowl.

"You don't forget certain things. You haven't."

"All that's left are memories," said Barigazzi acidly. "And there is no pleasure in raking over them."

"I am sorry, but I am afraid I am going to have to do some raking. Or some wading."

"Well then, it might be better to let the water levels drop," Torelli said. "Bit by bit, everything will become clearer."

Soneri looked at him and there appeared on the man's face the slightest, fleeting outline of a smile. "When the rivers drop, the waters turn clearer but they cover the riverbeds with sand."

"You're a man who knows how to dig about," Torelli said, in a tone which appeared to carry some kind of dark threat.

"You haven't told us if you've been to inspect the barge," Ghezzi said.

"I have. And the dinghy is missing."

"I knew it," Barigazzi jumped up. "There *was* someone at the helm. There never has been a barge which sailed under four bridges without crashing into one of them."

"The dinghy hasn't been found."

"You could always put out a message on the radio to ask them to look out for it," Vernizzi suggested. "The watchmen must have caught sight of it. Unless they abandoned it to the current."

"That seems the most likely to me," Barigazzi murmured. "But they must have used it first."

"Are you saying that whoever it was fled to the far side?"

Barigazzi stared at him to see if he was joking.

"So how did you get on board the barge?"

"Via the gangplank."

"Do you believe that if he had escaped on to the Emilia side, he would have taken the dinghy?"

"He could have taken it to get off further down the river, but still on the right bank."

The boatman shook his head. "Luzzara is the place with least surveillance, and the place hardest to keep under surveillance between Parma and Reggio."

"But on the far bank?"

"Nobody bothers with the inside stretch of the Luzzara bend. The river has never burst its banks there."

That could be right. Whoever was on the boat did not have much time to disappear. You needed a bit of time to get the boat into the water, to go with the current, paddle towards the Lombard shore downstream from Dosolo, then abandon the boat to the current and clamber over the embankment. The carabiniere on guard at Tonna's barge had told him that no more than twenty minutes had elapsed between the barge hitting the bank and the arrival of the search party. And by the same token, there had been no immediate inquiries made on the Emilia side of the river.

The music swelled to its dramatic climax and provided the perfect accompaniment to Soneri's thoughts as he imagined that flight, in the evening, on a river in spate, between embankments which had suddenly shrunk for someone looking up at them from midstream. He thought of one solitary, single-minded man clambering up, sliding about in the mud as he attempted to reach safety, wading up to his knees in filth, soaked through like marsh life, hoping to reach a friendly house as the veterans had done of old and to find people speaking the dialects of the Po.

He failed to notice that the four men were staring at him. The deaf barman was at his side, too discreet to make him aware of his presence. Finally he nodded, and Barigazzi once more held up fingers that were as twisted as old nails.

"Fortanina is the best thing in the lower Po valley, apart from Verdi and pork," Torelli said.

"And none better than what you get here," Vernizzi said.

The faint light and the red of the brickwork made the place look like a cellar. The windows were shuttered in the heavy darkness. Soneri was sunk in his thoughts, again imagining that flight.

"Luzzara, Dosolo… it could be around there…" he murmured in a voice they struggled to make out.

"These places are all one. The river doesn't divide: it brings people together," Barigazzi said.

"That's why I asked if you knew the partisans and the Kite."

"At my age, I sometimes think the mist over the Po has got into my head."

"Wine always clears the mind," the commissario retorted, looking around that bar where everything seemed redolent of the past. With a swift glance he took in Verdi's characters displayed on the walls, the Fortanina the customers were drinking, the bricks of a red that seemed permeated by pigs' blood, the Christ with the crossed legs.

"Don't get carried away by appearances," the boatman interrupted his thinking. "The past falls apart when you distrust the present."

"I don't get the impression that you've forgotten. This river, for example…"

Barigazzi interrupted him with a wave. "Don't go there. It's important to distinguish between experience and memory. You can fool yourself that you remember because it seems that everything is always the same, like the river perpetually switching between floods and low water. It's not true. Each time you start over from the beginning. Memories are worth something for two or three generations, then they disappear and others take their place. After fifty years, you are back where you started. I chased out the Fascists and now my grand-children are bringing them back. Then it will be their turn to end up on their arses."

"As happened to Tonna?"

"He ended up on his arse quite quickly. He didn't really have time to get a taste for it," Barigazzi said.

"He really stood out, did he?"

"He did his bit. More downriver than here. 'Barbisin' was a name that struck terror."

"How did he get on after the war?"

"He went up into the mountains around Brescia for a bit and worked as a driver, the same place he'd been in Mussolini's final days, under the Republic of Salò. When things calmed down, he returned, but he went back to sailing to make sure he stayed well away from the piazzas of the lower Po."

"They had it in for him?"

"Yes, according to the reports I heard. But as I've said, I was still a boy."

"But you joined the party quite young…"

"So what? We didn't care about Tonna. What did it matter to us if somebody went sailing up and down the Po and never found any peace. He didn't even put in here any more. The port in Cremona was all he had left, because one or two of his old colleagues were there. There were a couple of places in Polesine where some farmers who used to be in the Blackshirts would give him half a cargo a week as a favour. He hadn't even enough fuel to keep himself warm in winter. He used to light his stove with bits of rotten wood from the river."

"And how do you treat him now?"

Barigazzi stared at him in surprise, thinking the reply was obvious. "Don't you see? He doesn't speak and neither do we. That way we get along."

"Is there anyone in the village or nearby who has a grudge against him?"

"I've already told you. It's all down to a couple of poor old souls. Who wants to remember? Anyway, everybody's opinion is that he's just an old bastard weighed down by age and regrets, reduced to living out his days by going round in circles on the water. If he's not already dead, he'll die soon with no peace."

"I wasn't talking about politics. I meant, a grudge because of something that might have happened in recent years."

"He had no dealings with anybody. He never exchanged more than twenty words a day."

"Sometimes that can be enough..."

"The only person he spoke to was Maria of the sands," Ghezzi said.

The others glowered at him in a way that seemed to the commissario to convey the dark shadow of a reproach.

"Who's she?"

Once again the most fleeting of eye contact between the men gave Ghezzi authorization to proceed.

"She's a woman of about Tonna's age who has spent most of her life on an island in the Po, digging sand."

"So where does she live now?"

"In Casoni, two kilometres inland," the man said, pointing in a direction which was meant to indicate the plain. "She was the only one, apart from his niece, who made him welcome. And when the Po was high and the island was flooded he paid her back by going and rescuing her possessions."

"Does she manage to live far away from the river?"

"She's paralysed. She couldn't live on her own in the cabin any more. When she was younger, she was a kind of savage who spoke only dialect," Ghezzi said. "Now the island's not there any more. With all the dredging, they diverted the course of the stream and the river ate it up bit by bit."

"Even the Po devours what it has created. Everything is changing all the time. In the party, no more than twenty years ago, they taught us that history is on the march, towards a better future. Now, not only has optimism disappeared, but so has the party. Don't ask me to say that things are getting better. Just like the Po, we're marching towards the filth of some stinking sea," Barigazzi said.

He gulped back the last drops of Fortanina, slammed his bowl noisily down on the table and rose swiftly to his feet. He was on his way out when the other three got up to follow him, in silence.

5

THE MOBILE RANG while the Alfa was travelling through the mists of the lower Po at the speed of a horse-drawn carriage. This time, Angela's voice did no violence to his eardrums, and this of itself was sufficient to put him in a state of alarm.

"You need to keep your finger in the hole in the dyke and can't get away, is that it?"

"I'm doing my level best to get back, but the fog is so thick you could lean your bicycle against it."

"Don't worry. If you do get lost, the worst that could happen is that you'd end up in a fast food joint."

"I'd rather end up in a ditch."

"Don't overdo it."

"I'll content myself with a glass of Fortanina and some *spalla cotta.*"

"Poor thing! They'll hear your tummy rumbling all the way to the Alps. Do you know that Juvara has been searching high and low for you all day?"

"In some areas you can't get a signal. But how did you know that?"

"I was down at the police station. I've been handed a public defence case."

"When will I see you?"

"Forget it, it's almost ten o'clock. I don't like being kept hanging about by men. It's better the other way round. But if you'd asked me earlier…" she teased, leaving the suggestion hanging in the air.

"I was late because I had to question the men at the boat club. Today I went to the barge where I found a note that said something about a partisan. Perhaps that's the key to understanding the motive, but it's all very puzzling."

"I've never been on board a barge. Anyway, if you're in your office tomorrow, I'll see you there."

"Will you be defending anyone I caught?"

"No, calm down. It's a small-time dealer picked up by the drugs squad."

"Just as well."

"Pity. I'd have made you squirm," she said, mischief in her voice.

As soon as Angela was gone, he dialled Juvara's number.

"At long last!" the ispettore exclaimed. "I was about to send a search party along the Po."

Soneri peered into the mist which made it impossible for him to put on any speed. He was afraid he had completely lost his way, not only on the road but in the investigation he was leading. The sensation was heightened as he listened to the words of his assistant: "Nanetti and Alemanni were both looking for you. Nanetti says he has further results from the analysis of the blood found on the windowpane. It doesn't belong to anyone in the ward."

"And Alemanni?"

"I think he was after you for the same reason."

He felt his stomach tighten with the unpleasant sensation of having got it all wrong. He had set off along the Po searching for the ghosts of times past and for a missing man, while in the city that man's brother had unquestionably been a murder victim. "Did you tell them where I was?"

"Yes," Juvara said, with a tremble in his voice.

That tone told him all he needed to know and was in its own way more eloquent than any reproach. He had no wish to go on with the conversation. In annoyance, he pressed the accelerator, but then had to step smartly on the brake when the rear lights of a car suddenly loomed out of the darkness ahead of him.

When he got home, he chose to remain in the half dark in his kitchen, smoking his last cigar, his elbows on the table. Before he fell asleep, with the taste of the Fortanina still in his mouth, he remembered that this was the position often assumed by his father.

Alemanni did not detain him for more than a quarter of an hour. He informed him of the outcome of the tests on the broken window with a degree of pedantry worthy of an infant school teacher, which irritated Soneri, but he refrained at least from making comments on the conduct of the investigation. For his part, Soneri made no reference to the magistrate's earlier scepticism, but on the telephone Nanetti had set out in detail his impressions. The man must have been at least unconscious before being ejected from the window. There was no sign on the windowsill or on the radiator of any struggle, nor were there any fingerprints, a clear indication that he had not grabbed hold of anything or been able to resist. The only sign of any struggle was the indentation on the steel cabinet where there was the imprint of the rubber sole of one of Decimo's shoes. Furthermore, no-one had heard the thud, nor had they noted any unusual coming or going. Soneri was curious about the way the killer had struck the blow and how he had stunned his victim. Everything had gone smoothly until the impact with the windowpane and the sound of breaking glass. Then the escape through the ordinary hospital exit. The murderer was plainly a cold-blooded individual, so much so that he had moved off without conspicuous rush, merging in with patients and visitors.

"Juvara!" he yelled.

The ispettore arrived as the secretaries were putting forms in front of him for his signature.

"Interrogate the patients and the nurses in the wards frequented by Decimo Tonna," he said without raising his eyes from the clerical assistant's index finger as she showed him where his initials were to go. "I want to know all his movements in the last fortnight and anything he was talking about."

He was now in the grip of an unhealthy frenzy, and only somewhat later, in the peace of the half-deserted *Milord*, behind the smoke screen of his own cigar, calmed by the prospect of a plate of *tortelli* stuffed with herbs and *ricotta*, did he come to recognize that his anxiety was the product of curiosity aroused on the banks of the Po and capable of being satisfied only there. He brought to mind the faces of Barigazzi and the others, with that slightly contemptuous look they had. He was already aware of a pressing urge to return when his mobile rang. He hated having it ring in the middle of a meal, but he had forgotten to turn it off. The few other diners, hearing the strained tones of "Aida", turned in mild irritation in his direction. He uttered a peremptory "Hello" to silence it.

"Commissario, I'm in a consulting room at the hospital," Juvara stuttered.

"Have you broken your leg?" Soneri said, finding Juvara's preambles more and more tiresome.

"No, but the nurses on duty are telling me something I can't make sense of…"

"What can you not make sense of?" he said, stuffing a whole *tortello* into his mouth.

"They say that recently Decimo was extremely nervous and would stare suspiciously at everyone who turned up, and that once they saw him rush off when he noticed someone or other walk down the corridor."

"Did you get any idea who that person might have been?"

"No, nobody remembers. It was only a brief appearance."

Juvara's account had distracted his attention from the *tortelli*, and when he turned back to it, the dish had gone cold. He could not bear butter and cheese once they formed into lumps and lost the warmth of soul acquired in the oven.

Alceste stared at the plate as though he had espied a beetle on it. "It's what I always say. The sound of the mobile telephone turns good *ricotta* bad," was all he said.

By this time, Soneri was in a state of agitation. Juvara's report had created for him such a mêlée of competing scenarios that he could have been in a puppeteer's workshop. So as not to give way to mere conjecture, he got up and made his way to the hospital. He found the ispettore perched on a high stool in the canteen.

"When you get down from your roost, they'll take you straight off to the treatment room and case you in plaster," Soneri said, mildly mocking the ispettore's less than agile figure.

"I've been here all morning," Juvara said, "and I haven't broken a single bone yet. But something or someone is breaking my balls."

"It goes with the job. Who else could I annoy if I want to find out about the worries of the townee Tonna?"

"The sister's name is Luisa. She finishes her shift at two."

She was a pleasant woman, solid inside and out. "Was what I told your colleague not enough?" she said with a laugh.

She had received him in the off-duty room, where the odour of disinfectant hung heavy in the air.

"Did he seem anxious recently?"

The sister stared at him a few moments before replying.

"I would have said so, yes."

"What gave you that impression?"

"Normally," she said, "he stayed the whole morning but in the last couple of days he came and went as though in a state of distress. He spoke less than ever."

"Did you form any idea of what was on his mind?"

"I asked around. They told me there was some anniversary, some date looming, but they didn't know what it was for. Not even if that was what was bothering him."

"They didn't tell you anything else?"

"No," the sister said, "I would have preferred to go into it a bit more deeply, but the man who knew most about it died a few days ago."

"Was there any explanation of all that popping in and out several times a day?"

She stretched out her arms. "He would go away then come back. I don't know why. I got the impression he felt someone was pursuing him and that he was keeping on the move all the time so as not to be caught up with."

"Whereas normally, how did he behave?"

"He was much more calm. They'll have told you that he would stay here until the last patient had left, and sometimes he even waited till we were all leaving the consulting rooms and he would go out with us. We would often find him in the waiting room reading magazines, and it would take the cleaning ladies to persuade him it was time to go. The nursing staff thought of him as one of the family."

"What did he talk to the patients about?"

"He comforted them, he listened to them and at times took

a real interest in them, taking advantage of the fact that the doctors all knew him. There are a lot of elderly folk who come here and they never have anyone to talk to, but with Signor Tonna they were quite at ease."

"You say he had an anniversary coming up?"

"So it seems, but it might not have had anything to do with him."

As he took his leave of the sister, the commissario remembered Sartori. He walked along the wards in the direction of the nephrology unit, where he found the man he was looking for half asleep, needles in his arm and the machine buzzing. He appeared even more yellowish and wizened than before, but he turned a tired smile on Soneri.

"Any news?" he said, opening his eyes wide.

"Your friend Decimo didn't throw himself from the window. He was pushed."

Sartori, although plainly moved by the news, did not stir. He lay there in silence, staring at the ceiling.

"Is it true that he's been highly agitated recently? I mean in the last few days," the commissario said, in an attempt to rouse Sartori from his silence.

He watched as the old man moved his head very slightly in a sign of assent. Then, just as Soneri had resigned himself to not receiving an answer, he made out a feeble voice. "Forgive me, but I am deeply troubled."

"Did you know that there was some anniversary coming up for him?"

"He had spoken to me about it, but when I tried to discover more, he found a way, as he always did, of avoiding giving an answer to my questions. He was like that. If he didn't speak of his own accord, there was no way of getting anything out of him."

"What did he tell you about this anniversary?"

"It was plainly not something he was looking forward to. He referred to it with fear. All he told me was that he had received a letter."

"From whom?"

"I don't know. I do know that it had shaken him to the core. He became gloomy. The last time I set eyes on him, he asked if I had noticed any new faces around the ward. I told him that in addition to us long-term cases, there were always new faces in a hospital. I was joking, but he took it the wrong way. He didn't say anything, he went and sat beside the exit, where he could see anyone coming down the corridor."

The following day, Tonna had been defenestrated from the General Medical section on the third floor. Everything pointed to the likelihood that someone, perhaps the murderer, had been tailing him from department to department. Soneri was lost in his own train of thought, heedless of Sartori stretched out on his bed, and when he turned back to him, he found he had drifted off to sleep. He got out of the room just in time to avoid waking him with the triumphal march from "Aida".

"You still away fishing?" Nanetti began.

"You caught me on the hop with that news about the townee Tonna."

"So you're feeling pleased with yourself? What kind of face did Alemanni make?"

"He wanted to bawl me out for having gone searching for the river Tonna, but he had to hold back in case I had something up my sleeve."

"You missed your chance. Never let him get away with a single thing. Anyway, there's something new about the brother who fell out the window."

"What?"

"You remember the dent on the cupboard? Well, I can confirm that it came from one of Tonna's shoes, but it wasn't a strong blow. The steel is only a couple of millimetres thick, so it doesn't take much to leave a mark. Then the wound on the head. The doctor said it was caused by a heavy object, such as a club, but one with a pointed tip. More likely, something metal. Between the blow and the fall from the window, no more than two or three seconds elapsed, which is why there was no blood of Tonna's on the floor or on the windowsill."

"He was being hunted," Soneri said, translating his thoughts into words. "Someone had been following him from department to department. Someone who was very smart and discreet, who managed to remain unobserved by everyone. Perhaps the same person who had delivered to him a letter capable of unnerving him."

"That's your business, Commissario," Nanetti cut in.

A short time later, Soneri dialled Juvara's number. "Have you got Decimo's file to hand? Look up when he was born. Check his brother's dates as well." He heard the ispettore's keyboard click. Juvara's silence was eloquent testimony to his astonishment over the request. "In your opinion, was there some anniversary of Decimo's which could fall on one of the days leading up to his death?"

Juvara sighed, a sign that he had finally understood. "It's not his birthday, that's in September. Not the boatman's either. His is in June."

"I wish we knew what he was talking about…" the commissario muttered.

"The ward sister was able to report only one thing Tonna had said one of the last times he ate in the department, but she had no idea what he was referring to."

"What did he say?"

"They were talking about his health, about how he was the healthy one among all those sick people, but for some reason he took it the wrong way, got all upset, started mumbling that perhaps he would soon be going to 'the angels'. The sister said they all burst out laughing, but later, when she thought about it again, she couldn't make head nor tail of what he had been on about. Was it that all of our lives hang by a thread? Or something else?"

"And that's the only detail she can remember?"

"That's what stuck in her mind. There must be some reason, mustn't there?"

Soneri said nothing for a few moments. "Has Decimo's apartment been sealed off?"

"Yes, but if you want to get in, all you have to do is advise the magistrate."

Decimo Tonna had lived in a block of flats with a faded facade not too far from the hospital. Two rooms and a bathroom, and the all-pervasive smell of rotting food. The coffee pot had been left on the cooker, and the rooms were in a state of some disorder as though Decimo had had to rush off for an appointment. In the bedroom, Soneri's attention was drawn to the photograph of an elderly couple who must have been his parents and of a young woman, perhaps his niece. On the sideboard stood a picture of him as a young man, in a black shirt.

Soneri opened the drawers and started to go through them. One was filled with bills arranged year by year in an elastic band. The second contained pension documents, medical certificates and receipts. The apartment gave off the idea of a life lived barely above subsistence level. And the objects in the apartment, even if conserved with great care, were shabby. The mirrors, grown dark with age, the discoloured table covers, the threadbare curtains and the damp corners of the walls which were now the colour of a mountain hare, all spoke of poverty borne with dignity.

As he was going through the wardrobe, in which he found pairs of knickerbockers and a black shirt, the ringing of his mobile startled him. He ignored it for a while before answering.

"So whose house have you broken into this time?" Angela wanted to know, picking up on the absence of background noise.

"I'm engaged on a house search."

"More likely you're searching up the skirt of some lady, one of those who adore uniforms and men of action."

"I do not have a uniform, nor do I have any love of action."

"There's no doubting that, and no-one knows it better than I do."

"I'm in the house of Decimo Tonna, and I have not the faintest idea what I'm looking for."

"What a coincidence! I'm right downstairs!"

"How did you know I was here?"

"I've always been able to get round Juvara. Anyway, I'm coming up to join you."

The news caused him no little anxiety, in part caused by the fear of breaking regulations and in part by the arousal of desire. When Angela appeared before him a few moments later, it was the second which prevailed, and overwhelmingly. She tossed her coat on to a chair with studied nonchalance, approached Soneri and took hold of his collar. In her face, the commissario saw the same excitement which he too felt as he came into contact with his partner's body.

"Where?" he said, his imagination telling him where it would all end.

"In the living room. I don't trust sheets that other people have slept in," she said, casting a glance at the bed in the room they were in.

*

Soneri got to his feet feeling a little bruised. The excitement had passed, leaving him so relaxed and yielding that it required an effort to recapture the thoughts that had been in his mind before Angela made her appearance. It was she who brought him back to the investigation once they had their clothes on again, "Have you really no idea what you're looking for?"

"No," he said, combing his hair. "Maybe a letter containing some kind of threat."

"A recent threat?"

"I believe so, judging from Decimo's anxiety in his last couple of days."

Together they went over every piece of paper in the sideboard. They searched the clothes which seemed to have been worn in the recent past, examined a dressing gown left hanging behind the bedroom door, but they failed to turn up anything of any interest. They went back to the living room and it occurred to Soneri that if Alemanni had had any idea he was in Decimo's house with a woman, he would have mobilized every policeman in the city.

"There's nothing here," he said with unconcealed irritation, sticking the burned-out cigar back in his mouth.

"Either there's nothing here or else the thing we are looking for has been left in such an obvious place that it hasn't occurred to us to look there," Angela said.

He sat down, leaning his elbows on the table and remembered doing the same thing the previous evening in the half-light of his own kitchen. As he grew older, he tended to resemble his father more and more, a thought which made him more mellow. With a touch of nostalgia, he recalled getting up before sunrise on dark mornings in winter to do his homework, and his father greeting him as he picked up his wallet from the porcelain dish on the top of the fridge. He remembered that dish perfectly. It had a picture of the Mole

Antonelliana in Turin on it, and was always full of papers. There was a porcelain dish on the fridge in Decimo Tonna's house too. In it, along with laundry receipts and bus tickets, he found an envelope without stamp or address but which had been torn roughly open and had the words "Decimo Tonna" scrawled on it in blue ink. He opened it and found a sheet of lined paper taken out of a notebook: "57th anniversary", and underneath, "San Pellegrino section, square E, 3rd row, number 32."

"Would you feel threatened by a note like this?" Angela wondered aloud.

He had no idea how to reply. The two phrases belonged to a code he could not break, but the reference to the anniversary was unequivocal.

"The Tonna brothers were the object of virulent hatred by many people."

"Because—" But she could not finish the sentence before he interrupted her.

"Yes, they were Fascists. The boatman in particular must have been involved in some really nasty business down the valley. But these are old stories..."

"Well, all these things can hardly be considered faults nowadays, seeing that 'that lot' are back in power."

"Memory is not completely dead. Along the Po some species survive that are long extinct everywhere else," Soneri said with bitter irony.

After seeing Angela out, he thought again of the river and the flood. Perhaps the water had now gone down far enough to reveal the rims of the embankments over the floodplain. The case still seemed to him most amenable to solution if it were approached from the riverbanks, always provided that the killing of Decimo and the disappearance of Anteo were linked. But might they not be? He could not fathom Decimo.

It seemed that his life had been enclosed in an impenetrable shell. None of his neighbours had had any relationship with him beyond casual greetings. No-one ever stopped to exchange two words with him at a street corner. He did not drop into bars. Decimo's day consisted of getting up early in the morning, leaving the house and making his way to the hospital where he would spend the whole day talking to patients, moving from one ward to another. He was given lunch and dinner by the orderlies, who were so used to seeing him around that they regarded him as a relative or a carer. Every evening he went home where he shut himself away in his gloomy apartment. That was his life, year after year, ever since he had returned from abroad. It might be that in this way he had sought to conceal his very existence. In the hospital, where people think only of present illness and future uncertainty, he had found himself so much at ease that he had come to consider it his real home. He had been a man on the run long before the delivery of that note which had seemed to him like a death sentence. Or perhaps he was fleeing only from that message? The oddest thing was that it had come to him at a point when life would soon in any case be presenting him with the final reckoning.

In the police station, Juvara looked long and hard at the sheet of lined paper. "San Pellegrino section... sounds like a graveyard. Considering how he ended up, and the various threats..."

Soneri had had the same impression. But which graveyard? The mystery surrounding the brothers seemed as inscrutable as ever. Hardened by years on the run, they gave the impression of having raised a drawbridge on the outside world, one sailing the Po in solitude, the other choosing to live among aged, suffering humanity.

The telephone rang. "Commissario, it's Maresciallo Aricò. He wants a word with you," Juvara said, covering the mouthpiece with his hand.

Soneri nodded, pointing to his own telephone.

"Commissario, when will the forensic squad be down to examine the barge? I can't keep a patrol tied up day and night."

"Aren't your colleagues in Luzzara attending to it?"

"Now that the water is dropping, they've palmed it off on to me. There's been a robbery at Luzzara and they've got their hands full."

"Be patient for a couple of hours," Soneri said. "Any news?"

"Your good friends the communists have moved back into the boat club to clean up their flooded premises."

"They're not my friends," he said, annoyed at the maresciallo's laboured irony. "And I don't care if they are communists."

"A bunch of hotheads. It's only age that has calmed them down a bit, but they're as pig-headed as ever."

"They're all the same along the Po valley, otherwise the river would have carried them away like sand."

When he hung up, he felt a sense of relief. Aricò had given him the perfect excuse for going back to the places and people who most aroused his curiosity. He felt like a fisherman dozing on a boat yawing in the slow current, waiting for a tug on the line to shake him from his torpor, make him swing into action.

"I'm taking you out today, to Luzzara. We'll have a look at the barge," he told Nanetti.

"Just you and me on a boat," Nanetti said. "Like a honeymoon."

"And the carabinieri on the walkway to protect our intimacy."

"If it's all the same with you, I'll send along two of my men. I'm not keen on going to a place which is even wetter than this city."

"No, I want you and nobody else."

He heard Nanetti groan. His joints would play up for a week.

Half an hour later, Soneri presented himself to the officer standing guard on the barge. As he came through the town, he had noticed that the water level had dropped and even that Tonna's boat seemed to have sunk down behind the main embankment. The gangplank sloped steeply now towards the deck, though the sides of the floodplain had not yet emerged from the muddy waters. Inside, he found the light unchanged and thought to himself that the seasons, the sun and the mists, would remain forever excluded from this cabin and would never make any impact on the heavy atmosphere of gloomy solitude. His attention was once again drawn to the little wooden chest of drawers where Tonna kept his documents. He looked again at the dates of the sailings and at the cargoes of goods apparently transported up and down the river. The hold should have been packed with grain for the mills at Polesella, but he knew already that it was empty. He would in any case have had no trouble in working that out from the draught. He went back on to the deck and saw the young carabiniere standing in the mud of the embankment, smoking. He opened one of the hatch covers over the hold and switched on his torch. There was a ladder in the corner but something about it made it less than inviting. He made his reluctant descent into what seemed to him no more than a rat trap, being careful to lift the wooden ladder and jam it in the opening to stop the cover slamming shut. The moment he made a move inside that hole, he was assaulted by a dense, nauseating stench of sweaty armpits and groins, of damp and dirty clothes and of the breath of starving people. In one corner, there was a pile of rags and newspaper pages. Tonna had not been carrying grain. In that dank, airless hole it was impossible not to feel the presence of the multitudes who had been conveyed in it. Their breath had remained trapped inside.

Soneri put the ladder back in its place and clambered up again, closing the cover behind him. He went into the cabin and opened the log book once more. Tonna had made many voyages, but he had not carried the cargoes entered in that register, and yet, in an old box, the bills of lading with the description of the goods in question had been meticulously recorded. A minimum of four sailings a week between Cremona and the area around Rovigo. On the other hand, if he had not sailed as recorded, how could he have met the running costs of the barge whose engine swallowed litres and litres of fuel as it struggled upstream against the current? An accountant's punctiliousness was evident in Tonna's handwritten ledgers. Each purchase of fuel was listed in neat handwriting and on each occasion the sums appeared considerable.

He heard the unmistakeable, irregular footsteps of Nanetti as he paced about on the deck. It sounded like a rhythmless drip-drip from a branch shaken in the wind.

"That's it. You're not getting me on that gangplank a second time," he said.

"I'm sure once will always be good enough for you."

His colleague stared at him with good-humoured pique. "In this mess, I'd be hard put to find anything," he said, staring about him in disgust.

"Above all, check the hold," Soneri advised. "I've got an idea this barge was the least comfortable cruise ship ever seen on sea or river."

Nanetti studied him attentively, and from that look it was clear he had understood. "How do you get into the hold?"

The commissario came back on deck to guide him and as soon as Nanetti saw the hatch, he grimaced and threw back his head like a horse refusing a fence. "Now I'm sure of it. You really do want to see me spend my old age in a wheelchair."

Soneri helped him down a ladder that was fit only for a chicken hutch, but did not venture beyond the hatch. As soon as he saw his colleague get to work, he felt boredom come over him. "I'll leave you in the capable hands of the carabiniere," he called down.

A voice rang out from the depths: "You're a treacherous bastard. That man will lock me in and slip the mooring."

Soneri recommended Nanetti to the care of the officer on guard, and made his own way to the town. The road turned away from the embankment at certain points and cut inland between flooded fields. When he came in sight of the bell tower, a blue sign indicated the way to the Casoni residence. Instinctively he turned off the road, taking him further from the embankment. He had remembered about Maria of the sands.

There were no more than seven houses and one very grand building, which stood surrounded by trees and was higher than the bridge at Roccabianca. He entered the lobby and stood there a few moments looking around as various nurses came and went with trolleys which gave off a vague scent of camomile. "I'm Commissario Soneri, Parma police. I'm looking for Maria of the sands..."

"Who?" the nurse said, straining to make out what he was saying.

"I'm afraid I don't know her full name. I've been told that you have here a woman who used to live on an island and who answers to that name."

"Must be Signora Grignaffini," said the woman. "She's the only Maria here."

"Probably her, then."

"And you would like to speak to her?"

"I would, but if she is resting, I can come back."

The nurse gave a laugh. "She only speaks Mantuan dialect. But the woman in the bed next to her can translate, if she chooses to. She's half mad."

"Don't worry. I understand the dialect perfectly."

Maria of the sands was an old woman of forbidding appearance, overweight, surly and sullen, with long, dishevelled hair that had turned as grey as the dry sand of the Po. She could still have been on her island peering at boats passing on the horizon, apprehensive lest they attempt to moor there. The nurse went over to her and informed her that Soneri was a police officer. She spoke in dialect, but Maria seemed to pay no heed, so intently was her gaze fixed on the commissario.

"You've got her on a good day. If she hadn't wanted to talk to you, she would have already turned away."

Soneri pulled up a chair and sat facing the woman, who greeted him with a respectful but wary nod. It was clear she had spent her whole life in a little homeland of her own which had been continually invaded and finally swept away by the dredgers.

"I can understand your dialect. It's very like mine," the commissario said, inviting her to speak freely.

"So you're not a southerner?" she said, in the harsh intonation of the people of the Po.

Soneri shook his head.

"What do you want to know? In all my life, I've seen only boats and water."

"Did you know that Anteo has disappeared?"

"They told me."

"You knew him well. Do you have any idea what might have become of him?"

"He'll have fled in the direction of Brescia, same as after the war. Those communist dogs..."

"Who?"

The old woman looked up, her look filled with pride and hatred. "The ones that were in the partisans. A lot of them died, as God willed. Others got away after 1946, but before that they did all kinds of things."

"Are any of them still here?"

Maria made an affirmative sign with her hand. "Barigazzi stayed on, and it was him that brought along that gang of Reds. Twice they burned down my cabin, but the carabinieri didn't want to know. They know the Po well, and they know the right doors to knock all along the riverbanks." Maria's breasts were heaving with rage. In spite of her years, a savage force emanated from that body made almost masculine by labour.

"Barigazzi says that in the days of Mussolini he was only a boy."

"He was sixteen and went around with a pistol. It was him who killed Bardoni so as to take his boat which was moored at Stagno. Everybody knows that."

"So how did Anteo get away?"

"I've told you. For a couple of years he was in Val Camonica."

"And later?"

"Fortunately the waters calmed down, but he was always on the alert. He sailed by night and slept by day."

"Was there some particular reason why they had it in for him?"

"When you're talking about a war, there is always a reason for hating. The Fascists did their round-ups, and the other side ran off like rabbits, but then they struck back treacherously." The woman grew more embittered as she spoke.

"As far as you remember, did Tonna take part in the reprisals?"

"How should I know? I spent years on my island, never moving off it. Only the floods could make me leave. The world is so evil, it's better to stay huddled in a corner."

"Why did Anteo come to see you?"

Only after speaking these words did Soneri realize that he had touched a very private nerve.

The old woman bridled, but immediately pulled herself together. "Neither of us spoke very much, but we were always in agreement. During the day, while he was asleep, I kept watch. He trusted me, especially since we were on an island in the middle of the Po."

"So he felt threatened, even in recent times?"

"I told him to trust nobody, but he always said the world had changed. He even started going to the club that Barigazzi went to, saying that it was time to draw a line under the past. He said we were all poor old folk who should be getting ready to leave everything behind, and that we should toss all our grudges into the Po. He came to see me whenever he could and always asked me to come with him on his barge. I told him that at his age he should be thinking of moving on to dry land. So, together... but he was not happy with his feet on the ground, he preferred to be afloat. He used to say that the years he had spent in the mountains had been harder for him than the war, because he had had to live between rocks and peaks. That was one of the reasons he came to see me on my island. The only kind of land he could put up with was land surrounded by water."

"You could have made a new life for yourselves somewhere near the sea."

"We thought about that, but he was not fond of water with no flow, or water that battered against the walls. He wanted the reliable water of the river, water that knows where it's going. He even had a plan for restructuring his barge and making it into a house where we could live when it wasn't possible to live at my place. But then they came and even swept away the island, so here I am now and I don't know where he is."

"Who destroyed the island?"

"The people in the co-operative. The communists," she said, almost spitting.

"Did they attack with the dredgers?"

"There was no need to attack. All they had to do was modify the course of the stream so as to make it erode the island. It disappeared under my feet, metre by metre. The co-operative knew what it was doing alright. They had their ways and means of obtaining a licence to dredge sand in a place that could only ever give them a return of half of what they'd spent. They paid a fortune just to get rid of the island. When finally I had to leave, they were all lined up along the embankment celebrating. As I went by, they were chanting 'Bandiera Rossa', and they'd hung a real red banner from the jib of the dredger."

The old woman had turned livid and her skin had taken on the colour of silt. The patient in the next bed looked at her in fear and began to scream. Two male nurses took hold of her by her arms, while Maria cast a glance of pure contempt in her direction. It was obvious that she would have gladly struck her across the face. Immediately afterwards, Soneri found himself the object of equally harsh looks from the two men in white coats. He went up to Maria, patted her gently on the back and made his way out.

6

ONCE AGAIN THE strains of "Aida". Even before Nanetti could begin speaking, Soneri heard his laboured breath.

"Have you been swimming across the Po?"

"To get me back on to the embankment across that gangway, they had to call out an extra patrol. We're going down big with the carabinieri!"

"Don't you worry. You're not known as a man of action, but you do represent the intellectual branch of the inquiry."

"You could spare me these little jibes. You make me feel ready for a care home."

"What did you make of the barge?"

"There was all kinds of rubbish in the hold. There must have been a whole army of poor buggers down there. Including children."

"Tonna was not transporting grain of any kind – or anything else. His cargo was illegal immigrants," the commissario said.

"Got any proof?" Nanetti said with his usual scientific punctiliousness.

"No, but it seems quite clear to me. He went up and down from the mouth of the river using as cover bills of lading drawn up by some compliant wholesale merchant. Officially he was transporting grain, but in fact he was carrying people who had to be kept out of sight. The ideal cover, the more you think about it: from the Adriatic, where the ships dock, to the industrial heart of the country where it is much easier to get fixed up. The whole thing done by a mode of transport which is much less risky than lorries or trains. No-one checks anything on the Po."

"He'd found a way of living and maintaining his barge," Nanetti said. "I've also made some other discoveries which I'll tell you about later."

As he put his mobile back in his pocket, Soneri wondered what the trafficking in illegal immigrants had to do with the disappearance of Tonna. He was still gathering information about him and his life without managing to make headway over where he was or who had killed his brother. He walked over to the embankment. Now that the floods had subsided and the Po was growing less turbulent day by day and settling back into its own riverbed, gangs of workmen were removing the sandbags.

The boat club was as feverish as a building site. Ghezzi, Vernizzi and Torelli were hard at work carrying buckets back and forth, while Barigazzi stood leaning on a shovel, observing the river. Soneri came up behind him, catching him unawares. "I bet that once you would have seen me when I was still on the embankment."

The old man turned round, his expression a mixture of anger and apprehension. "Why do you have to rub salt in the wound? I'm still lucid enough to know that the years are catching up on me."

"It's only lack of exercise," Soneri said in an attempt to play things down. "There are no more threats now."

Barigazzi looked at him in puzzlement and from his eyes the commissario understood that he considered him a threat.

"The floodplain's not really visible yet," he said, changing subject.

"You're wrong there," Barigazzi said, pointing to a longitudinal wrinkle across the current. "The floodplain is no more than half a metre under."

"So tomorrow it will appear and part the waters," Soneri ventured.

"Some time tonight, around four o'clock. The level of the water is dropping by nearly ten centimetres an hour. The cold reduces it."

"How long will it take for the floodplain to dry out?"

"If they get the water pumps started up to drain the water from the houses, it should take less than a week, but it'll be springtime before they're really dry. Otherwise, we'd need about a month of freezing weather," Barigazzi said, continuing to look out over the slow-moving current.

"You've already cleaned up your club, I see."

"Almost. The walls are still soaking and we'll have to wait for the air to do its work for us. Unfortunately," he said, pointing into the distance towards the bank on the Lombard side, "the *fumara*, the mist, is drawing in."

The sky over the river appeared swollen and the air heavy. Barigazzi, with one hand still on the handle of the shovel, seemed to be waiting for the mist to arrive, an event which had occurred thousands of times, but which had not lost its power to surprise.

"I'd like to know where it's born," Soneri said.

"Everywhere and nowhere, like those of us who move in the heart of it."

The faint autumn sun clouded over, making it possible to stare at it directly. The river blended with the sky, as does the winter snow on the hills, and it was at that moment that a long, dark shape made its appearance, forcing its way upstream and beginning the slow manoeuvre of mooring. As it passed in front of them, a solid stretch of bank concealed its outlines. The engine spluttered quietly with a noise similar to cooking *polenta*.

"He's mooring against the current," Barigazzi told him, answering a quizzical gesture the commissario had made with his chin. "He'll go a bit further up and then manoeuvre sideways into the port."

After a few minutes, with the movements of some lazy, languid fish, Tonna's barge began slowly to turn, showing its side. Finally it made its approach crabwise until the hull came to rest against the cushion of old tyres hanging from the coping stones. Two men emerged from the cabin, threw the hawsers on to the land, disembarked and made them fast to the iron rings.

"The final journey," Soneri suggested.

Barigazzi's glance was eloquent, but he said nothing.

"Who are they?" asked the commissario, pointing to the boatmen.

"People from Luzzara," Barigazzi said evasively. "And they know their business. A perfect bit of manoeuvring. Tonna himself couldn't have done better."

It began to get dark, and Gianna appeared at the door of the club.

"I'll see you at the bar, in *Il Sordo*," Soneri said as he turned to go, seeming to confirm a previously made appointment. Barigazzi did not move or utter a word, but he raised his free hand in assent.

Smoking his cigar, the commissario passed along the colonnades in the town. The offices of the carabinieri were wrapped in mist, but on the first floor he saw a light burning at the maresciallo's window. The guard at the door showed him into the two duty rooms, heavy with the smell of reheated minestrone. Aricò was chilled to the bone and cursed the mist and the Po, while every so often the radio transmitted some communications from the radio car.

"They've brought the barge into the port," the commissario said.

"So that's that, then. Thank God!"

Soneri would have liked to tell him that it was his duty to investigate the disappearance of Anteo, but he held himself back because Aricò's lack of interest afforded him more liberty of movement.

"Any news?"

"None," the maresciallo said in his nasal voice. "I'm afraid he's come to a bad end."

"I never believed he'd simply fled."

Aricò sighed deeply. "Neither did I."

"Do you have any idea what Tonna carried in his various cruises up and down the river?"

Aricò was plainly taken aback. "Grain and various other assorted goods. The barge was not equipped for containers."

"That was not all."

"And what else, then?"

"Have you ever heard word of illegal immigrants being landed along the river?"

"Not around here. Near Cremona and Piacenza perhaps."

"Did you ever check up on Tonna?"

"What was there to check up on? An old man with a barge that had seen better days?" the maresciallo protested. He had taken Soneri's questions as a criticism. "Do you really think he put in here with a crowd of people in the hold? He would have disembarked them further down, wouldn't he? Certainly not at a landing stage."

"I'm only asking you to make inquiries with your colleagues in the stations along the Po. You do understand, Aricò,"

Soneri said, drawing close to the other as though in complicity, "this is a nasty business, and I wouldn't rule out the possibility that the motive may be found here... seeing as we're both convinced he didn't run off."

The maresciallo, reassured, was still nodding his head as the commissario left his office. A few seconds later, as he was crossing the mist-covered town, he went over that hypothesis in his mind and felt it crumble away bit by bit. He didn't know why, but something about it did not convince him. Principally, he didn't understand what Decimo could have had to do with the whole business.

The niece was behind the bar as usual. She had the familiar, slightly down-at-heel look of middle-aged women who have let themselves go. Her clinging skirt drew attention to her broad, flabby, matronly hips, while her hair would have required bleaching if it was ever again to be viewed as blonde. She came over to the commissario, placing her folded arms on the bar as though she were leaning out of a window. The gesture caused her to push up her breasts, making them bulge out of her low-cut blouse. Soneri could not avoid looking at her. In spite of everything, she gave the impression of a woman in the rude health of a mare.

"I would like to talk to you about that phone call."

She stared at him vacuously.

"I mean the one from the guy who was looking for your uncle, Barbisin."

Something seemed to light up in her face: a faint, vague light. "I don't know anything apart from what I've already told you."

"When he came off the boat, did he just bring you his dirty clothes to wash or did he spend time in the town?"

"Recently he would be here for a couple of hours."

"Would he drop in to the bar to see you?"

"No, absolutely not. He never set foot in here. He would come to my house."

"And then?"

"He would always arrive very early in the morning. No problem for me, I get up early to open the bar. We would have breakfast together, then he would go off for a walk."

"Where?"

"Oh, I don't know... Towards the oratory of San Matteo along the embankment."

"Why there?"

"Old people are generally fond of the places they used to go to when they were young. Our family contributed to the restoration of the oratory and once, when there were more people here than there are now, they used to say mass for this quarter of the town."

"Was the oratory the only place he went?"

"Sometimes he would visit Don Firmino in the parish house."

"Was he very religious?"

"He became so as he grew older. I couldn't tell you why," the woman said as though this fact was somehow inconvenient.

"Did you notice anything else about this change? I mean, something he said, some change in his behaviour that might have explained the reasons, the motives behind it?"

As he put the question, he saw Claretta looking at him with a kind of irritated bewilderment. He found himself staring into an obtuse face, and there seemed no way of making any headway with her. They stood saying nothing, looking at each other for a while, until some young people who had arrived in a large, black B.M.W. came into the bar.

Even later, as he walked under the colonnade in the direction of the parish house, the commissario continued to see in his mind's eye that obtuse expression. It was the disorientation of a person used to thinking only in material terms, who quite suddenly finds herself obliged to deal with an abstraction, with something which has no weight, no shape, and no price.

As he stood face to face with Don Firmino, he would have liked to explain in detail what was on his mind, but he remembered he was a police officer. The priest, on the other hand, had the combative air of someone brought up in the days when the Reds would do anything to make his life difficult. He was a chubby man, but his hands betrayed someone more accustomed to handling a spade than an aspersorium.

"I'm very worried about Anteo," he said. "Disappearing in the Po valley is simply impossible. Only the river can keep you hidden, but it nearly always gives back what it has taken."

"So there's nothing for it but to wait?"

"I don't know about that," Don Firmino said quickly. "I'm going on intuition."

"Unfortunately, that's all I can do too," Soneri said. "I came to you hoping that you could help me to understand."

"I don't know if I can help you in any way."

"Lately, Anteo came to see you quite often, is that not so?"

The priest drew himself upright, assuming a solemn pose, but all he said was, "Yes."

"The impression I am getting is not of a particularly devout man. What was it that encouraged him to come back to the Church?"

"There's always a moment when we become aware that it's time to draw a line under things, to make your final reckoning. It's my belief that that moment had arrived even for Anteo.

He came to see me the first time in May. I was surprised, but I felt the joy that only a priest can feel when he sees someone return to the Church."

"Did he feel death was near?"

"It would be only natural if he felt that way. He was about eighty. But that doesn't matter. Have you any idea how many people die without having faced the need for repentance?"

"Did he repent the life he had led?"

"That, among other things. Anyone who has been through a war inevitably will carry on his shoulders a weight which sooner or later he will look to shed. And when your strength begins to diminish... No-one emerged unscathed from the times he had had to live through..."

"Tonna was a Fascist, an activist, a Blackshirt..."

Don Firmino sighed deeply. "Don't delude yourself that the other side..."

"But he's the one who has disappeared."

"I understand your curiosity, but what does the past have to do with it? More than fifty years have gone by."

"As I told you, I'm working only on suppositions. There's a lot to be taken into account."

"He did have some sense of remorse, that is true," the priest said hesitantly, as though that sentence had been dragged from somewhere deep inside him.

"What for?"

Don Firmino gave another sigh before looking at a point halfway up the wall where a crucifix was hanging. "For having been a member of a corps notorious for its atrocities. Once he spoke to me about burning down a house, but I don't know what he was referring to. Maybe it was an act of reprisal, or perhaps a punitive expedition. There were many partisans in these parts."

Soneri thought of the many fires he had seen in his years

with the police force. The crackle of the flames, the floors collapsing suddenly after being weakened by the heat and the windows exploding like eyes pulled out of their sockets. A burning house is an insult to memory. "Do you remember where the house was?"

Don Firmino raised his eyebrows. "No, he never told me."

"Is that the only grave matter he ever spoke to you about?"

"In general, he felt guilty for the outrages which had been committed around here by the Blackshirts."

They sat facing each other in silence in the low-beamed room where the parish priest received the faithful on Saturday afternoons. At a certain point, Don Firmino removed his *biretta* to reveal a head almost totally bald and as pale as the underside of a snake. For some seconds his few remaining hairs seemed to move about in agitation. After smoothing them with one hand, the priest threw his hat into a corner of the sofa.

"Was he preparing for death?" the commissario insisted.

Don Firmino spread out his arms: "There are many old people here, but none of them behaved like him. Those who came to church when they were young have continued to come, but those who never set foot across its threshold have not changed."

"Do you think someone was pursuing him for certain things which had happened in the past?"

Once again the priest revealed himself incapable of replying. "I do understand your curiosity, but it is different from mine. What I was looking for was something inner, while you are looking for something external."

"Sometimes it's necessary to look inside to understand what is going on outside."

"I can tell you that Anteo was very troubled, but he had found the path to peace. In the last few weeks he had seemed to me much more serene than usual. He told me he would give up sailing and that the barge would become his home once he had restored it. He liked the idea of a house-boat, like the ones he had seen in Amsterdam. It also seemed to him a good compromise. He would give up spending whole nights at the tiller, but he would not abandon the water and his barge."

"Did he ever speak to you about Maria?"

"He was a widower and he tried to make a new life for himself. However, neither he nor she were really the marrying kind. Both of them preferred to go their own way, like cats."

"Did he ever refer to a telephone call? Somebody who was searching for him, using the nickname he had had in his Fascist days?"

"Yes, he did mention that to me."

"Was he agitated about this?"

"No, he had attained a state of serenity. He felt that his life was drawing to a close. Once he even confessed to me that he was at an age when it was possible to die without recriminations."

"But did you get the impression that he was treating the telephone call as a threat?"

"No," the priest said. "In my opinion, he knew exactly who was looking for him. He might even have thought that the person wanted to harm him, but he was ready for anything. He seemed uninterested in any kind of precaution because he had abandoned himself completely to the will of God."

An elderly woman appeared at the door behind the priest and observed the commissario with a certain distrust, turning her face slightly away from him. Soneri supposed that, apart from being displeased with unannounced visits, she did not care for the smell of cigar smoke.

"It's time for the catechism class," Don Firmino murmured wearily.

The commissario bade him farewell and took his leave.

He chose a roundabout route. He walked towards the embankment through an area some distance from the houses with their tidy gardens, lined up one alongside the other like a chessboard. An icy breeze accompanied the mist, pushing it upstream. Soneri turned onto a track which led to the road alongside the dyke. The river was entirely shrouded by a blanket of greyness which took on even darker colours among the poplar trees which stood in water up to the level of their branches.

He lit a cigar, and as he began to walk back towards the town his thoughts turned to Anteo as he had been described by Don Firmino: serene and at peace after a life on the run. Who could say if the transport of illegal immigrants had been intended to finance the rebuilding of his barge, to make it into a home where he could settle? Not even the telephone call had troubled him – at least in the priest's opinion – and yet it appeared to be the only unforeseen element in an old age filled with guilt which he was striving to expiate on the benches of the church, head bowed, in sight of a statue of San Giovanni encircled by lighted candles, or in meetings with Don Firmino for confessions face-to-face or for conversations of half an hour, an hour, or more. He could not imagine Tonna talking very much. Perhaps it was the priest who took the lead.

He came in sight of the first houses in the town, all huddled under the embankment. From somewhere beyond the stone-crushing plant, he thought he could make out the rhythmic swish of oars. He stopped to listen and picked up the sound more clearly: a boat was moving among the poplars, between

the large embankment and the floodplain which was now beginning to emerge here and there, making the waters even
more lifeless on this side. He tried to see more clearly. He
turned back across grass flattened by sandbags where, away
from the sun, patches on the ground as white as onions had
begun to appear. The noise of the eddying water could be
heard more distinctly. He crouched in the undergrowth and
waited until he thought he could sense something emerging
from the shadows. A figure was rowing a small boat, standing upright, using one oar in the style of a gondolier, passing
through the poplars at the level of the branches. One stroke to
propel the craft forward and then a long pause: it might have
been a hunter, but this was not the hunting season. The commissario rose a little to lessen the pressure on his legs but at
that moment a pheasant took flight noisily from the river side
of the dyke, screeching as it flew low over the water.

The boatman took another couple of strokes, pushing the
boat in the direction of a wide inlet and carrying himself out
of sight. Soneri waited, attempting to work out the direction
the boatman had taken, but he did not hear anything more.
He had disappeared into the mist and must have been sculling his oar astern under the water, like a fin. He must have
positioned the boat so that he could take advantage of the
current, patiently allowing himself to be pulled along by it.
The commissario would have given anything to be able to
swim after him.

Soneri arrived at the jetty. He saw both the little pennant
over the boat club waving once more in the wind and the
beacon-lamp facing into the thick, swirling mist. The temperature had dropped still further and it was beginning to freeze.
He was fastening up his duffel coat when he heard the strains
of "Aida" from one of his pockets.

"Your good friend Alemanni is telling everyone in the

prosecutor's office that you're getting nowhere," were the words with which Angela assailed him.

The magistrate's name caused him to shiver more than did the icy breeze blowing along the embankment. "He's got it in for me because I proved that Decimo's death was no suicide."

"He's gone and leaked something to the newspapers too, and they're all saying that the investigation is in a blind alley."

Soneri let out something like a roar and cursed himself for not having been the first to go to the press with the story of the murder. He regretted having done anything to spare the magistrate's blushes. Grinding his teeth, he swore under his breath.

"Calm down," Angela said. "In a few months the *presidente del tribunale* will pension him off and allow him to live out his days in his club. They won't even trust him with the most straightforward inquiry. The Tonna case will be his last," she said. Soneri bitterly regretted his ill luck. "Anyway, get ready: One of these days I'm going to drop in on you. So work out how you're going to welcome me. I'm already fed up with the Po valley, and if I make the effort to come, I won't be best pleased if I end up being let down. That barge..."

"It's right in front of a very busy boat club."

"You're a commissario, are you not? So it's up to you to find the solution."

He would have been delighted to. Not the solution to the problem of taking Angela below deck on the barge, thereby gifting her the excitement of making love in an unusual place, but to the dilemma of discovering who was the solitary boatman on the waterway and what he was up to. The man had been at risk of being intercepted by the carabinieri, who were keeping an eye on the flooded houses beyond the embankment, but then, with that mist, they would never have caught a boatman skilled in the ways of the Po, not even with a speedboat.

He felt uneasy, and as night spread over the valley already darkened by the mist he was nagged by the thought of another day gone by with nothing to show for it. He was beginning to wonder whether the doubts insinuated here and there in the columns of the newspapers could at any moment be transformed into headlines. He could already picture Alemanni in triumph, foaming at the mouth, his vengeance complete as he resigned from the profession with a sensational parting shot.

His ill humour was still on him when he arrived under the colonnades, and did not leave him even when he was at the door of *Il Sordo*. Hunger had been gnawing at him for some hours, so the usual plate of *spalla cotta* and glass of Fortanina were not now likely to be sufficient. There were only a few customers, and a muted "Otello" seemed to be rising from the darkness of the cellar.

He sat down in front of the cross-legged Christ and placed his elbows on the table, bowing his head slightly in a posture which appeared almost devout. The hazy image of the boatman was still in his mind, and so caught up was he that he did not hear the deaf landlord come up beside him. He looked up at him. His rolled-up sleeves exposed enormous, hairy forearms and he was wearing a waistcoat which could scarcely contain his paunch. His face was dominated by his big lips and by a look which seemed to give off a kind of mysterious malevolence. That evening too he had his hearing aid switched off. Soneri picked up the menu and pointed to the *pasta con fagioli*.

By the time Barigazzi arrived, almost all the tables were filled with people playing cards. The old man still had his working boots on as well as the heavy-duty overalls worn by dockers. "Good choice," he complimented Soneri, pointing to his dish.

"I have a good nose for food. Better than for investigations."

"You need patience," the old man consoled him. "It's a rare gift. Everybody's in such a rush nowadays."

"If only it were a question of patience and nothing else… Here you all are, convinced that the game's up for Tonna, but no-one can say how or why."

"Do you believe there is any other solution?"

"Possibly not. But someone knows something and is saying nothing."

"Tonna didn't have many friends in the village… Nobody got close to him."

"Except for Don Firmino and Maria of the sands. She's outraged with you lot," Soneri said. "Because you took away her island."

"Do you think we don't know! Her beloved little island!" Barigazzi said in a rasping voice. "She was a Fascist spy and had two villagers shot. And that wasn't all. She started spying on people who went up and down the Po. We should have drowned her," he said, making a signal to the landlord with his thick thumb.

"Whose house was it that the Fascists torched?"

Barigazzi stared at him, pushing his hat back on his head. "Nothing was torched on this side," he said at last.

"And on the Lombard side?"

"I have no idea. You don't concern yourself with fires when there's a river in between."

He raised a glass of Lambrusco which was as dark as black pudding. The commissario did the same, and when both had put their glasses down, he said: "Have there been any robberies in the flooded houses?"

"We'll find out when the river level drops, but I don't think there's much to steal around here."

"This evening I saw a boat among the poplars, in the inlet beyond the stone-crushing plant."

Barigazzi assumed a puzzled expression, and noticing Soneri staring hard at him he made an effort to appear calm. "Obviously somebody is still out hunting. After a flood, the embankments swarm with insects which attract pheasants and grouse."

"There was one pheasant, but the hunter made off as soon as I caused it to get up."

Barigazzi said nothing, then changed the subject: "What did that savage tell you?" he said, meaning Maria.

"She said that, through the co-operative, you obtained licences to dig up the sand deliberately so as to shift the course of the water, so that it would erode her island. And that when she was forced off the little land she had, you made her walk in front of you while you chanted 'Bandiera Rossa'."

"Those were memorable moments, like when we shaved her head after the war," Barigazzi exulted, evidently still bent on revenge.

"Did she and Anteo live as man and wife?"

"Two Fascist bastards, and she the worst of the two."

Someone had turned up the volume of "Otello", which occasionally drowned out the hubbub in the room.

"I don't believe it was a hunter," Soneri said, returning to the subject which was foremost in his mind.

"Who do you think would be going down to the floodplain in the dark in this season?" Barigazzi said. "It could have been someone going back to see their house. There are some people who tie their boats to the bars on the window and move upstairs. The water didn't get that high."

"He wouldn't have made off."

The old man sat a moment in thought. The wine glass seemed to disappear inside his huge oarsman's hand.

"There are some sinister characters along the Po. They keep away from everybody else, like beasts in the woods. The only time you run into them is when your paths cross, but then each goes in his own direction," he said, but with little conviction.

The commissario had the impression that Barigazzi was just as curious about the episode. He was about to take out his mobile and call Maresciallo Aricò, but he thought better of it. He would play this his own way, and was more persuaded that this was the right course as he looked into the old man's face, where a trace of surprise was still evident.

"Don't brood too long over it," Barigazzi said in an attempt to conceal his own embarrassment. "Little by little, with the onset of cold, the waters will go down and become clearer. At that point, all will be revealed."

It was not the first time Soneri had heard that said, but the old man had spoken with a kind of sneer, curling his moustache like a grandfather playing with his grandchildren.

Soneri, as when he almost jumped into the flood to pursue the boatman, or when a few seconds earlier he had been about to call Aricò, now felt his instinct at odds with his self-control. Giving in to instinct would have meant taking Barigazzi by the scruff of the neck and shaking him. As a young ispettore he would have sprung out of his seat and threatened him. He was not at his best in those moments, and by now he had learned to stay calm, to take it easy and not betray his intentions. He could not be sure if this was down to experience or middle-aged cowardice, but he had decided to suspend his enquiries on that topic.

The volume of "Otello" was turned up even more as the din within the room rose. The atmosphere was growing more heated as second bottles were consumed and the general merriment increased. Every so often one of the customers would rise from his seat to accompany the tenor and give voice to as much of the aria as he could recall. It was said that the landlord kept his hearing aid switched off precisely so as not to hear the voices of great singers drowned out by over-excited tenors under the influence of wine. He had been listening to that noise for forty years. At the climax of the opera, Soneri became aware of other dissonant notes, those of "Aida" from his mobile.

"Where are you, in a theatre?" Juvara said, somewhat simple-mindedly.

"Do you really think I would be in a theatre?"

"I can hear music..."

"I'm eating in a place where they love opera," Soneri said irritably, wondering whether Juvara could tell an operatic aria from a Gregorian chant.

"Commissario, we can't solve that puzzle."

"You mean the note?"

"Exactly. The only thing we're sure about is that we're dealing with a graveyard. There is nothing else like it divided into lines, squares and sections."

"And as it happens, Decimo is dead..."

"The problem is that even small cemeteries have this same kind of sub-division and in the Po valley there are hundreds of them."

"So how are you going about it?"

"We're going through them one by one. I mean, those in the provinces on the banks of the Po."

"And so far no match?"

"Once or twice, but they correspond to people who died many years ago and there is no apparent connection."

"Well, I'm afraid that's the only way of dealing with it," Soneri said briskly.

"That much we can agree on," Juvara snorted, and was gone.

7

HE WAS IN his car in front of the *Italia*, whose shutters had been lowered, and the piercing hoot of an owl reached him from down by the river. Owls called to the dead, he remembered being told. As he drove up the embankment, the bird appeared from among the poplar trees and its call seemed to be aimed at the lamp over the boat club, a faint light shimmering in the mists and looking like an illumination at a vigil or at the recitation of the rosary. He thought, giving his imagination rein, that the owl was chanting for all the lives sacrificed on the river, perhaps even for Tonna, who might be somewhere underwater, or on the sandbanks or in the muddy depths of some inlet.

The mist was less dense now, diluting the still darkness of the autumn night. As he drove towards the city, Soneri could not escape that final vision of the sleeping town, sunk in the gloom of the embankment's long shadow, with the hoot of the owl hovering over everything like a preacher's warning, solemn and sinister in the silence. "When the waters drop, everything will be revealed," Barigazzi had said, twisting his moustache. What did he mean – that it was only a question of time? Or that there was something he knew? Or was it just long experience?

That question was still with him as he came back to his

house and it remained with him when, standing in the half-light at the window overlooking the street, he let his mind wander over what emerged from the turmoil of sensations accumulated in the course of the day. Every so often, from the stew of conjectures simmering in his mind, a single, perfectly formed thought bubbled to the surface. When will the water drain from the inlets and the floodplain? "One month if there is a freeze, or less if they set the pumps to work," had been Barigazzi's judgment. He did not know why, but he expected some development, something that would lead somewhere, from that kind of prediction. He fell asleep clinging to that hope.

He awoke to the sound of his mobile which he had forgotten to switch off before he went to bed. He could not tolerate noise on first waking, but then he could not tolerate anything much at that time, not even finding himself next to a woman who wanted to touch him and talk to him. Every awakening was like coming anew into the world, and inside himself he screamed like a newborn babe wrenched from his mother's womb. Perhaps that was why he mistook Nanetti for a midwife.

"The damp hurts my bones, but it damages your character," Nanetti said, in response to Soneri's complaining.

Soneri said nothing to that so Nanetti went on, "The first results of the tests on the barge are in – they should help you work out what happened that night."

"You may be a disappointment with gangplanks, but you're in a class of your own with microscopes," Soneri said, in an effort to revive their cordial dealings.

"Try to keep Alemanni well away from any contact with the press. He's dispensing pessimism right, left and centre and making sure that it is us who will be held responsible if this business degenerates into a fiasco."

"Tell me what the results say," Soneri said, fearing a return of his black humour.

"It's a hundred per cent certain that there was someone on board the barge on its final voyage to Luzzara. And someone who was not the owner. Someone who left his fingerprints alongside the older ones belonging to Anteo Tonna."

"Only one?"

"Yes. A man, tall and well built judging from the shoes he was wearing and from his weight as deduced from the footprints below deck. The same ones that were found on deck, near to where the dinghy was attached."

"You're sure Tonna's fingerprints were all earlier ones?"

"The last person in the wheelhouse was not Anteo, I'm sure of it. The traces of him that we've found are not from the same timeframe as those of the other person. No doubt about that," Nanetti said.

Which meant that if Tonna had been murdered, the crime had not been committed on the barge and that the killer, or his accomplice, had simulated the boatman's escape by leaving the dinghy at the embankment at Luzzara. This gave him the first nucleus of certainty around which he could wrap some facts.

"I hope it may be of use in sorting out the thousands of suppositions you've got in your head," Nanetti said.

"No question," Soneri said. "I now know that five hundred of them can be discarded but that five hundred of them might still be valid."

He had slept longer than normal and was conscious, as he downed his *caffè latte*, that the silence of dawn had already passed. What Nanetti said about Alemanni caused his anxiety levels to jump. The grey light and the roar of the traffic came in simultaneously from outside. He walked towards the police station, chewing on his depression, feeling like an engine that was too cold to start.

Juvara, with two assistants to give him a hand, was already at work in his office, clapping the dust from old telephone directories and making calls.

"Any luck?"

The ispettore shook his head. "In Cremona there's a man who died in '86. I have checked up but he doesn't appear to have anything to do with the Tonnas. In Pomponesco…"

Soneri cut him off with a gesture. He lit his cigar and leaned back against the cabinet. What cemetery could it be? If indeed it was a cemetery.

Once again the mobile broke into his train of thought.

"Hello!" he barked.

"A Doberman would be more polite."

"Ah, Angela?" Soneri said, in a gentler tone.

"You remember me?"

"Please don't. It's too early for that."

"And don't you come the tough guy with me, Commissario. I'm not the kind of woman who lets herself be pushed about," she snarled. "Or maybe you're muddling me with some other angelic Angela who wouldn't raise a whimper if she were insulted."

"And how many angelic males do you have fluttering around you?"

"Carry on in this vein and you will very soon be seeing all the angels you can use."

Soneri froze. Hadn't he heard that phrase somewhere before?

"Hey! Are you still there? Did you get frightened when I raised my voice?"

He needed silence to concentrate, but Angela, chattering away in his ear, would not relent. He held the telephone at arm's length. He could hear the faint voice buzzing away inoffensively like a bee in a blossom while he concentrated on where he had heard that remark. In the yard below, an officer in the white coat of the forensic squad passed by, and then he remembered: the nursing sister, Decimo's friend. She was the one who had said that he was worried about seeing "the angels".

He put the telephone back to his ear. "Do you know of a place called 'the Angels'?" His tone was so serious that Angela replied at once. "In Mantua. It's a cemetery."

Of course, Angela was from Mantua. "No woman is more precious than you," he said, and abruptly ended the conversation.

Juvara could not fail to notice his state of euphoria.

"You can stop all of that," Soneri announced. "I've found the cemetery."

The ispettore looked at him in amazement, put down his papers and dismissed the two assistants with a jerk of his chin. But before he could seek an explanation, his superior had vanished.

Within a few minutes, Soneri was driving towards the lower Po valley. The houses were beginning to peep out of the mist, taking shape slowly, like the pieces in his investigation. It occurred to him that all of his inquiries were leading to the Po, towards that flat land where the sky was never visible. And he had little faith in coincidences.

Mantua always gave him the impression of land that had risen from a huge bog. It was said that graves there could not be dug deeper than one metre lest the bodies ended up buried in water. On the other hand, it seemed to him bizarre that with all the lands of the plain available, they piled the dead one on top of the other like stacks of Parmesan cheese.

He asked for information about the San Pellegrino section. It was quite a recent wing, with bouquets of artificial flowers and the marble still shiny. It occurred to him that although his job brought him frequently into contact with death, this was the first time that an investigation had taken him to a cemetery. He usually had to occupy himself with the crueller aspects of death, never with its more peaceful, silent side. The unseemly poses of corpses were invariably a yell of rage, and a commissario was called on to deliver the vengeance of law. Once the case had been neatly filed away, he had never had occasion to go and see where the victims ended up, not even those whose lives he had combed through with an investigator's disrespectful zeal.

When he arrived in front of the smooth, marble plaque without name or date, he felt torn between surprise and disappointment, the same feelings he had once felt when his pistol jammed as he was about to fire on a man. The burial niche in the wall was empty. As was the one next to it. He checked again: square E, row 3, number 32. The crossword puzzle of the dead each time led him to the same conclusion, to the afterlife's unfilled box. Then he looked over at one side and intuition provided him with the solution, as intuition can sometimes supply the correct word from the opening letters alone. There was a photograph of a woman with a severe countenance: Desolina Tonna of Magnani, and just below: "Husband, daughter, brothers and sisters."

He reached the graveyard's administrative office just before it was due to close. The clerk on the information desk was seated in front of a computer screen and over his shoulder the commissario could see that he was engrossed in a video game. The office was there to field enquiries about where the dead were buried, although the dead that Soneri was inquiring about were in all probability not there, or at least not yet.

"I'd like to know who owns the burial places thirty-two and thirty-three in square E, third row, the San Pellegrino section."

He expected the official to object on the grounds of confidentiality, so without waiting for an answer, he held up his police identity card.

The man appeared to choke on the words he was on the brink of uttering, and turned to his keyboard. "Number thirty-two has been acquired by one Decimo Tonna and thirty-three by one Anteo Tonna."

It was all he needed to know.

He did not go back to the police station. Once he had crossed the Po by the Casalmaggiore bridge, he turned along the road which followed the course of the river on the Emilia side. As he was getting out of his car, Juvara called him.

"The note was a threat," he told Juvara. "It explains why Decimo was so frightened."

"Why?"

"It corresponds to the burial places which the Tonna brothers had acquired beside their sister years ago. You understand now?"

"I do. The killer was well informed about their lives."

"He must have been somebody from the locality."

"But how did you work out that it was the Mantua cemetery you were looking for?"

"Oh that…" Soneri muttered evasively. "It was all to do with the angels. That's what they call it in these parts."

Juvara had no idea what Soneri meant, but he was thankful to be relieved of the tedious task he had been set.

The Tonnas' niece was not in the bar. Soneri found himself face to face with a tall young man with long hair and one earring.

"You must be the matelot who didn't quite make it, or have I got that wrong?"

The young man stared at him vacuously, before replying: "I didn't like it, so I gave it up."

He did not seem very bright. Perhaps he took after his mother.

"Is your mother—?"

"No, she went into town." The boy interrupted him curtly, as if to suggest that the conversation was at an end.

Although he had nothing particular in mind to ask, Soneri chose to persist. He had never had much time for braggarts, but there was fun to be had with them. "You didn't fancy life on the river, then?" he said, deliberately mocking.

"No, maybe a bit at first, but then…" The boy was obviously annoyed.

Half a dozen young people were in the bar, their backs towards them and each one absorbed in a video game. The one behind the bar was not much different from the others.

"What's your name?"

"Romano."

Names with Fascist connotations seemed to be a family tradition, although the long hair and earring would hardly have been congenial to Anteo.

"You didn't like the life or you didn't like your uncle Anteo?"

"I am not cut out for the solitary life, and anyway, the river is always the same."

"And yet you carried a lot of cargoes. I've been having a look at the rosters… you can't have been short of cash."

Romano gave him a swift, nervous glance. He had the air of a pupil who could not answer the teacher's question. "The barge is very old and wouldn't have been able to struggle on much longer. The engine eats oil and it needed no end of care and attention… it couldn't have gone on even if my uncle…"

Soneri thought he picked up a trace of antipathy. He looked

out and saw some big, shiny cars parked in a row, an image of the affluence which had invaded the Po valley like a flood. "Were you ever aware of your uncle having received threats? Maybe money problems?"

"He alone had dealings with the clients. He didn't even have any competition because, considering the times we're living in and the few landing stages left, it's much more convenient to transport stuff in lorries. He didn't realize he was out of date."

"Is that why you left?"

"In part. Who's going to put their money in barges? They've had their day. Don't forget, my uncle was around eighty."

"Did you try to persuade him to settle down on dry land?"

"My mother tried to get me to do it several times, but he would just lose his temper. He said that it was his life and he liked it that way. After a bit, I said good-bye. I couldn't stay and rot in the middle of a river. I don't like the Po and I'm not interested in it. And it is a threat. And then all this stuff about its legends and its beauty... young people nowadays couldn't care less and shove off."

"Will you leave too?"

"As long as the bar is here, no. I've done my best to bring it up to date, with things that people of my age like," he said, looking over at the video games with their flashing lights and loud music. "In this town, there's nothing to do but play card games in the *Italia* and drink Fortanina in *Il Sordo*, where you've got the added attraction of the same old moans and groans from Verdi."

In the background Soneri heard the irritating, repetitive strains of the video games. "Do you know Barigazzi, Ghezzi and the rest of them?"

Romano gave a disgusted scowl. "Shitty communists!" he hissed.

"At least you agree with your uncle on that one."

"A bunch of losers who only believe in taxes and stopping other people from getting on in life. If it was up to them, we'd still be going up and down in big boats. They hate us because we own something. Look, they call us shopkeepers, but they're gushing with sympathy for those foreign beggars who turn up here and start stealing. My uncle was always on the other side. He had his barge and he was always his own boss."

These were the only sentences Romano spoke with any spontaneity. They were fired out like a belch, having plainly been rehearsed for some time in a brain not much given to rumination.

Soneri got to his feet. Everything now seemed clear to him, but he was not sure if it had much to do with the investigation. He strolled down towards the embankment until, leaving the colonnade behind him, he heard the water pumps at work.

Barigazzi told him that the pumps had been going for a couple of hours. They had arrived that morning from Parma and it had taken some time to get them set up in the best operational position. "A waste of effort," he said.

The chug-chug of the diesel engines seemed to cause the inlets to shake, and sent up clouds of smoke. To one side, he noticed Aricò in earnest conversation with a group of about twenty people. "Who are they?" he said.

"The ones who were evacuated from their houses in the floodplain," Barigazzi said. "It's for their sake that this whole shambles is under way, but if they don't erect some kind of breakwater across the river upstream of the port, they'll never drain anything. The pump that can empty the Po has yet to be invented."

Vernizzi joined them to say that the dredger and the excavators were placed sideways across the river to close off the floodplain. Barigazzi spat on the grass and that seemed to be his verdict.

"They want to go back to their houses," Soneri said.

"Do they really believe that merely getting the water out will solve their problems? The walls are soaked, so when it freezes, they'll crack. Houses don't dry out here in the Po valley in winter."

"Wouldn't you do the same?"

"If you buy a house on the flat lands, you've got to allow for the fact that things will not always go well. Sooner or later, the Po's going to come and pay you a little visit."

Aricò was perspiring. He had pushed his cap to the back of his head, exposing the beads of sweat on his forehead. The crowd who clustered round him, pacified by seeing the pumps at work, had allowed him a moment's peace. The people forced out of their homes had moved on to the embankment to watch the water being drained out litre by litre and poured back into the riverbed. Soneri too made his way up to the elevated road, leaving the town centre behind him. Having reached the same point where he had been the previous evening, he crouched among the branches which had been so damaged by the current. He moved to halfway down the embankment and studied the poplar trees with the water lapping around them.

In the silence, the inlet looked like an immense pot from which thin streaks of vapour were beginning to rise, as invisible as the lines used in fishing for barbel. The Canadian poplars made the autumnal twilight draw in more quickly. Squatting on his heels, he waited, rolling the extinguished cigar around his mouth. He lit it, but held the glowing end towards him, as his grandfather had done at the front. He took wartime precautions, but he did not expect to see a warship with cannons, only a solitary boat in a strip of dead water. The light faded at the same pace as the mist thickened. It seemed to him that the time had come.

Soneri became aware of its presence, hearing it before he saw it. He heard the low swishing sound, as when water is poured from a bucket over gravel, then made out the profile of a boatman rowing with few, slow strokes in a rhythm mastered by long familiarity with the oar. Undoubtedly it was the same man as the night before, and if he was coming back, it was a sign that he had not noticed anything on the previous occasion. The commissario let him approach until the boat was in line with the stone-crusher. A few more strokes and he could have called out to him, maybe even have looked him in the face, but suddenly the man shifted his oar to the other side of the boat and changed tack. He seemed to want to go back, even if he was only making for the centre of the poplar wood. The tree trunks stood in geometrically regular lines and diagonals, dividing equally all that water between the two embankments.

Soneri kept his eyes fixed on the boatman, who gave the impression of circling round like a buzzard on a warm afternoon in summer but then, unexpectedly, he jabbed his oar against a trunk to stop the boat, which stayed where it was, swaying slightly. He looked as though he were peering hard into the flood water which, in the absence of any current, was completely still. Soneri looked too and noted that the stagnation, by freeing the water of the clouds of sand, had caused it to lose its iron-grey colour as well.

The man dipped his oar to the right and set off again in the direction of the riverbank where Soneri was waiting. When he was ten metres away, the commissario rose to his feet and called out, causing the boatman to turn rapidly. He remained very still from the neck up. The boat swayed slightly without making him lose his balance. Soneri had the impression that for a few moments the boatman was undecided whether to flee or draw alongside him. When he realized that he was close enough to be recognized, he gave a couple of energetic strokes to direct the boat towards the great embankment. The commissario walked a few steps in the squelching mud, keeping his feet well apart to avoid tumbling into the river. The boatman drew closer, until he was almost on the grass.

He said not a word, restricting himself to jerking his chin in a way that implied a question. He was elderly, but still full of energy and pride. His enormous hands were like Barigazzi's, in whose fist glasses could disappear. He now observed Soneri from the shell of the boat, his eyes grey and piercing, with the strong hint of a challenge.

"A strange hour to be out between the embankments."

"Every hour is a good hour. The thing is to know where you are going."

"And where were you making for?"

"I'm here to see how well the pumps are working. I've put some stakes in the ground."

"Has it dropped much?" Soneri said.

"Five centimetres. Nothing much. But the water is still coming in over the barrier upstream of the port. I'll have to adjust it."

"Where do you moor your boat?"

"At the port. Where else with the waters this low?"

"How about if we arrange to meet in *Il Sordo*?"

The man thought it over for a moment, the intensity of his stare obscured in the gathering dusk.

"No, not there. We can meet in the *Italia* in thirty minutes."

"You think you can make it in that time?"

"Listen, policeman, I know the Po better than you know the inside of your police station."

*

Being in the large, single room of the restaurant felt like being inside a refectory. The loud voices, the smoke and the crush made the meeting oddly discreet. There was too much going on and too much to overhear to allow people to take notice of anything. The commissario made his entrance and occupied one of the few free tables no bigger than a window recess. Only when he was sitting down did he see that the boatman was waiting for him at the bar, where he had already ordered a white wine. He caught sight of Soneri and made his way over, followed by someone else, evidently a colleague. When they arrived at the table, Soneri eyed them up and down as training required, then gave them a sign to sit.

"This is my lawyer," the boatman said.

Soneri took in his bulk and the skin made leathery by the sun on the Po. He did not look like a lawyer.

"What made you think I was a policeman?"

"Your type is easily picked out," the man said. "I've a lot of experience of them."

The second man stretched out a hand with the dimensions of a small shovel. "Arnaldo Fereoli, but everyone around here calls me Vaeven. It's dialect for someone who comes and goes."

"I know the dialect. Do you have a barge too?"

"A *magano*."

Soneri turned to the first man who, without offering his hand, said: "Dino Melegari, or Dinon to the people around here."

Melegari was built on a monumental scale. Soneri had not appreciated the sheer bulk of the man when he was in the boat, but now that he was there in front of him, he seemed as overwhelming as the statues of Hercules and Antaeus outside the questura. "Will you join me? A drop of wine?"

"I never say no to another glass."

They were served by a tiny, silent, serious-looking girl who seemed just out of school.

"Will they do any good?" Soneri asked, meaning the pumps, which were still droning away on the other side of the embankment.

Dinon stretched out his great hands so wide that he almost touched his neighbours. If he closed them too suddenly he might crush the table. "The plain is low and the water is going down. They had to do something to satisfy the people who were evacuated from their homes."

"What is the level now?"

"Can't you see from the poplars? A couple of metres."

Vaeven had pulled up the sleeves of his pullover, revealing a hammer and sickle tattoo on his forearm. It was the right time to ask: "Did you know Tonna?"

The two men exchanged glances. Their expressions implied that they thought they were being tricked. "By reputation," Dinon said.

"As a boatman, or because of his Fascism?"

"What do you think?" Dinon said, pushing back the rim of his beret with his knuckles. "Will one or the other not do for you?"

"I know he has left some painful memories."

"A number of widows and orphans," the boatman said sardonically. "But nowadays people have short memories."

"But you remember very well."

"We're old enough to have known him."

"I believe it's all ended badly for him."

"Maybe he set off with the engine not running to take advantage of the wind, lost control of the barge and ended up running aground against the embankment. He would have been deeply ashamed. His reputation as a fine sailor was all he had left."

"He had nothing else but the barge," Vaeven said. "He

couldn't have lived with the idea that he'd made a mistake that would make a novice cringe."

Soneri thought this over for a few moments as he sipped his Malvasia. The notion of his having fled out of shame had not occurred to him. It might even be plausible. After all, it could just have been the way out he had been searching for. But if that was the truth, what was he, the commissario, doing there on the Po, hunting down a phantom when a real crime had been committed in the city? The jeering face of Alemanni – all skull-like features and receding white hair – was imprinted on his mind.

"Who was 'the Kite'?" he said, shaking away these jarring thoughts.

The two looked at each other. "We're not actually under arrest, I take it," Dinon protested. "Tell us what you want and we'll save a lot of time."

He was staring at Soneri with those clear, piercing eyes. Soneri took his time lighting his cigar. He wanted to let the accumulated animosity evaporate. "I've told you I have reason to suspect that Tonna is dead. They've already got rid of his brother."

"What's all that got to do with the so-called 'Kite'?"

"We found a note on Tonna's barge which referred to some decision concerning him."

"Must have been one of the partisans. But there were so many of them," Vaeven said.

"If that's true, you would have known him," Soneri said firmly.

"We weren't here then. We were too well known and they'd have picked us out immediately. In '43, we were up on Monte Caio."

"Have you ever heard tell of this 'Kite'?"

"There were all kinds who passed this way," Dinon said, to

quash any further discussion. "There were followers of General Badoglio, as well as members of the Garibaldi Resistance group. They came from Lombardy, from the Veneto or up from the Gothic Line. And then there was the other lot, the G.A.P., and nobody had any idea who they were. They wouldn't have given away their undercover names even to their own families."

"Perhaps Tonna had killed—"

"Nothing more likely," Dinon interrupted him. "And it wouldn't have been the only time."

Soneri signalled to the waitress to bring another bottle and when he had refilled the glasses, he confronted them: "I believe you both know exactly who this 'Kite' is."

Vaeven now pushed his hat to the back of his head with his knuckles, put one elbow on the table and leaned forward, causing the table to tilt to one side: "Listen, Commissario, I got to know lots of you police types back in 1960 when we took to the streets to stop Tambroni becoming prime minister. So you're not going to catch me out."

Soneri said nothing and the other took it as a surrender, but instead of attacking, he retreated, relaxing against the back of his seat. They remained in that position until the commissario decided to drop the subject. The equilibrium underlying their exchange was as precarious as the currents of the Po.

"You've stayed in the party?"

"Always. We've never changed our banner. Ours has the hammer and sickle," Vaeven said forcibly, pulling up his sleeve to show off his tattoo.

"Are you saying that others…"

The man raised his right hand as though he were going to toss something over his shoulder. "The majority has changed. Nowadays they're cosying up to the priests and the churchy lot. They've got their co-operatives and strike deals with the bosses."

"Barigazzi as well?"

"He's getting on now, but the people he has around him… they've watered everything down. They used to be Lambrusco, but they're very thin wine now."

"Do the two of you still sail?"

"We do some fishing as a hobby. I've got an old *magano* which is holding up well."

"What did Tonna transport?"

"They say he carried odds and ends, but what was really below, nobody knows. There are no borders or customs along the Po."

It was dark now, nearly time for dinner, and the bar was emptying. Dinon rose to his feet, slowly stretching his giant body. Each of his movements was deliberate, as though he were keeping his balance on a boat on the river. "Commissario, what are you looking for?" he asked, when the conversation seemed over.

Soneri was thrown by the question. He had lowered his guard and that question reopened the door on all his doubts, because he was not sure himself what he was looking for. For a second time he felt lost, and all the while the boatman kept his steely gaze on him. There was in him a certainty which had probably never faltered. There was no trace of doubt in his eyes. Soneri felt a twinge of envy.

"I'm looking for Tonna," he said, but he had voiced the first thought that came into his mind.

The other two stared harder at him and then left the *Italia* without another word.

At that hour, the town was deserted. The only noise that cut through the mist was the unchanging sound of the water pumps. Behind the embankment, the floodlights trained twin beams, two shining circles made almost solid by the enveloping mists, on to the floodplain at the points where the pumps were draining the water away. He felt the full weight of the question: was he wasting his time in a town indifferent to the fate of a boatman who had been a leading figure in an age long gone? Not even his family wanted to understand. For them, too, Tonna had been dead for some time. He belonged to a past that no-one wished, or was able, to remember – the old from abhorrence and the young from ignorance.

He walked under the colonnade leading to *Il Sordo*, and on the far side of the street he heard the click of heels, a woman's heels. He stopped but could see no-one. He went on walking but again heard from under the arches the steps of someone who seemed to be playing hide-and-seek with him. He stepped into the middle of the road and shouted, "Come out, whoever you are!"

Angela appeared from behind a pillar and walked towards him, imitating a streetwalker.

"Stop that," he said with a smile. "This is a small town and people talk."

"I can see the headline and the photograph already. The commissario and his lady friend."

"I'm not important enough for the gossip columns. The stuff Alemanni is planting with the journalists is ample for the time being."

"They're getting all hot and bothered now about your absences. Juvara is running out of things to say. He tells them that you're away, pursuing leads, and he has no idea when you'll be back."

"How did you get here?"

"I came down when it was still light and followed you until you went into that bar."

"I had someone to meet."

"And two bottles of Malvasia to down."

"I can't stand vegetarians and teetotallers."

Angela started unbuttoning her shirt, but Soneri pulled her close to him to make her stop.

"Please, don't hit me. I'm feeling very fragile tonight," he begged her in a voice weighed down with anxiety.

Suddenly recognizing his vulnerability, she returned his look, gave him a tender hug and a kiss. "You're irresistible when you surrender," she whispered in his ear. "But do remember that you owe me one. Remember? That barge and only us on board making..."

"What are you talking about? There might still be people at the boat club."

"So much the better. More exciting."

Resistance was pointless, but as they walked on, Soneri felt ill at ease in the unaccustomed role of a fragile man looking for consolation from a woman, yet if he was disconcerted at first, he rediscovered his self-assurance in assuming the more usual role of taking the necessary precautions to avoid being seen by the members of the club, whose shadowy outlines were visible as they passed in front of the brightly lit windows. They climbed up the embankment and came down at a dark corner of the yard. Once more the commissario was acting as guide to Angela.

They proceeded cautiously in the dark on the far side, away from the lamp light, in the shelter of the slope. There were no steps there alongside the club, so they had to make their way on the riverbank itself.

"I've got high heels on," Angela murmured.

Soneri cursed under his breath. In addition to vegetarians and teetotallers, he now had to cope with an insane woman. He lifted her in his arms and began the descent, while she whispered ironical flatteries, "How strong you are!" and such like, punctuated with melodramatic sighs.

"Carry on with that nonsense, and I'll drop you in the Po."

They reached the bottom, out of sight of the club. They ran the risk that someone might come outside for a pee and catch sight of them on the landing stage. The noise from the pumps mixed with the splash of the water as it gushed over the embankment from the field was particularly loud there, in contrast to the river which flowed silently by. Whoever had set off in the barge on the night of the flood had in all probability taken the same route, unseen by Barigazzi and the others.

Soneri put the gangplank in place and helped Angela across before following her. When he was safely on board himself, he used the perch pole to carefully reposition the plank on the quay. They went down below, and Angela made an immediate beeline for the cabin.

"I want the captain's bunk," she said, peremptorily.

They lay in each other's arms for a while until the barge was rocked by bigger waves and the mutter of voices made itself heard alongside. A craft was passing close to the jetty, causing Soneri some alarm. The cavernous roar of its engine, only partially drowned out by the noise of the pumps, died away as it drew alongside the barge. The commissario leapt up from the bunk. He tried to pull on his clothes, but Angela held him by the arm and made him lie back on the mattress. Every time he attempted to raise his head to listen, she gripped him firmly round the neck and pulled him over to her. Outside, an engine was turning over and someone was talking. Then the barge rocked gently and feet were heard on the deck.

"They're coming down," Soneri said, struggling to free himself from her embrace. She clasped him more tightly with both her arms and legs, forcing him to stay where he was and concentrate on not making a sound.

Up above, someone was walking about. The commissario tried to picture what was happening on deck, and remembered with relief that an hour earlier he had been meticulous about closing the wheelhouse door from the inside. Shortly afterwards, he heard the rusty creak of the doorhandle as it was tried a couple of times. Someone was attempting to break in. The footsteps rang out again, passed directly over their heads and then went towards the side of the barge. Moments passed, and then the engine revved up again and moved away.

"That is the most exciting situation I have ever been in," Angela said, close to ecstasy.

He stared at her. "Do you think we'll ever be able to meet in bed at home, between two bedside tables, with a picture of the Madonna hanging above the headboard?"

"If ever we do, that will mean it's all over."

Soneri went back up to the wheelhouse, pushed open the door and stepped out on to the deck. He jumped on to the jetty to put the gangplank in place. The two of them climbed back up the incline which they had earlier descended, and came out on the dark side of the square. There was no-one left in the boat club. The lights were off and the shutters drawn. Whoever had come aboard the barge had probably taken the club's closing time into account.

"Who do you think it was?"

"I have no idea. I think they were there looking for Tonna. He'd been keeping bad company."

"Well, I am indebted to whoever it was. That was unforgettable."

"I would be interested to see how you would react if someone did catch us during one of your mad moments."

"I wouldn't turn a hair. Are you or are you not the commissario of police?" she said, giving him another hug. She pulled away and looked squarely at him, trying to read his thoughts. "Did you not like it, or is there something else buzzing about in that head of yours?"

"I'm thinking about the people who came aboard."

8

ONCE THEY WERE back in the city, he had attempted to persuade Angela to come to his apartment, but she had refused. "You're bound to have two horrible little bedside tables and a Madonna over the bed," she had said as they parted.

In spite of that, within ten minutes he had settled into his usual routine and even felt relieved at being able to sleep on his own, but his state of agitation had him awake once again before dawn. The city was still noiseless in the mist and he stared out at it through the glass door on to the balcony. He knew that his journeys down to the Po valley could not go on much longer, and that this was perhaps the last day he could justify being absent from the police station to pursue a line of inquiry which might be only secondary or possibly irrelevant. He could already hear Alemanni's victory chants, further exacerbated by the echo which they would produce in the reprimands of his own chief, the questore: a quartet of shrill, menacing violins.

Instead, the first music he heard was the equally irritating "Aida".

"Commissario, thank goodness you're up early," Aricò began.

"These Tonna brothers don't allow me much sleep."

"Nor me. Last night someone set fire to the bar belonging to the bargeman's niece."

"At what time, exactly?" Soneri said, immediately relating this event to his night-time visit to the barge.

"Around three. There's no doubt the fire was started deliberately. They found a burned-out petrol can under the bar."

"Did anyone see anything?"

"What do you think? The baker called us when he went down around four and saw the smoke."

"Was it an act of hooliganism or something more serious?"

"Professionals, Commissario. They made a thorough job of it. There's nothing much left," continued the maresciallo, before adding: "I called you first before getting the others involved… I'm giving you this chance. I know how things are between us and the magistrates."

"Thanks, Aricò," Soneri said, "I'll be there in half an hour."

As he drove through the even thicker dawn mist, he thought gratefully of the maresciallo. Soneri had had to get the questore out of bed to report everything to him, and his superior, still half asleep, had been unable to respond with anything more than a series of *Madonna santa!*s each time he asked for more time or for the chance to carry out further inquiries. He finally arrived at the conclusion which had seemed evident to Soneri for at least an hour: it was a very serious business, the like of which had never before been seen, could well be the work of extortionists. It might even be that Anteo had been threatened by the gang who had engaged him to transport the illegal immigrants. Maybe he was transporting other things as well and had not kept his side of the bargain, but if he had been killed, why were they still coming after him? Perhaps another lot had got rid of him, or possibly it was all a set-up, a so-called accident so he could make off with the money after selling a cargo of drugs? It was in any case exceedingly strange that this should have happened exactly one day before the murder of his brother.

He parked in front of the *Italia* as the mist was lifting from over the embankment. The pumps were still roaring and the commissario was tempted to go and see how far the water level on the floodplain had dropped, but a gust of wind brought the smell of burning to his nostrils and focused his attention on the cluster of houses in the old town. From a distance, what remained of the bar gave the impression of a black eye. A coating of black had discoloured the facade of the house up to the first floor, and there was no need to go too close to realize that in the interior nothing had been saved. It occurred to him that black had been a constant in the history of that family, more for evil than for good. The firefighters had gone into the building with their hoses and had shored up the ceiling. Now they were directing jets of water at the centre of the room where embers were still smouldering. On the pavement, a slight distance away from onlookers, Tonna's niece – with an overcoat over her dressing gown – stood with her son.

Soneri lit a cigar and went over to join Aricò beside his van. "You had a good nose for this Tonna…"

The commissario brushed the remark aside with a wave of his hand. "Aricò," he said, putting his mouth beside the maresciallo's ear, "this one is for you. This is my chance to pay back my debts for this morning."

This time it was Aricò's turn not to overdo things. After a brief pause, he said, "The question is, why should you hand it over to me?"

"My sense is that the fire has nothing to do with the disappearance of Anteo Tonna. He had various other pieces of business outstanding."

"Commissario, are you trying to give me a headache? After a sleepless night, with this pile of charcoal here, you're in the mood for talking in riddles?"

Aricò was right. Rather than talking to the maresciallo,

Soneri was simply thinking aloud. "It's like this: Tonna was transporting illegal immigrants. The cargoes of grain which appear on the registers were only a cover."

Aricò turned more serious and pulled the peak of his cap over his eyes.

"He owed something to the traffickers, whoever they were, and that's why they came after him. When they didn't find him, they left a little warning. So, they think he's still alive and they believe he's giving them the run-around."

"Are you sure that's the way it is?"

"It can be, yes. But I suspect there's more to it than that," said Soneri. "But I'm giving you a free hand. The matter of the illegal immigrants is your case."

Aricò pushed his cap further back and leaned on the door of the van, peering into the dark cavity of the burned-out bar. Soneri left the piazza in the direction of the jetty. He climbed up the embankment and when he was near the elevated road, he heard the buzz of the engines. At the entrance to the club he could see Barigazzi in knee-high boots. He went down the slope to the yard.

"You're not over in the piazza?"

"Been there already."

"What do you think?"

"It's never happened before that they set fire to a bar or restaurant. When something new happens, there's something sinister behind it," the man muttered, making no effort to disguise his pessimism.

"Is the niece's family clean?"

"They go about their own business, same as everybody else. Money is the only religion here nowadays. The husband of Tonna's niece is a right-wing councillor. I mean the new right wing, the shopkeepers' right wing, one which has taken off its black shirt and put on a tie."

Barigazzi spat on the road as he always did when he disapproved of something, expressing unease at living in a world which was too deeply changed. All that remained for him was the Po, his landscape, the mist and that little corner of his past which opened up inside the doors of *Il Sordo*.

"I met Dinon sculling among the poplars," Soneri said. "He said he was checking how far the water had gone down."

The old man looked at him in amazement. "No, he would have been checking on the memorial to the partisans. The river damages it every time."

"Do you mean to say there's a memorial on the floodplain?"

"Always has been. A monument to the comrades who fought along the Po."

"And Dinon takes care of it?"

"Him and that group of his who call themselves orthodox communists, and who believe they're the only ones with the right credentials for the custody of the monument. In fact, we do it too. We're well mannered towards each other and choose different days."

"How many are there besides Dinon and Vaeven?"

"Very few now," Barigazzi said in a derisive tone. "A tiny group of nostalgics who meet every so often in an old shoemaker's shop to adore the bust of Stalin."

"So much the better for them. At least they've lived their lives hoping for the revolution. It was worse for Tonna who had only memories and frustrations to live on."

"Tell me the truth," Barigazzi said. "He was in deep trouble, wasn't he?"

"How do you know that?"

"Along the Po everybody knows everybody else, word gets around. From what I hear, he didn't carry very much grain. However, he did a lot of boating and a barge like that costs a lot of money. In other words, the money must have come from somewhere."

"I have to agree with you," Soneri said. "This mist covers more and more mysteries."

"The valley is wide and there are fewer and fewer people about. There are houses where nobody knows what's in them, nor even who lives there."

The commissario turned away. "How much water is there left on the floodplain?"

"A metre and a half. You'll see the bottom by this afternoon."

Even where they were standing, the air was still heavy with the smell of burning. The smoke had mingled with the mist and together they formed a cloud which hung over the village. What had happened to the bar had galvanized everyone and this made things easier for the commissario. The questore would spend days chairing meetings and the press would pay no more heed to the toxic leaks from Alemanni.

"What would you say to going out over the floodplain in your boat?"

"We'd risk getting stuck in the middle, or beached on a sandbank or banging into a tree trunk. It's a fishing boat that I've got..." Barigazzi said.

"If there were two of us, we could manage."

"What has brought on this appetite for a bit of tourism?"

"You started it. Did you not tell me to wait until the waters were less muddy?"

Barigazzi fixed a sharp, penetrating look on him, but he said nothing. Only when the commissario was ten steps away did he shout after him, "Come immediately after lunch, before the waters drop too far."

Soneri walked towards *Il Sordo*, through air still rank with the stench of the embers which swept up the streets and under the arches. He was passed by large saloon cars, their lights flashing. He recognized the chauffeurs from the prefettura. He too had been summoned to a meeting in the questura, together with the questore, the prefetto and the mayors of the towns on the plain. Official anxiety had returned to the levels it had been at when the Po was threatening the houses.

Before going into the *osteria*, he called Juvara. "Have they left you all on your own? They're all here."

"More or less... Is this fire going to help clear things up?"

"Yes, but only up to a point."

"What does that mean? The questore is persuaded that it's the work of the gang that did for the Tonna brothers."

"If they had killed them, why would they have torched his niece's bar?"

"Maybe she was mixed up in it too..."

'Tonna was carrying illegal immigrants from the delta up to the cities on either side of the river. Some hours before they burned the bar down, they came looking for him on the barge. That means they thought he was still alive and double-crossing them. They didn't destroy the boat because it might still be useful. There's no safer or easier way to deliver immigrants into the heart of the industrial zones than by transferring them from one vessel to another offshore in the delta without the inconvenience of berthing. Minimum risk and maximum profit."

"Commissario, you have to go and tell this to the questore. They're all convinced that this means people-trafficking has arrived in these parts and that the two brothers were bumped off by a bunch of gangsters."

The ispettore was right. He knew the kerfuffle that they could get into at headquarters every time something out of the ordinary, like this, happened. There was the risk of them opening a new, useless line of inquiry. In addition, he thought that Aricò would certainly have sent in a report on Anteo Tonna's trafficking and at that point the circle was closed. He kept his mobile in his hand for a few minutes, unsure whether to call the questore immediately or to wait. The meeting in the questura was at 4.00 that afternoon. Perhaps he would manage to get down to the floodplain and back in time.

The landlord in the bar was wearing his hearing aid, but the means of communication were not much different. Soneri had to make use of the sign language he had learned from Barigazzi. There was no-one in the *osteria* and perhaps that was why the owner had his hearing aid switched on. Watching him shuffle between the tables, it occurred to Soneri that he must know a great deal about life in the town, about Tonna and about the past. Perhaps he even knew the Kite. It was for this reason that he had asked Barigazzi to take him out on the floodplain. He wanted to examine the monument and read what was inscribed on the marble.

As he made his way to the jetty, the Fortanina wine was still bubbling in his stomach. Barigazzi was waiting for him.

"We'd better get a move on," the old man said. "By this evening the water will be too low and I might not manage to get the boat back to the jetty."

They stepped aboard and, as a precaution, Soneri sat down while Barigazzi set his feet wide apart on the bottom boards, a position which allowed him to manoeuvre without moving his upper body one centimetre. They arrived at a point a little beyond the pumps, disembarked, raised the boat with the winch and lowered it carefully on to the other side, into the waters of the flooded plain.

"You see? The undergrowth is beginning to appear," Barigazzi said, pointing to the first branches emerging from the water.

"There's enough to keep us afloat," the commissario said.

"Not everywhere. The land on these plains is irregular and there are no navigation lanes."

The light was very faint, even though the poplar trees were totally bare. The mist seemed to be trapped in that spiderwork of branches, or perhaps the shade was caused by the embankments which shut off that stretch of flooded land. They passed the great outline of the stone-crushing plant, with its gantries and enormous skips, a kingdom of rust and mud on which the water had spread the fresh stain of its passage. With a few quick strokes, Barigazzi rowed through the trees which would remain damp until the first foliage appeared. The thrusts of the oar made the boat skim along smoothly, and when necessary, the old man turned the oar on its side behind the stern, using it as a rudder to give more precise direction.

At a certain point, Barigazzi stopped rowing and, standing quite still, without uttering a word, raised his arm with his index finger outstretched. Soneri saw a low column of white marble emerge from the water like a fleshless bone, its colour clashing with the surrounds.

"We can't go too close," the boatman muttered, "because it's not very deep there and the monument is planted on a raised piece of land."

They approached as near as possible until the bottom of the hull rubbed against the sand. Soneri made out the words clearly: TO THE PARTISANS OF ALL FORMATIONS WHO FOUGHT AND DIED HERE OPPOSING BARBARISM. There was nothing else.

"Who erected it?" he asked.

"The old Party," Barigazzi said, "when we were all still united."

"Why here where the water comes and goes?"

"The floodplain was the place where the partisans were

able to move more easily. Once it was full of trees and under-growth, but when needed there was the Po to get them out of trouble."

A sense of mystery emanated from the monument and from the spot on which it stood. The commissario reread the words engraved on the marble and became aware of the contrast be-tween their solemn ring and the dialect speech of Barigazzi. It was at that moment that he recalled the words uttered by Tonna's niece about the telephone call and some mysterious person looking for Barbisin, her uncle. The man had spoken excellent dialect, but had stumbled over his Italian which he pronounced with a foreign accent.

Barigazzi began to circle the monument. In the stillness, mud had settled and the water was now much clearer. Son-eri looked for other marks on the marble, but there was no inscription save the one on the side facing the Po. The com-missario leaned out of the craft to touch the marble, risking losing his balance. He moved back in and looked over the side of the boat.

There was something dark below, something which, even in its vague outline, seemed to him like a body. He had seen so many that it was sufficient for him to take one more look to be sure. A body which must have been held down by a weight. The hem of something that looked like a cloak was moving gently with the undulation caused by the boat. The commis-sario stood up, turned to Barigazzi and pointed to the shape beneath them: "He didn't get very far."

At first the boatman did not say a word but then he mur-mured: "I never thought that he had run off."

Soneri took his mobile from the pocket of his duffel coat and dialled the number of the forensic squad.

"You'll have to come back to the Po," he said to Nanetti. "And this time you're going to get your arse wet."

He then called Aricò. It was the officer who replied and told him that the maresciallo was in bed.

"Get him up. Tell him we've found Tonna's corpse."

"Right away," the officer said, swallowing hard before hanging up.

Soneri sat back down in the boat and looked over at Barigazzi to seek his advice. In reply, the other man stared back and shook his head. "We couldn't manage with just the two of us. It must be tied down and we'd have to go underwater to cut the ropes. It's not going to be easy, because as soon as anybody touches the bottom he'll disturb the mud and then he'll see nothing."

"How long will they take?" the commissario said, looking over at the pumps.

"By tomorrow morning there'll be nothing but a few puddles."

"Push over to the embankment," Soneri said. "I'll take the short cut."

Barigazzi took the boat to the bank, between two bushes. Soneri jumped out, rocking the boat so violently that the old man had to press down with his oar so as not to capsize. "People who move that awkwardly always end up at the bottom," he shouted to Soneri before moving off among the poplar trees.

As soon as he was out of earshot the commissario took out his mobile and called the questore. He would ruin the afternoon ceremonial of tea and cakes, with secretaries scurrying about and the inevitable grand orations against organized crime. The mincing secretary was exasperatingly obstructive until Soneri, with the vaguely menacing tone he used with criminals, told him in no uncertain terms to put him through to the questore.

A fresh burst of *Madonna santa!*s with audible exclamation marks. "Of course, go right ahead... Yes, yes, all the necessary inquiries into the case... Certainly, mobilize the forensic squad... and the frogmen..." And, finally: "Keep me informed!"

His superior evidently had no inclination to muddy his shoes. The commissario's had a double layer of earth clinging to each side, allowing the pebbles on the pathway to attach themselves. He crouched, as he had done the preceding afternoon while waiting for Dinon Melegari's boat. The light was failing minute by minute like a fade-out on a cinema screen, and down there, where the bright marble was now emerging, the water was doing its work, eating away at the body of Anteo Tonna. He had spent his life on the water and now he was under its surface.

The first to arrive was Aricò, his light flashing. The commissario asked him to switch it off for fear of attracting too many onlookers.

The maresciallo had an ugly face resembling a map where the severe contours of mountains and unforgiving valleys alternated. "How much water is he under?"

"A metre, perhaps less. But he's tied down. Someone'll need to go in and cut the ropes."

"I'll call the divers; even in this town there are people with wetsuits."

For a few moments, the commissario pondered the best solution – to wait until the following morning when the pumps would have emptied the water from the plain, or else to bring the body up right away – but even as he was thinking it over, Aricò was already talking to someone who was promising to be there in a quarter of an hour. He felt a sudden, terrible unwillingness to move the body. He was afraid that he might miss something, that a piece of evidence might be destroyed. He looked around for Nanetti, but in the gathering darkness there was no sign of him.

When the diver went under, he could see only a couple of metres in front of him, at least until Aricò aimed the police car lights into the water. The monument was now halfway out of the water, shining white. The diver walked towards it slowly so as not to disturb the sludge. He then went down on his knees, switched on a strong torch which he fixed to his forehead and plunged his head into the water. From the embankment, Soneri watched the illuminated water bubble and the hem of Tonna's cloak come to the surface. Then, with the slowness of bread starting to rise, the whole body came up, swollen with water, back first, legs wide apart, rotating slowly. The diver took hold of one shoulder and manoeuvred it to the bank.

Only when they were at the top of the embankment and could lay the body on a plastic sheet did they roll it over onto its back. They were confronted with a waxen face, eaten away by the water and encrusted with slime. But it was him. When the commissario shifted his glance from the forehead, he realized that half the skull was missing. A deep cavity gaped open at the top, looking like a cut in an over-ripe watermelon.

He tried to bring to mind the image of Decimo's head, but his memory was blocked by the body in front of him, bones disjointed, stretched out under a yellow sheet. Then it dawned on him. He did not need to be an anatomist to recognize that there was a link between those two smashed skulls.

"A savage blow," the maresciallo said.

"Indeed," Soneri mumbled, "and not the first I've seen."

"I imagine," said the other, without grasping the reference to Decimo.

It was now pitch black. Only the commissario, Aricò and the officer remained beside the corpse. Not far off, the diver, still in his wetsuit, looked like a strange river fish, dripping with slime. The only light came from the headlights of the police car, around which wisps of mist were swirling. The smell of burning still hung in the air.

"We have to inform the ambulance men and the magistrate before removing the body," the officer said.

Aricò turned towards the commissario, who nodded. At that moment, a car approached along the embankment road and when it was only a few metres away, Soneri recognized the vehicle belonging to the forensic squad. Before Nanetti could get out, the commissario turned in the dark towards Aricò. "Is there a chapel near here?"

In reply, the maresciallo pointed along the embankment into the darkness, but Soneri understood perfectly. He remembered having passed it.

When he turned back to look at the corpse, he saw Nanetti already bent over it with a little torch which gave out a light as white as the full moon. He recognized the procedures of the forensic squad, as unchanging as any ritual. With a grimace of pain and a creak of his joints, his colleague got to his feet. "I suppose you have already noticed the blindingly obvious?" he said, indicating the head. "Apart from that, I haven't much to say just now, but at a guess it would seem to me that he died on the same day that he disappeared."

"It would be better to move him at the earliest opportunity to a cold slab in the morgue," Aricò said.

"Agreed," Soneri said with a glance at Nanetti, who nodded before saying: "The killer must have made his calculations very carefully. What better way to cancel out the traces of a crime than a flood on the Po?"

It had never occurred to the commissario that the murderer might have taken into account the rise in the river level before making his move, that he might have waited for the waters to overflow on to the plains, fill them and cover over the scene of the crime. He noticed that Aricò and Nanetti were staring at him strangely. When he was thinking, his face must have assumed a particular expression, as everyone noticed it. Angela would always say: "What's the matter, what are you thinking about?"

Fortunately the blue flashing lights of the ambulance arriving attracted everybody's attention. Before it pulled up, the commissario took a last look around him: Aricò, the officer, Nanetti and himself standing there, in the mist, beside a corpse swollen with water. It was like a scene from a gangster movie.

It was only when the scent of the *pasta con fagioli* worked its way into his nostrils that he remembered about the meeting in the questura. It had completely slipped his mind, but then the questore had completely forgotten about the murder.

"So you've won," Nanetti said, looking around at the walls of *Il Sordo* with that curiosity for detail which he showed when examining corpses or cartridge shells.

"Won what?"

"With Alemanni. He said you were chasing fireflies..."

"Alemanni has never understood anything. He should have been a lawyer."

"What do you think about it now?"

"That the motive is not one of the usual ones."

"Why so?"

Soneri looked up at the cross-legged Christ but was unable to translate into words the dance of phantoms, intuitions and conjectures inside his head. "It's all to do with something that happened a long time ago. Or perhaps that was only a pre-liminary. On the barge I found a note which said something about the killing of a partisan."

"That was more than fifty years ago..."

"That's true, but I have the impression that time passed in vain for the Tonna brothers. Perhaps out of an extreme regard for consistency, or perhaps out of shame, their minds remained the same as when they were in their twenties. It's strange, in a world of whitened sepulchres."

Nanetti tucked away four spoonfuls of the pasta as though he were shovelling sand. Then he raised his eyes and said, "That's to their credit."

"The price they paid was an isolated life. Decimo pretended he started living when he was forty. His brother spent his days on his own on a barge, willing to deal with people-traffickers, anything to keep him afloat."

"You're sure they've got nothing to do with it?"

"Yes. They thought they were the only threat facing Tonna, but I'm afraid..."

As he spoke to Nanetti, his conviction that he was dealing with an unusual and almost unfathomable crime gathered strength. He was reminded of the death of a well-known criminal many years previously. He had been under threat from all sides, but died in the most banal of ways, falling off a ladder trying to break into an apartment.

"If it was the same person who killed the two brothers," Nanetti broke in, "it means that in the morning he deposed of Decimo and in the evening Anteo. But was the latter not the main target?"

"Certainly," Soneri said, deep in thought. "And why kill Decimo in a hospital, with all the risks that involved? And anyway, are we sure we've got them in the right order?"

"We'll find out from the post-mortem."

"He obviously meant to kill them both, and it seems that both of them were aware of the threat."

Nanetti put his spoon down on the empty plate and stretched out his arms. He never followed his colleague in his suppositions. The only things which interested him were evidence and proof, and the only hard facts at that moment were corpses, two brothers, killed in the same way.

Soneri made a sign to the landlord to bring a plate of *spalla cotta*. The restaurant was beginning to fill up, but there was no sign either of Barigazzi or of the others from the boat club. Nanetti kept looking around until he noticed, tucked away in a corner behind him, the notches marking the height of the water and the date of the flood. "Just thinking about all that water makes my arthritis play up."

"Think of Tonna, underwater for days."

"A damp patch was the least of his problems. If anything, the water stopped him from decomposing too rapidly. And besides, on the floodplain, there are no pike."

In fact even the fish had left Tonna's body untouched. Soneri was contemplating other corpses which had been eaten away by marauding fish and left disfigured as though rubbed by sandpaper, when Nanetti surprised him with an unsuspected knowledge of the Po and its fauna. "I've looked it all up," he said. "I also know that in these parts, over on the Cremona side, there's a submerged village which re-emerges only when the water is very low."

"You don't remember where?"

"No, but it must be right in front of where we are now, on the far side. I think all you've got to do is ask. The land reclamation programme in the post-war period modified the course of the river, and the village itself was moved a couple of kilometres inland."

Soneri reflected on this for a moment and began to feel welling up inside him a sense of unease which was more like deep rancour. It was like a mild pressure on a part of his head he would not have been able to identify too precisely. For days, he had been moving around on the embankments and speaking to the local people without finding out about that sunken village. It annoyed him that Nanetti had simply turned up one evening with a new piece of information. He felt a fool, even if he was not sure that those few miserable hovels whose very existence he had been ignorant of were genuinely important. Perhaps not, but then why was he in such an ill humour?

The barman came over with the *spalla cotta* and Soneri was tempted to ask him about those submerged houses, but saw he had removed the hearing aid. And anyway, he would not have told him even if he had heard perfectly. Soneri concealed his thoughts by acting for a moment as head waiter, dividing the *spalla cotta* between the two plates and pouring the Fortanina into both glasses. Nanetti let him get on with it, and when they were about to eat, he said, "This story of the underwater village has really made an impression on you, hasn't it?"

He expressed himself with such moderation that the commissario calmed down, surprising even himself with his sudden change of mood.

"Absolutely nobody spoke to me about it," he said, while the possibility that there was a reason for that superimposed itself on what he said.

"It's still on old maps from the Fascist era. It was in the middle of a marsh," Nanetti said, "and the Fascist officials refused to initiate the reclamation programme in that zone because, so they said, it was a nest of Reds. The work was done under De Gasperi after the war."

Soneri remembered Nanetti's passion for topography and for old maps of any kind, military or civil. In his cellar at home he had a pile of them, which his wife described as the finest woodworm farm in the province.

"And this village was inhabited until they altered the course of the river?"

"I just don't know," Nanetti said, "but I believe so, considering it was rebuilt from scratch further inland on the plain."

He did not know why, but the story interested him. "What was the name of the village?"

"San Quirico. It seems no-one actually lives in the reconstructed houses. The children of the original owners keep them as second homes."

Soneri continued to think about the walls over which the Po slowly flowed. How many people had been happy or sad in that place? How many personal stories were buried under the water there? He was not sure why, but he imagined that some of these stories were connected to the case of the Tonna brothers. This idea frightened him, but his curiosity was aroused by the fact that no-one had ever told him about that place, even though it was only a stone's throw from the boat club. Perhaps on clear days you could even make it out beyond the bend in the river.

Nanetti got up and when the two of them were under the colonnade, the stench of burning still in the air, Soneri concluded to himself that the inquiry would need to start afresh from Anteo's corpse, from the facts in other words, the one thing that counted, as Nanetti always insisted.

"Tomorrow you're going to have a horde of journalists on your back, and Alemanni will be in a rage," Nanetti said before getting into his car.

The commissario gave a forced smile, clenching his extinguished cigar between his teeth. If he had paid heed only to the facts, he would never have set foot near the Po.

9

THE FREEZING FOG had left a fine film of frost on the car roof. Clouds of minute crystals floated through the air, while the drop in temperature had caused the grasses and plants in the fields to stiffen. Alongside him, the little villas with their overhanging roofs reminded Soneri of Christmas cards. As he was going along a stretch of completely white road, his mobile rang.

"I didn't see you at the meeting," the questore began, in a tone which was intended to convey a reproach, but he was too weak a man to make it felt.

"I was stuck with a corpse," Soneri said.

The silence was so long that it seemed for a moment as though they had been cut off. "I would have liked to speak to you about that, among other things." The questore was attempting to make up lost ground. "Tomorrow we're going to have the press on our backs."

"I'd prefer to steer clear of that."

"We'll have to give them some account of this new turn in the investigation," the questore said with greater feeling.

"Yes, sir," the commissario said. "But you know how to deal with these things much better than I do. Anyway, there's not a lot to say. We fished the body up this afternoon. Its skull had been cracked open in the same way as the brother's, and he was probably killed on the same day as he disappeared. The body had been secured underwater, next to the monument to the partisans on the floodplain beside the stone-crushing plant, not very far from the jetty. That's all there is to it."

From the long pause, the commissario guessed that his superior was taking notes on one of those sheets of notepaper headed QUESTURA which he kept in front of him at every meeting. He could even picture the pen with the pointed stem which he kept propped upright like an aerial in a kind of inkwell on his desk. He was equally sure that the questore would not pursue the topic. No-one ever appealed in vain to his vanity. Soneri did not have anything against journalists, who after all did the same sort of job as he did, but he never knew how to deal with their questions, so he evaded them by claiming judicial confidentiality and appealing to the complexity of the investigation. They would certainly want to know how he had worked out where the corpse was hidden. What could he say? That it was a matter of intuition? Or a hunch? Would he be able to transform something so fleeting and complex into a coherent answer? In his head, clouds without form and without geometry were blowing about. He could not squeeze them inside any rational perimeter – not that he had ever tried. It seemed to him as impossible a task as giving shape to the mist. There he was, splashing about like a gudgeon in the Po, and that was enough for him. It was all he needed to be able to get on with his job.

Now he felt drawn by the same inexplicable force towards the submerged village, and it was already in his mind that the freeze, with the dry days which accompanied it, would lower the water level to a point where the walls of the old San Quirico would be uncovered, making it possible for him to wander along a kind of Venetian *calle* surrounded by the ghosts of houses. The investigation was moving in time to the rhythms of the Po, of waters which rose and fell, endlessly changing the outline of the riverbank.

The car almost skidded on a stretch of road which was like a sheet of glass. He was badly shaken and this stopped him hearing the strains of "Aida" which had been ringing out for a few moments in his duffel-coat pocket.

"Where did you end up?" Angela said.

"I almost ended up in the ditch."

"You must be very distracted..."

"The ice and the tyres are as smooth as each other."

"Do you know that the carabinieri have mounted a huge inquiry into the trafficking of illegal immigrants?" she asked him.

"How do you know that?"

"A colleague is defending an Albanian pimp who's been bringing girls here to work on the streets, and he let me read the report. It seems they've uncovered a sizeable trafficking racket, and they even know how the girls are brought here."

"Did you see if Maresciallo Aricò was involved?"

"He's quoted frequently, but with all the big egos in the provincial command, if he's looking to get any credit, he can forget it. He'll be left with the crumbs at best."

The commissario let out a cry of fury. The maresciallo had been beavering away on his own initiative for some time, but he had been leading the commissario astray, either by acting the fool, or by spinning his tale about the lack of resources.

"Don't forget that you're in my debt over a certain discovery which has turned out to be very important for your inquiry," Angela warned him in a mock-threatening tone.

"So what?"

"So, Commissario, debts must be paid. Or would you rather I let the information leak out to your rivals in the carabinieri?"

"Fair enough," Soneri said, with a touch of resignation in his voice, "but don't ask for the impossible."

"The impossible! Quite the reverse, I promise you. Only the most possible of things. In fact, we've already achieved it!"

"You mean on the barge again?"

"I liked it very much."

"It's too risky. We got away with it once, but a second time…"

"You just don't get it, do you? No risk, no fun. Be prepared. As soon as I have a free moment, that is. It's one date you had better not forget… and when it comes to collecting dues, I'm completely unscrupulous."

"I'll take you for a drive along the embankment, down the river."

He heard a kind of shriek down the line. "You can't rise above banalities. The people who write those little sentimental ditties in chocolate wrappers should consult you. What you're talking about is the ante-chamber of conjugal love, a quick screw on a Saturday night in the double bed with freshly laundered sheets. I promise you, I'll never do it between your two loathsome bedside tables," she hissed.

It had, in fact, never happened. There was the one occasion when Angela had suddenly had the urge to reprise a situation from one of Boccaccio's stories, which had her chatting from a window with a friend below and the commissario behind her, invisible from the street.

Later, at home, in the half-light of his rooms, he thought that it was his good fortune not to be pursued by one of those clingy women who aspire to the role of wife. Perhaps that was why he was so fond of Angela.

He woke in the same half-light as the night before. The freezing fog had transformed the trees into white lace, the only vivid tone in the part of the city he could see from the kitchen window. With the blanket of clouds covering the skies, there was not much difference between the shimmering light of day and the light coming from the lamp-posts at night: it all resembled a northern dusk. He drank his *caffè latte* and then began to assemble in his mind the things he had to do. The central heating pipes, filling with warm water, gave a gurgle and a noise like the sound of digestive fluids, which made him think of the water pumps on the Po. Was everything dried out? By the time he put his coffee cup in the sink, he had already taken his decision. He wanted to return to the Po and at that time in the morning he would not encounter much traffic in the city.

He called Juvara when he was at the wheel, and instructed him to go to the mortuary where, in a couple of hours, they would be doing the post-mortem on Anteo Tonna. He did not expect much to emerge from that examination. What he had deduced from observing the corpse was not likely to be very different from what would be obtained by cutting it open. He tossed his mobile on to the seat beside him and concentrated on his driving. The Po valley was white in every direction. The hoar frost had attached itself to each hanging branch, making them seem thicker and endowing them with new colours, a spectacle that raised his spirits as much as the first snow of winter.

He travelled along the embankment, stopping where the previous day they had lifted Anteo's body on to the bank. It was still possible to make out the darker mark on the ground where the corpse had been laid. The commissario got out and looked over the floodplain and noted that all that was left were a few large pools covered by layers of ice. Elsewhere the ground seemed to have been thickened in the cold which had hardened the surface mud into a crust. It was only at that point that he became conscious of the silence. The mist and the white of the frost gave a certain solemnity to the surrounding countryside. They had switched off the pumps when the engines were only sucking in air. The freezing weather would finish the job.

He heard a tractor approach on the elevated road, but he had to let it draw close before he could make out one of the inhabitants of the floodplain coming back in order to work on his house, now reduced to a mud dyke. He would begin again, as those people there always did: giving new life to land made yet more fertile by the deposits from the river, spreading fresh gravel on the pathways and removing the sand from doors and walls.

Soneri parked at the boat club. There was no-one there yet and the locked door had the melancholy colour of aged straw. He got out of his car and called Juvara again. "Are you at the mortuary?"

"Yes, but it hasn't got under way yet. The police doctor said it would begin at nine."

"Never mind about the post-mortem," Soneri told him. "Go over to the Istituto Storico della Resistenza and ask if they know anything about a partisan who was called 'the Kite'."

He deduced from a long silence that Juvara was somewhat taken aback.

"Are you still there?" he barked.

Juvara hastened to register his attention with a few grunts. "O.K., I'm on my way," he said.

Soneri collected that Juvara was not pleased, and this annoyed him. He could not stand people who required their day to be mapped out in every detail from early morning, especially in a job like his. He detested diaries. He himself could never imagine what he would be doing one hour later, and lived from moment to moment without giving thought to the future. Things occurred according to a sequence which was rarely logical. It was useless to indulge in conjecture, since the prospect shifted as rapidly as it did for high-wire acrobats. His days were a process of continual adaptation to change, as was the case that morning on the banks of the Po. Rather than observing a body being cut open, he was looking at falling water levels which were funnelling the river back into its customary riverbed, and which were now so low that the riverbed itself seemed to him like a cavity in a gum from which a tooth had just been extracted.

He did not hear Barigazzi arrive and, when he turned round, he found him standing motionless behind him in the middle of the yard.

"Once you would have been on the jetty well before now," Soneri said.

"And how do you know that?"

"Boats have been going up and down the river for quite a while now."

Barigazzi said nothing, but made for the club and put a key in the door. The commissario stayed where he was, watching the current. He was happily wondering where San Quirico might have been. Straight ahead, Nanetti had said, so he looked into the middle distance, his gaze suspended somewhere between the water and the mist.

"Come on in, it's warmer in here," Barigazzi's voice shouted from the club.

Soneri went in and stood in front of a cast-iron stove where the flames were already roaring. From the windows it was no longer possible to see the barge, which had dropped with the waters. Barigazzi came over and stood beside him at the window.

"San Quirico must be straight ahead," Soneri said, pointing. The old man remained silent for a few moments before saying: "It's a bit further down the valley, just before Gussola."

"How many people used to live there?"

"Forty or so. It was a small village."

It was only then that he thought of a certain parallel which had been troubling him without his understanding why: the village, like Anteo Tonna, was underwater. And both were dead.

"Of those who used to live there, are there any still hereabouts?"

Barigazzi looked at him nervously. He was making an obviously unsuccessful effort to grasp what was behind these questions. "There are one or two up and down the Po valley, but they're very old. The people who lived there were a pretty odd lot."

"They were all communists, I've been told."

"Strange characters, the sort you find in marshlands," Barigazzi said uneasily. "Turned savage by the water and prey to malaria. People always on the verge of madness, after generations of intermarriage. Even the Fascists left them alone. And then the land reform programme wiped San Quirico off the map."

"Can you still see the ruins of the houses today?"

"A couple more days and they'll be sticking out of the water. It happens every time the level drops. They say that on misty nights when this happens you can still hear the voices of the people who lived in those houses. But it's only a legend. Maybe it's the wind whistling over the stones dislodged by the current. Others say it's because in San Quirico they never buried their dead. They threw them into the river with a rock tied to their waists. Water to water."

Soneri briefly reflected that this practice was probably not so different from what had happened many years previously all along the banks of the river: men eaten by fish and fish eaten by men. The same substance forever feeding off itself in an eternal cycle. And then his thoughts went back to Anteo Tonna, buried underwater by a boulder from the stone-crushing plant, but pinned, in his case, to the shallow, provisional floor of the flat lands where even the fish feel the precariousness of the sluggish, underwater currents, and for that reason do not stay there for long.

"It was not by chance that he was found there," he said, staring straight ahead at the window, where the mists of the Po and a faint reflection of his face were superimposed on the glass.

He noticed that Barigazzi had turned to observe him, apparently bemused, as though he feared the commissario were talking in a delirium, but Soneri himself continued to look out at the horizon over the river, where for many days now the line between land and sky had been lost. It seemed obvious to him that the killer had had a certain taste for symbolism. Consciously or not, everyone did. Every pre-meditated murder followed the ritual of a theatrical production. Plainly there were some actors who performed their parts well; and others, less well. The problem was to identify the gifted ones.

To which category did the man who had killed Tonna belong? Soneri imagined him to be a well-focused, brazen type. Who else would plan a murder in a hospital ward, with all the risks he was bound to incur? And then there was the corpse on the floodplain, put there precisely so that it would be found beside the monument to the partisans. An ordinary killer or a professional hit man would have tossed it into deeper waters, weighed down with a stone, in common with the practice for funerals at San Quirico.

Many things simply did not add up while others seemed to be talking to him, but in a language which was as yet indecipherable.

His mobile telephone brought him back to himself. "They killed him on the day of his disappearance, between eight and ten in the evening," Nanetti informed him, with no preliminary greeting.

"So the barge set off without him."

"Exactly. That whole business of the barge was to put us off the scent."

"Was there anything else apart from the blow to the head?"

"Nothing. The body was otherwise unmarked. He was still a vigorous man in spite of his age."

So, whoever had killed Decimo in the morning had killed Anteo in the evening. He must have known his two victims well. Above all, he must have been aware that the boatman – who rarely left his barge – would not have known about his brother's death or else he would have taken precautions. In any case, the brothers had only occasional contact and Anteo was a man accustomed to threats.

Barigazzi switched on the radio, but now that the water was low the look-outs along the embankment had nothing to report to each other. In a silence broken only by the low buzz of the loudspeaker, the click of the door handle made itself heard. Dinon Melegari stood framed in the doorway. As soon as he saw the commissario he hesitated as though he would rather turn back, but he decided to come in, with obvious reluctance, looking past Soneri at Barigazzi. When the commissario fixed his eyes on him, interrogating him with his stare, Dinon pointed an outstretched index finger at Barigazzi who, although evidently taken aback, returned his glance. With no more than that exchange, the two men established a kind of complicity.

"I came for the boats," Melegari said, embarrassed. "Now that the waters are so low, I thought that it would be better to drag them ashore. The winch is working, isn't it?"

"You're right. The boats are on the sand." Barigazzi was doing a better job of masking his feelings.

"White wine?"

Melegari nodded, as did the commissario. The three men then found themselves around a table while a silence as cold as the frost outside made conversation impossible.

"Will the inlets freeze over?" Soneri said.

The others looked up, wondering who was expected to answer this. "Only if it lasts a week. By the banks on the northern side," Barigazzi mumbled, looking at Dinon, and in that exchange the commissario perceived a coded message.

He remained obstinately at the table, asking off-hand questions about the Po, about the levels of the water and the boats. After a time Dinon got up, almost banging his head on the light which hung over the table. "I'll go and have a look at the boat."

After he had left, Soneri said: "An unexpected visitor."

Barigazzi said nothing, but got to his feet and took the bottle away. He came back for the glasses.

"The split in the Left has been resolved, then?" the commissario said.

The old man shrugged and tried to make light of the issue. "He drops in every so often. He's required to inform us about what he's doing at the jetty. That's what the regulations say. And then he pays a fee for the boat."

The commissario got up. It seemed to him pointless to go on. It was enough for him that evidently Melegari had come to speak to Barigazzi, perhaps about matters which concerned the Tonna brothers. He felt his distrust of him increasing, and this told him that he was getting close to something important.

He gave a curt nod to Barigazzi and went out, walking

along the pebbly track which led to the jetty, where half of the boats had been left. On a large *magano* he saw Melegari testing the current with an oar. Melegari saw Soneri too, but pretended not to.

He crossed the river at Torricella, then turned on to the wrong road, but made it to Gussola by lunchtime. There was no great difference between the two banks of the river: the same low houses in rows, the same churches with that distinctive, blood-red Baroque typical of the Po valley. Juvara interrupted Soneri's contemplation of a kind of cathedral with *salame-* coloured bricks, on which almost half a century of humidity had left its deposits. "There's no Kite in our part of the valley," he said. "There are two of them, and they both fought on the Apennines along the Gothic line."

Soneri thought this over for a few minutes. "Cast your net wider. Check with the Resistance archives in Mantua, Cremona and Reggio. He must have been somewhere, this Kite."

"Do you want me to look on the internet?"

"Look anywhere you like. Maybe the killer will pop up on your screen."

It was not Juvara's idleness which annoyed him as much as the intrusion of these new-fangled investigative techniques. He detected some vague threat in them, even though he knew perfectly well that it was the fear of feeling redundant which really upset him. At his age, this had become a matter of some delicacy.

He found a seat at a very ordinary restaurant, which did however promise a *stracotto d'asinina* with genuine credentials. The television was talking about what journalists were now calling "the murder on the Po". A roomful of lorry drivers, office workers and shopkeepers had stopped eating and were glued to the screen, but Soneri was beginning to feel some unease at not being where logic dictated he should be. He saw the questore behind a microphone, with four officers in yellow jackets marked "Polizia" – worn especially for the cameras – and a group of journalists with their notebooks, and there he was in a country *trattoria* which had nothing to do with the investigation, along the misty banks of the Po, searching for a phantom village which had long since been swallowed up by the waters. Once again, he was overwhelmed by a feeling of insecurity arising from his invariable role as an outsider, but he comforted himself with the thought that perhaps that was why he was able to see things from the correct angle.

The riverbank was now one long beach littered with the flotsam and jetsam of the flood. He approached, hoping to see if the first stone or the first wall of the sunken village might be emerging. Perhaps it was too early. Barigazzi had said that it would take another couple of days' freeze to bring the waters right down. He walked along the stretch of sand where he saw trails of old footsteps and the tracks of dogs which had been sniffing out the faint scents left by the encroaching water.

His intuition suggested to him that there was an uneven section of riverbed at the point where the ruins of San Quirico ought to be. There the surface of the water broke up into eddies and curled and twisted like a lazy reptile. He stood a few moments peering into the deeper solitude until it occurred to him that if he really wanted to give some sense to his wanderings, he should make his way inland and go from house to house making inquiries, risking the wrath of guard dogs.

New San Quirico, a soulless place without a centre, thrown up haphazardly across a defunct road, was far worse than anything he could have imagined. He would have sooner owned an underwater house than one of those anonymous villas prematurely aged by the mists. He wandered for a few minutes among shut-up houses, past huts with rusty steel roofs containing only odds and ends no longer useful in city dwellings. The village appeared to be deserted, but at least half a dozen dogs barked somewhere in the mist, though there was no way of knowing where exactly they were. For ten minutes he did not come across a single trace of another human being, but then he noticed a low house with a woodshed under the balcony and a garden covered with sheets of plastic as protection against the frost. Outside it, half-concealed by a glass-fronted veranda framed by gilt aluminium, an old man sat on a wooden bench looking out on to the roadway. He was wearing a heavy overcoat and leaned both hands on a walking stick. He had plainly been there for some time, but it was not clear what he was looking at, unless it was the mist itself as it deposited a sprinkling of ice particles.

Soneri got out of his car and gestured to him, but the old man made no move. He rang the bell, causing the man to turn towards the door to see if anyone in the house had heard. A small dog, which must have been sleeping behind the house, came scampering towards the commissario, growling. He waited until a light was switched on inside. The old man remained motionless, as though under a glass case in a museum. The front door opened and an old woman came out. She exchanged some words with the man. The man gave a start and rose to his feet. The veranda window opened and the commissario introduced himself.

"My husband doesn't see too well," the woman said. "He's got cataracts."

The dry heat of the wood fire greeted him and the old man's eyes began to follow him, picking up his voice and tracking his passage across the veranda.

"I'm looking for someone who once lived in San Quirico on the Po," the commissario began.

The man nodded and his wife explained that he had been the miller.

"When did you come here?"

"Immediately after the war, when the reclamation schemes got under way."

"The Fascists had excluded you from their reconstruction programmes…"

"They knew things were bad for us and left us up to our arses in the water."

"Were you sorry to come here?"

"No, here you can live like a human being." It was the wife who spoke.

"You can't see the Po," the man said with heart-felt regret.

Soneri guessed that, in his lonely afternoons on that veranda, the cataracts and the mist forced him to imagine the banks of the river, the flat lands, the inlets and even the fish.

"Were they all communists in San Quirico?"

"For the most part," the man said, as his pupils stopped roaming and he cast his clouded gaze towards the floor.

A silence fell over the kitchen, now in half-light, the best conditions for cataract sufferers. The commissario felt embarrassed. He was not making a favourable impression, asking for information from two elderly people who had little inclination to dwell on a grim past. The woman came to his rescue. Breaking the silence in which the two men sat facing each other, she said: "We paid a heavy price for that."

The Fascists. She could not be talking of anything else.

"What did they do to you?"

"Reprisals, round-ups. Fortunately we could always hear them coming from a long way off and we were able to make our escape along the Po. Sometimes they burned down houses, although there was not much to burn. They even set fire to my home, but we managed to get there just in time. There being no shortage of water."

"Were there any partisans among you?"

"Yes, but they stayed away so as not to get their families involved. All that were left were women, old folk and children."

The man made an effort to focus on the commissario, but his eyes were too weak and stared up towards the ceiling, having been misled by the shadows.

"So there were not many people killed, is that so?" Soneri said cautiously, thinking of what San Quirico must have been like, a mass of grey stone suspended over the water, at the mercy of the currents.

"Life's hardships took many more," the woman said.

There followed another silence which seemed all the more profound in that house with its dimmed lights, oppressed by a cellar-like darkness. Just as it was becoming embarrassing and Soneri was about to take their unwillingness to speak as a sign that it was time for him to leave, the man said: "The worst thing was when they burned the Ghinelli house, and the women..." The sentence was moving to its climax, but he stopped. His wife made a gesture expressing her displeasure, turned her face away, overcome by the horror brought on by the recollections.

"Was he a partisan?" Soneri said.

"He was killed near Parma. In '44, I think."

"And the women?"

The old couple looked at each other, and something like a reproach came into the woman's eyes. Memories from a far-distant time, long buried and now being hauled out, must have been bitter.

"They... I don't know how to say it. They used them," the

man said. "There were so many of them. One of the women couldn't bear the shame and threw herself in the Po near the whirlpools. The rest of them disappeared and were never seen again."

"What was left for them there?" the old woman wondered. "Their house had been pulled down, and the little they had was destroyed."

"What about the brother in the partisans?"

"A brave man who was afraid of nothing. Always in the thick of things, whatever the danger. But nothing more was heard of the Ghinelli family after the war."

"Was there anyone in the partisans from San Quirico who was called 'the Kite'?"

The old man looked up, trying to locate Soneri's face, but he turned the wrong way and ended up peering at the lamp, whose light forced him to look down. Instead, palms upwards, he stretched out hands as calloused as hard clay. "There were so many names. The Resistance fighters... the partisans in that formation, what was it called, the Gruppo di Azione Patriottica, kept changing names all the time."

They heard the sound of a car drawing up outside. It seemed extraordinary that anyone would willingly come back so late to such a place, but a middle-aged, rather stocky man smelling of iron and oil made his entrance. "My son," the woman said.

The commissario looked closely at him and formed a picture of a deeper solitude yet: two old people with an unmarried son destined to remain on his own and to grow old in a place like this. No-one had invested anything in the future of San Quirico.

As he was taking his leave, all three came out on to the veranda with its glass front and gilt aluminium frame, and from behind the glass the old man gazed at things that were not there. From the window of his car, Soneri kept his eyes on them, still together, until the mist swallowed them up.

The darkness fell quickly as he tried to find his way back on to the main road. After a while, he fell in behind a lorry and resolved to return to the police station. When he entered the office, Juvara looked up in surprise. "Did you turn off your mobile to avoid the journalists?"

Soneri took out his telephone and saw it had no battery left. He must have switched it on by mistake. "Have you been trying for long?"

"Three hours," Juvara said timidly.

The commissario would have apologized but could not find the words.

"I wanted to reach you to let you know," the ispettore said, "that I've found out who the Kite was."

"Where?"

"In the Resistance archive in Mantua. He was from Viadana and a member of the Garibaldi Brigade."

"What was his real name?"

"Libero Gorni. Born 1924, died aged twenty."

"Where?"

Juvara consulted his notebook, running an eye down the page. "Captured during a skirmish on the banks of the Po, province of Parma, near Torricella," he said, reading word for word the note he had copied out exactly as he had found it. "He was shot at Sissa four days later, in spite of an attempt to save him by a prisoner exchange."

"Nothing else?"

"In the original exchange of fire, two partisans fell: Ivan Varoli and Spartaco Ghinelli."

"Get back on to the archive and see if these two or any other members of the partisan group had relatives among the combatants. Ask if they are known to be still alive and if so, where they can be found."

Seated in front of the commissario's desk, his great belly wedged between the arms of the chair, the ispettore favoured his superior with a puzzled glance. "You don't really think," he stuttered. "It's more than sixty years ago..."

Soneri made no reply. He was not sure himself about what he had just told Juvara he wanted done.

"It's because of the note. The one that referred to this Kite. It has to mean something."

The moment Soneri was left on his own, the telephone rang. He lifted the receiver impatiently and heard the voice of the questore. The attention lavished on him by the television crews had obviously acted on him like amphetamines. His ego had swelled, as was clear from the waves of rounded rhetorical frills, each as neatly finished as an embroidered quilt. There were even grand words of praise for Soneri, more for having left the stage to him alone than for his having had the intuition to conduct an investigation along the banks of the Po in the first place.

When he put the telephone down Soneri should have been pleased, but instead he was nagged by a sense of unease. No-one was more aware than he that the conclusion was not yet within sight. He lit a cigar and tried to calm himself, but at that moment the strains of "Aida" rang out. He sat indecisively for a moment, the mobile in his hand, until the noise irritated him so much that he decided to press the button.

"Commissario, I'm ready to collect payment of your debt."

"Angela, could we not just spend the evening in town? I'll take you to dinner."

"It's a long time since you called me by my name. Pity the only places you know are places to eat in. You measure out your life in restaurants."

"We could go macrobiotic or vegetarian."

"No. I prefer to be afloat."

There was no changing her mind. They would only quarrel and he had no appetite for a barrage of wounding remarks. As it was, his mood was upsetting him more than any ulcer.

"But there'll be people at the boat club until ten. Can't we just stop off somewhere for a bite to eat?"

"No, you know I love running risks."

"We'll go in your car. Mine's too recognizable."

Walking under the arches of the town, along the less-travelled streets so as not to be seen, made him feel like a teenager again. Angela, hugging him close, went on tiptoe to avoid making any noise with her heels.

"Be ready for criticism," she warned in a whisper.

"Haven't I had enough already?"

"All my criticisms are good-natured. I might bark a lot, you know, but I don't bite. I meant from your superiors."

"The questore has just been showering me with praise."

"Wait until you hear what he has to say when the carabinieri get the headlines in the papers for the anti-trafficking operation. I heard the prosecutor who's taken charge of the inquiry talking in the corridor before a trial... it looks like a major breakthrough."

Soneri cursed himself for having given Aricò so much rope. Angela understood and held him closer. She made him stop and looked him squarely in the face. "Are you sure you're on the right track?"

"At this stage it is impossible to be sure."

"If you're talking like that, it means that deep down you *are* sure," she replied, giving his jacket lapels a little tug.

When they were in sight of the embankment, they clambered up the side away from the yard. Below, the club gave off a yellow light from windows through which they could see dark shadows. They climbed back down, keeping to the asphalt path on the far side. They stopped in their tracks when the door of the club opened for a moment and Gianna stretched out an arm to shake a duster, but they then proceeded towards the jetty. This time the ground was frozen hard and the barge was even lower in the water. The gangplank was hanging perilously low.

They moved from the captain's berth to the matelot's quarters, but then Angela wanted to try the wheelhouse. Later they began to feel the cold and got dressed. Soneri glanced at the clock and noticed the little hand almost at one. When he climbed back up to the wheelhouse, he saw three men walk by on the jetty. From his gait, he recognized Barigazzi with Dino, unmistakeable because of his girth, beside him. He could not identify the third man, who was tall, and his head swayed as he walked. Their route took them away from the jetty towards a pathway on either side of which little houses had been built on raised columns.

"We're trapped," Soneri said to Angela, gesturing with his chin in the direction of the moorings and looking at her in gentle reproof.

"Don't you dare tell me it wasn't worthwhile," she said menacingly. "If you ever solve this case, it will all be down to me," she added, drawing close to warm herself.

Soneri tried to control his annoyance at the contact. He could not bear having anyone too close to him when he was thinking. He was now engrossed in working out what those three could be up to, but his head was clouded by the same mist as the one into which the three had vanished. If Dinon and Barigazzi were the first two, could the third man be Vaeven Fereoli?

"I'll have to go and see," he said with a decisiveness in part due to his discomfort over his proximity to Angela.

She held him back, clinging to the hem of his duffel coat. "You must take care," she said, indicating the road with her glance.

Two outlines slowly emerged some twenty metres from them. The commissario pushed Angela's head down to hide her, even if in the mist and with no light other than the small lamp a little way off it would not have been easy to make them out through the window. When they passed a few metres from the barge's cabin, Soneri recognized Dinon and Barigazzi, on their own, walking one beside the other with the nonchalance of fish in a shoal. They strolled slowly by and took the steps leading up to the boat club. The other man must have stopped off in one of the fishermen's cottages below the embankment.

"You see, it was worthwhile after all," Angela said with ironic malice as she stood up.

Soneri took her in his arms, and that was something that he rarely did.

10

JUVARA HAD LEFT him more confused than before. Libero Gorni, known as "the Kite", had faced a Fascist firing squad at Sissa on 23 November, 1944. In the encounter on the Po floodplain, both Ivan Varoli and Spartaco Ghinelli had died. Ghinelli was a native of San Quirico, one of the family whose house had been burned down and whose women had been raped by the Blackshirts.

"This much is clear, isn't it?" Soneri asked the ispettore, who continued to rifle through a pile of papers with scribbled notes in the margins.

Juvara nodded, but he continued to consult the pages, seizing hold of one of them as though he had been searching for it for days. The commissario listened again to a summary reconstruction of the battle which had been read to him the day before, finally focusing on the description provided by the partisans who had retrieved the bodies:... *The two who fell on the battlefield had been so badly disfigured by gunshot and stab wounds that they could be identified by their comrades only after an examination of the objects they had about their person. Varoli possessed false documents ever since he belonged to the Gruppo di Azione Patriottica. The Blackshirts had fallen on their bodies with ferocity, which might be evidence of how much they dreaded the Garibaldi Brigade ...*

"Have you checked to see if Ghinelli and Varoli have relatives still alive?"

"Ghinelli's brothers and sisters are all dead. One sister committed suicide in the Po, a brother took his life in South America."

"What about Varoli? And the relatives of the Kite?"

"Varoli... Varoli..." Juvara repeated, fumbling among the paper on the desk in front of him. "Here we are. One sister died in Turin seven years ago. Gorni, the Kite that is, had no relatives. He was brought up by the Sisters of the Child Jesus, before being sent to work as a farmhand when he was eleven."

Soneri mused on how little life had given to an unloved boy who died in his twentieth year, but this thought gave way to the consideration of the *cul de sac* into which history had turned. If the killing of the Kite had been in some obscure way a precedent for the death of Tonna, who could have remembered and avenged that event if everyone involved had already gone on to another world? And in that other world, were there already reports circulating about those days? Memory buried by ignorance and by a frivolous, doltish affluence... what had he achieved by his early death?

He noticed that Juvara was staring at him, but fortunately he did not ask him those insufferable questions: "What's the matter? What are you thinking about?" When he finished brooding and came back to the facts of the case, he asked, "Were there any grandchildren?"

"There were three grandchildren, all girls, on the Varoli side, and five, including two males, on the Ghinelli side."

"What do they do? Where do they live?" Soneri said impatiently, but he had set Juvara rummaging even more frantically among the documents.

"Jobs: nothing out of the ordinary. One of the grandsons

has been living in Switzerland for forty years, the other died in a car accident twelve years ago."

The commissario sensed that these questions and the ispettore's exhaustive answers were not helping him much. It seemed that the crimes had been committed by someone for whom time had stood still, as it had for the Tonna brothers.

With his thoughts leaping from one contradiction to the next, he opened the newspaper. The front page was given over entirely to the developments in the inquiry conducted by Aricò and the carabinieri from three provinces: HUMAN TRAFFICKING BEHIND THE TONNA CRIME? one headline wanted to know. He read the statements of the carabinieri commander and some magistrates, each expressing the conviction that they were on the right track. He felt Angela's grim warnings come true. His own superior would no doubt be vacillating, and Soneri would be left high and dry to defend an inquiry which risked sliding into depths of improbability or into obscure aspects of a history of deaths which no-one any longer remembered.

Juvara looked up to see Soneri stride so decisively into the corridor that he had no time to stop him; by the time he got himself out of his chair and round the other side of the desk, the commissario had disappeared.

Shortly afterwards, as he travelled through the mist, Soneri tried to imagine those corpses defaced and deformed by bullet and knife wounds. The Fascists, doubtless motivated by detestation and a thirst for vengeance, must have fallen on them after the battle with appalling ferocity. Perhaps they had been searching for them for some time, to make them pay. Perhaps it was Tonna himself who had been guiding them, he who knew the Po so intimately.

His mobile rang. Juvara's voice was, as usual, trembling when he had to make use of a mechanism he knew the commissario detested.

"I saw you running off, but I didn't have time to..."

"The sprint was never your strong point."

"Listen, I wanted to tell you something that I forgot earlier on. A small detail, just to fill you in."

"What is it?"

"In the firefight, there were three Fascists killed as well, but one of them, a man from Brescia, they never found his body. The story went that he might have fallen into the Po and that his body got caught up in the sands or was devoured by the fish."

Soneri drove on in the mist, deep in thought. The encounter between the two embankments took place in mid-November. In the first days of the same month they had burned down the houses at San Quirico... and that body that was never found... the circulation of documents among the partisans of the G.A.P. ... the dead bodies savaged by knives... "A murky business", the partisan bulletins had defined it some years later as they strove to reconstruct what had happened along the Po, perhaps on a day of mists like today.

On the way, he saw signs for San Quirico and turned on to the high, narrow road with a ditch on either side which ran above the countryside. He found the old man in the same position as on the previous occasion, as though he had not moved in the interim. He was still staring straight ahead, hands cupped over his walking stick. His wife saw the commissario and opened the door without a word of greeting. When he was close beside him, the old man became aware of his presence and began to explore the space around in search of him, but when Soneri took a seat beside him, he turned to peer once again into the mist. The woman stayed to observe them for a few moments, and then discreetly withdrew.

"Do you remember the battle of '44, the one that took place in the floodplain between the embankments?"

The old man abruptly raised one arm. It was obvious that he remembered it perfectly.

"Was it ever known with certainty what happened?"

"The only people who know that were those who were there, but they are all dead."

"Did you, any of you, ever speak about it in the past?"

"There was a lot of talk, yes," replied the man, still gazing in front of him into the mist. "Do you think we wouldn't have spoken about it? On the feast of All Souls, the Fascists had burned down the houses in San Quirico and the Blackshirts marched up and down the plains of the Po like masters. People accused the partisans of staying in hiding, like rabbits. It was then that Ghinelli and the others decided to make them pay."

"An ambush?"

"Along the embankment, near Torricella. They thought they had the Po to help them retreat, and the brush on the floodplain to hide them. They knew them both intimately."

"Was Ghinelli in command?"

"He was the most decisive one. It was his idea to carry out the ambush. The other commanders were not much in agreement because it might have exposed civilians to reprisals. And anyway, it was very risky."

"Why were they defaced in that way?"

The old man raised both hands as he had done previously, letting go of the walking stick which fell against him. "Nobody knows, nobody was ever able to explain that. Perhaps they had accounts to settle with Ghinelli and the others from earlier times. Hatred added to hatred, but none of the Blackshirts ever admitted to having desecrated the dead, and anyway there was the mist all around, like today. Sometimes that's your salvation, other times it's your destruction. Like life itself, you never know if it's going to protect you or not. It went very badly for poor Gorni, who had got separated from the rest and was making his way back under the embankment on foot. They came out of nowhere."

"Is he the one they called 'the Kite'?"

"As far as I knew he was called 'Arrow', but the partisans around here changed their names all the time."

They remained in silence for a few minutes. After the last sentence the old man made a circling gesture with his hands, indicating some kind of confusion, so the commissario said: "So nobody ever found out anything about the Fascist who went missing?"

The man shook his head.

"He was from Brescia..." was all he could say, but then, after a pause, he added: "Maybe he was injured and ended up in the Po as he tried to make his escape. They're mountain people and they drown easily."

"But the body was never found..."

"Normally the river always restores what it has taken, but around here they say that someone who has not learned to swim when he's alive doesn't float when he's dead."

Soneri tried to imagine what was going through the old man's mind, what he was watching in that mist he had been observing day after day as though it were a screen on which a nostalgic film of past years was being projected.

"Very few people know what happens in the mist," he said. "And the question is whether those few people have any inclination to tell. In this case the matter is closed."

It was not the first time that Soneri found himself facing the irremediable. Death was the most unwavering of all forms of reticence. "Perhaps that's why there are so many rumours going around..."

The old man repeated the jerky gesture with his hand. "There are some people who even say that maybe one of those who was there did not die," he said, apparently to fill the silence.

The hypothesis aroused Soneri's interest and once again set his imagination working overtime, but not at the same rate as that of the old man who the moment he stopped talking began once again to observe with a sort of avidity the grey emptiness that surrounded him. Soneri too did his best to absorb himself in an imaginary film, staring into a space stretching from somewhere above the low roofs of the houses before them to unfathomable depths in which it was possible to glimpse everything or nothing. He was trying to stage in his mind all that might have occurred under the main embankment on that land won back from the water, where everything appears precarious.

The ambush, shadows facing shadows, the rounds of gunfire shot at random at ghosts made of air and little else, the awareness of the dying that they were falling without knowing the identity of their killers, the flight in any direction for refuge in the same mist which had made the ambush possible, then the silence after the gunfire in the damp air which had served to muffle the shots, the attempt to listen for the enemy in every blade of grass that rustled, the stumbling over corpses, and the undergrowth growing more dense in a world of dancing wisps of mist. Anything at all could have happened, including the possibility that one of them had not died and so… perhaps then the ferocity perpetrated on the bodies should not be attributed to Fascist vengeance. But after seeing the body of the Kite savaged by the torture so minutely described in the partisans' bulletins, who could give credence to any conflicting hypothesis? Eyes pushed in by relentless punching, face swollen and dark like garnet-coloured quince and made to look like sausage meat. And finally the burns, the fingernails wrenched out, the testicles a bloody mess.

Certainly no-one had been identified. It required the intervention of the entire Garibaldi detachment to decide which corpse was which. The pike could not have done worse in a month. And then there was the question of the man from Brescia who had disappeared. A missing body represents an unsolved case, always and everywhere. He was thinking of all this when he turned gently to the old man and saw him concentrate on that unmoving grey.

"What do you think happened?"

"It always seemed strange to me."

"You don't believe that it was the Blackshirts?"

The old man shook his head. "They only did those things in their barracks. They wanted to look bold, but in fact they were shit-scared. They were terrified, and anyway, in '44 they knew their time was up."

Soneri made no reply and the silence seemed to him deep enough to enable him to hear the sound of the specks of ice falling one by one on the dry leaves. He rose to his feet quite abruptly, as he always did. The old man was startled and turned to look and see where he was. The mist over his eyes must have been populated by something new superimposed on his recollections. When he felt the commissario's hand on his shoulder, he turned rapidly and tried to stare at him with eyes which were now filled only with apparitions.

"You know how to peer into the depths," Soneri said, preparing to leave. It was a sentence which might have seemed foolish or jeering, but that was not how it was meant.

He parked outside the *Italia* to let it be known he had arrived. Up on the embankment, looking down at the boat club, he felt a kind of resentment. He felt alienated from that world which seemed to be betraying him, but as he thought over all that was going on, some form of childish pride filled his breast and made him feel as though he were reverting to his childhood days. He climbed back down towards the centre where, in front of Anteo's niece's bar, the labourers were hard at work fixing up the facade of the building which had been blackened by the flames. The woman stood looking on in the same pose as when she was behind the bar, arms folded to support her heavy breasts.

"When do you plan to open up again?" Soneri said.

"In two weeks, if everything goes according to plan," the woman replied, without turning towards him.

"That telephone call..." the commissario said, "I mean the one from that man who was looking for your uncle... and who spoke dialect very well but was not sure of his Italian... you said he had a foreign accent, maybe Spanish... or Portuguese."

Showing no interest, the woman made a movement with her chin as if to say: "So what?"

"I want to get it right. He said that he was looking for Barbisin?"

The only reply he received was a kind of gesture of assent, once more with her chin, and an expression of mild irritation.

"I've explained it all to you, haven't I? He didn't speak in dialect all the time. When I picked up the phone and said 'Hello', he hesitated for a moment and then asked in Italian if that was the Tonna household. Maybe he thought he'd got the wrong number. I asked him if it was my uncle he was looking for, and then he began to speak in dialect."

"Did you answer in dialect?"

"No, I have always used Italian. I hardly ever speak in

dialect," she said, with an edge of contempt in her voice towards customs which no doubt reminded her of the peasant origins she preferred to leave behind her.

"When was the last time your son sailed with the old man?"

"He's right there, go and ask him," the woman said, growing more and more hostile and pointing to the boy standing under the scaffolding.

Soneri walked over to where the boy was, lighting a cigar to calm himself. He smoked as he listened to the labourers cursing the frost which made their hands numb.

"When was the last time you went on the river with your uncle?"

"A week before he died," the boy said. "I remember it well because we went down together and then went to my mother's house. That happened only once a week."

"Did you ever notice anything unusual when you passed other boats on the river?"

"On the Po, people always behave in the same way. They exchange a few words or signs of greeting. There's hardly ever time for more than a couple of words."

"Did your uncle have that sort of time?"

"Generally it was other people who asked him something and he would answer them. He had a reputation as a good sailor and his advice was always useful."

"Was there anyone who avoided you, or who would not greet you?"

The boy looked about him as though unsure whether to reply. "The communists," he said in a voice barely above a whisper.

"Who?" Soneri said, even if he already guessed all he needed to know.

"People like Melegari and that other one…What's his name? Vaeven. If we'd had a smaller vessel instead of a barge, they'd have rammed us."

"Did they move about a lot?"

"We met them several times. Sometimes with other people."

"Did you recognize these other people?"

"No, they always kept their distance. They have a *magano* which can move very fast."

"One person or more?"

"Almost always one."

"Were they fishing?"

"Who knows? I've never seen them fishing, but I think they travelled quite far. They used their boat instead of a car. I don't think they had a licence to drive a car."

"What about Barigazzi, did you ever bump into him?"

"He doesn't move about very much," the boy said, shrugging. "And he nearly always stays close in. He's only got an old boat."

"And what do you plan to do with the barge now?"

"As soon I can I'll ask the shipyards to give me an estimate, because I'd like to anchor it at the jetty and convert it into a bar for the summer season. It's the only way to make use of it now."

Soneri stood in silence. He imagined the barge with its engine shut down for good, a stopping-off point for couples on a trip up the Po, and he thought of certain former colleagues who had ended up as porters in blocks of flats to supplement their pensions. At his age, he was only too aware of the prospect of hard times ahead. To chase away those grim thoughts, he turned suddenly towards the boy, taking the cigar from his mouth as he did so. "Maybe it would be better to sell it as scrap."

It was getting dark and a freezing fog was coming down once more from the skies. Under the arches, he took out his mobile and called Juvara. "Check up on the records of the telephone company and see if you can work out where that call to Tonna's niece came from. The one made a week before they killed him."

"No problem," the ispettore said. "Have you seen what the prefetto told the newspapers?"

The commissario replied that he had not, but he could sense trouble ahead.

"He said that the police will be investigating the trafficking because it's highly probable that that was the motive for the Tonna murder."

"They can investigate to their heart's content!" Soneri said angrily. And when Juvara said nothing, intimidated as he was by the commissario's tone, the latter made an attempt to sound cordial and said: "Cheer up, I'll call you later."

He walked back to the jetty. The road was white with hoar frost, while from the skies flakes continued to fall as slowly as the flow of the current when the water level was low. He went down towards the yard, took the track leading to the fishermen's cottages and then turned to the stairs leading to the moorings. Melegari's *magano* was not there, but the ropes which had been thrown on to the concrete quay were clearly in evidence. The other boats, including Barigazzi's, had been covered with tarpaulins. Along the riverbank, a row of stakes had been driven in to measure how quickly the water was falling.

He returned towards the yard just as the big light was being switched on. He was passing the fishermen's cottages when his mobile rang. In the silence, he had the impression that his "Aida" had put the whitened branches and the buildings on stilts on the alert.

The commissario put the telephone to his ear. He knew from the number that it was Juvara.

"I've checked. The call you asked about came from the Fidenza district, from Zibello. I didn't go through the official channels, but I was able to make use of our mole inside the company."

"Did he tell you the time?"

"It lasted from 7.44 to 7.46."

Soneri ended the call as he reached the yard. He walked round the club and as he was about to go in he saw the carabinieri van pull up. Aricò was wearing a coat down to his knees, and he seemed to be in uniform.

"Being in the newspapers at last has done wonders for you," Soneri said.

"Orders from above, the television people turned up today," the maresciallo mumbled.

"Did you tell the journalists how Tonna was killed?"

"You don't believe this story of the trafficking of illegal immigrants?"

"The trafficking, yes, I believe that."

The maresciallo fell silent, deep in thought, before adding: "I don't really believe either that..."

"The magistrate spoke to the press and now it seems that everybody has embraced this idea of the traffickers' revenge," Soneri said.

"They've cottoned on to the one certain fact. Put yourself in their shoes. What would you do? These two murders have remained unsolved for some time now. If nothing else, this story will help to calm public disquiet."

Unwittingly, Aricò had put his finger on the wound. The only certainty was the trafficking, and to make matters worse, it originated largely from the commissario's own investigations.

"Have you managed to reconstruct the traffickers' organization?" Soneri said, feeling annoyance grow inside him as he spoke.

"We're nearly there. We've only one or two points to verify," he said. Pointing to the door of the club, he went on: "I've come to piece together the barge's movements in the last month from here to other ports along the river."

"It won't be too difficult. They keep meticulous records," Soneri said distractedly.

Aricò frowned. "They used to keep meticulous records, but it seems that for the last two months they forgot to keep any account at all of the river traffic. But it shouldn't be too difficult to put it all together, granted that so few of them carry any cargo," he said in a tone in which the commissario detected something halfway between seriousness and malice.

"Who worked the river apart from Tonna?"

"Melegari and the one called Vaeven. Whose boat is registered in the name of a fishing co-operative, which – it transpires – is inactive. At Torricella there's not much indication of activity but I've sent an officer to check the registers in the ports in the provinces of Reggio, Mantua, Cremona and Piacenza. Over the last month, it seems that the *magano* has moored on several occasions in each of them, but here it's put in only three times."

"He has to be involved in the same line of business as Tonna," the commissario said and began to move on. But he had only gone a couple of steps when the maresciallo said: "Don't you want to come in?"

Soneri thought, and then said, "You have more important questions to ask."

He clambered over the embankment in big strides, and turned into the colonnaded street. From *Il Sordo* he heard a tipsy "Rigoletto", perhaps a consequence of the singer's second bottle. There was only one table occupied, all British by the sound of them; perhaps they had been on a Verdi pilgrimage and had lost their way in the mist. The landlord had no problem in making himself understood in sign language, since he was accustomed to doing so with those who spoke his own language.

Soneri ate his pumpkin *tortelli* and *stracotto d'asinina* and then, after some gesticulating, succeeded in having the landlord cut and parcel up some pieces of *culatello* and some slivers of well-matured parmesan, which he slipped into the wide pockets of his duffel coat. He went out, leaving both Rigoletto and the Duke of Mantua behind him.

Out on the grass of the embankment, the cold seemed even more biting than in the town. In front of him he could see the fishermen's cottages and, further down, the port with the moorings, and over to the right the boat club whose great light was, at that distance, no more than a blur in the mist. Thinking over the conversation with Aricò put him in a better mood. The meal helped too, especially now that he was losing the calories in the battle against the freezing cold. He had no means of knowing if the *magano* would turn up, but it was worth waiting at least until after midnight. Was this yet another voyage which would leave no trace in the club's records?

He wrapped his coat more tightly around him, put on a woollen cap, checked that his mobile was switched off and began feeding himself with pieces of parmesan and slices of *culatello* at the rhythm of someone poking the fire. Shortly after eleven o'clock, he saw the lights of the club being switched off and heard stray snatches of conversation between people moving from the yard towards the embankment. He thought he could make out the shadows of four people as they climbed towards the elevated road: perhaps Barigazzi, Ghezzi, Vernizzi and Torelli going home to bed.

When the town bell struck twelve, the commissario contemplated giving in to the cold. Ten minutes later, he tried to rise, only to find his legs stiff and all feeling gone from his feet. The hoar frost had covered him all over like icing on a cake, but before he had taken a few steps he began to hear a distant rumble, and as it became louder he clearly recognized the diesel engine of Melegari's *magano*.

He saw the prow light as it drew up to the mooring, and then heard a muffled thud as the craft bumped against the tyres on the coping stones. A man leapt ashore to take hold of the hawsers. When he came into the strip of light emanating from the prow, the commissario saw that it was Vaeven. The engine and the light were then both switched off and Soneri waited for Melegari to disembark, even if in the darkness he would find it difficult to make out his imposing bulk. Shortly afterwards, lighting his way with a torch, Melegari appeared with a third man of robust build, slightly bent and with a shuffling gait. Soneri believed that this was the man he had seen between Barigazzi and Dinon near the fishermen's cottages a couple of evenings earlier.

As the three made their way towards the club, the commissario kept watch on them for as long as he could. He could only make out shadows, but for the moment what interested him was the direction those shadows were taking. They proceeded slowly and would shortly disappear from view at the point where the road curved round parallel to the embankment. Perhaps he would hear their footsteps crunch on the gravel hardened by the frost. He thought of following them, but he risked being given away by the frozen grass, so he decided to let them move off but to keep them in sight until they reached the yard, when he could move on to the road and track them in the fog.

It was some time before they reappeared. He had the impression of hearing first footsteps and then the sound of something bumping against a wooden object, perhaps an oar striking the hull of a boat, and then nothing until he saw Melegari and Vaeven striding back towards the yard. The yellowing light of the huge lamp now lit them up very distinctly, but the third man was no longer with them. He must have gone into one of the cottages whose door could not be seen from where Soneri was, even if it seemed to him impossible that the man would spend the night in such a place. He went down towards the path, slipping on the icy embankment as he did so. The fog and the dark made it difficult to explore that chessboard of gardens and yards which acted as antechambers to the fishermen's cottages. All he could see were pieces of old furniture piled up, fenced plots that might have been gardens, and a few upturned boats. He did his best to compare his memories with the kind of photographic negative he now saw. What had become of that stooped, apparently elderly man who dragged his feet as he walked?

He made his way back towards the town, walking more quickly to warm himself up. The *Italia* was in darkness with even the light on the sign outside switched off, while between the houses the streetlights were dimmed by the patchy fog. Over the whole scene, the hoar frost cast a frozen mantle. He walked along the streets in the middle of the road rather than under the low colonnades. He came to the piazza which contained the bar owned by Tonna's niece and turned back into the alleyways. It was there that he came upon Melegari's shop, where Barigazzi had told him the old communists of the town gathered around the bust of Stalin. The front was no more than a grey metal shutter with a faded sign above it: SHOEMAKER. He looked up to see a couple of windows with the shutters open.

He took a few steps and turned back to look once again at those windows which seemed to him like the staring eyes of a corpse. He was still puzzling over that peculiarity when he realized he had reached his own car parked in front of the *Italia*, and he understood. Melegari had not gone home. When they disembarked from the *magano*, they had been convinced they would find the town deserted. The two men had left their friend in the cottage, but they had then noticed the commissario's car which was easily visible from the elevated roadway. At that point, Melegari and his friend must have suspected something was up and had not come back to their houses – an old precaution from their activist days when they had clashes with the police.

Once home, he managed only a couple of hours' sleep. All he felt was a kind of grim determination. The light of the late autumn dawn was as faint as at night-time, but the cold was more intense.

Things were already on the move in the town. Some lights could be glimpsed through the still-closed shutters, and shop-keepers were beginning to unload merchandise from vans. The lights were on in the newsagent's, and as he passed, Soneri glanced at the hoardings:

MURDER ON THE PO

ANTEO TONNA KILLED BY TRAFFICKERS

He decided against buying the newspaper. He did not want to begin the day in low spirits.

He parked in an out-of-the-way spot and walked towards the jetty. He climbed over the embankment and came back down into the yard. Over the water, the clear glow of a timid dawn began to appear. He passed the cottages and walked straight over to the moorings. The space occupied by the *magano* was empty and the hawsers had been thrown on to the coping stones as on the day before. The commissario was disappointed and even duped, but at least he knew that the men sensed they were being watched. They had accepted their parts and were performing their assigned roles.

He wandered among the cottages, his path taking him along the avenue between on one side the entrances to the dwellings and on the other the slope at the bottom of which the river flowed. In the ashen light, he gazed at various constructions which had been thrown together with cheap, left-over materials, strange pieces of architecture with the common feature that they were all built on stilts to keep them above the water. All around lay old boats, wheels of farm carts and barbecues for the summer. He examined them one by one until he came to a detail which attracted his attention: two footsteps imprinted on the thin layer of hoar frost which had settled the night before on the avenue alongside one of those raised dwellings, footsteps which stopped abruptly near the road.

The commissario reflected on this and when he looked up at the embankment he noticed that the cottage was one of those which was invisible from where he had been standing the evening before. He went back to examine more closely those solitary footprints which came to a stop at an invisible wall. He walked along the path and climbed the steps to the upper level. A covered balcony ran round the perimeter of the dwelling, and from there on a summer evening, provided the observer used a good insecticide, the view of the Po must have had a certain charm. He tried to peer between the cracks in the shutters, but he could see only darkness within. However, he felt a draught coming from somewhere, a sign that the windows had not been closed.

It was not difficult to undo the catch. As he had anticipated, he saw before him a room where the plants had been brought in to shelter them from the frost, an oleander, geraniums and a lemon bush half covered in cellophane. The commissario breathed in the dust-filled air, while spiders' webs clung to his face. He opened the door in the room and found himself in a corridor. His torch lit up a row of boots and a single shelf above which there was a mirror. He pressed the light switch and there appeared walls abandoned to the damp, with various doors opening off them. The one directly facing Soneri led into a kitchen which contained everything needed to prepare a meal. A calendar open at the month of September was hanging from a hook, and on the other side there were doors giving on to first a bathroom and then two bedrooms, one of which contained a perfectly made double bed which gave off an odour of camphor, while in the centre of the second stood a camp bed and beside it an electric heater.

Soneri approached the heater with all the caution of a bomb-disposal expert. It was still plugged in, but it was switched off. It was warmer in that room and everything led him to suppose that it had been occupied until a short time before, but the occupant could not have slept for long, four or five hours at the most. He examined every corner of the room. There were no more than odds and ends, a few things left over from the summer, a couple of magazines and assorted objects stuffed into a cupboard without order or neatness. Only one thing appeared to have been left there recently, a box of pills for high blood pressure. He opened it, but there was nothing inside.

He went back into the corridor and saw that the exit had been closed but not bolted. Whoever had gone out last had simply pulled the door to behind him, as did Soneri. He closed the shutters from the inside of the room with the plants and went out through the main door. When he was at the bottom of the stairs, he made his way towards the road by the shortest path, but it was then that he came across the footprints once more. If he were to continue in the same direction, he was bound to leave his own prints, because the wind had caused the hoar frost to cover the pathway. Unthinkingly, he had done what the person in the house the night before had done, but whoever it was must have noticed he was leaving traces and had turned back on his steps, picking his way between the stilts beneath the house towards a point in the driveway untouched by the hoar frost. But in the dark he had failed to notice a couple of footprints.

On the street, Soneri lit his cigar and tried to put these facts into some kind of order. Someone was living in hiding here but had been able to move about the Po with the complicity of a circle of orthodox communists who had remained faithful to Stalin. All this after the murder of two old Fascists. It might still have been 1946…

From the yard he noticed the figure of Barigazzi going down to check the stakes. He followed the old man as he set about his work. When he came up behind him, Barigazzi spun round and stared at him, a quizzical expression on his face.

"If it goes on like this," Soneri said, pointing to the water, "even the fish are going to have a hard job of it."

"The water is very low," Barigazzi said, as though he had expected a different kind of question.

They walked along, leaving footprints side by side in the muddy sand just above the waterline.

"Whose is the third cottage along from the mooring berths?"

"It's Vaeven's," he said with a sigh that conceded he had known the commissario would get to that point.

They went back up towards the beacon. Soneri patiently followed Barigazzi who seemed in a state of resignation. The partisans, like the Kite in those days in 1944, must have walked in the same way as they were led to the wall. When they reached the front of the boat club, the old man walked straight ahead up to the elevated roadway. The commissario caught up with him, both still lost in their own thoughts.

When they were in sight of the monument, Barigazzi

stopped and turned to Soneri, evidently angry. "Look, I've got nothing to do with them. To my mind they're all mad, with Stalin and all those meetings…"

"Stalin has nothing to do with it. They're threatening you because of the registers," Soneri said after a brief pause.

"What really upsets them is the business with the diesel," Barigazzi said in a voice two tones below his normal speech. "They're making illegal use of agricultural oil because it costs less. If too many trips appeared on the register, the police would check the files with the fuel records and might start wondering how they covered such distances with so little naphtha."

The explanation was plausible. After all, the *magano* was registered in the name of a co-operative of fishermen.

"There are other illegal immigrants apart from the ones Tonna was transporting," the commissario said.

Barigazzi walked with his head down, and looked up only when the oratory which Anteo had been visiting almost every week in recent times emerged from the mist. Its darker shadow in the surrounding greyness brought them to a halt, and without Soneri's having applied any more pressure, the old man seemed to feel his back was against the wall.

"Do you think I don't know that? But I don't know what they're really up to. They're hardly going to come and explain it all to me."

"Melegari frightens you. I recognized as much that time he came to the clubhouse and saw me there."

"There are some people who can make themselves clear without issuing threats. They go about their own business, but they know that I know who they are."

"And yet they're all old now," the commissario murmured.

Barigazzi walked around the tiny chapel, glancing in at the little altar where the flame of the sanctuary lamp was flickering. Behind the chapel, in a sheltered corner and by a kind of apse, a rosemary plant was growing.

The old man plucked off a sprig, rubbed the herbs into the palm of his hand and smelled it. "A little miracle," he said. "Next to the river, with these winters and fog six months a year... and yet it survives. The walls of the oratory protect it from the north and east winds, and the embankment from the rains from the west. The only air which gets in is the gentle wind from the south. Ten metres away, it would be killed off by the frost, but here it can live."

There was some implication, lost to Soneri, in Barigazzi's words. Soneri did as the old man had done and inhaled the scent. In the misty frost which suppressed all smells, he could detect an aroma of springtime.

"It's the only green thing which has remained," Barigazzi said.

The hoar frost had not reached that spot, and nor had the waters which gushed through the coypu burrows in times of flood. The plant was sheltered just as Barigazzi had explained.

"There are certain spots not even winter can reach," he said. "And the weather, I really mean the seasons, seem to stop and merge into one."

The commissario nodded absent-mindedly, both of them focusing on the rosemary. There was nothing else to look at now that the frost-whitened herb had the colour of the mist itself.

"Did Tonna take care of it?"

Barigazzi stared at him with eyes made watery by the cold. "It needed more than one man. He came only once a week, more for San Matteo than for anything else," he said, nodding towards the entrance through which the statue of the saint could be seen.

"He had turned religious in his latter years..."

The old man gave the faintest of smiles in which cynicism and wisdom could both be read. "He was preparing himself for death."

"Not everybody gets that chance."

Barigazzi picked up the allusion. "No, they don't. When you are young, you live thinking only of your body. When you're old, you dedicate your time to your soul. At least the communists have remained consistent. They denied God when they were young and they go on denying him now that they're old."

"It was not only old age that was a threat for him," the commissario said. "And recently the danger was anything but undefined."

"Some things you know better than me. Like all those journeys. I know the *magano* sets sail and arrives back at the strangest of times, but as to what they're doing... The river gives and the river takes, and around here that's all there is to it. It gives you what you need to live and then takes your life. The same water which gives you food to eat also leaves you starving. People move away from the river and then come back to it, and those who live on its banks have no choice."

What he said still had about it some veiled allusion, sufficient to leave Soneri disconcerted. He seemed to be listening to a sermon from an old priest in a country parish giving a commentary on the Scriptures, the same source, after all, that Barigazzi must have learned from.

In that sort of greenhouse where the rosemary grew, even the grass seemed more green and more lush. Was that why Barigazzi had brought him there? To make him understand that there were particular conditions there, impossible to reproduce elsewhere? And therefore in the town too... in a bend of the river Po, communists still faithful to Stalin and hardline Fascists could survive, just as the rosemary could survive between the walls and the embankment?

The old man turned to move away from that protective shell and face the frost again.

"At this rate," he said, "the inlets of stagnant water will freeze over, and when it turns mild again, sheets of ice will break loose and the hulls of the boats will be at risk."

"That will be when the *magano* will have to put in somewhere or other," Soneri said.

"And when that happens, you'll get to know the whole crew."

II

ARICÒ RECEIVED HIM as usual in the first-floor office overlooking the embankment. The telephone rang continually with calls from journalists eager for news of developments in the case of "The Murder on the Po". Finally he got up to shout an order down the stairwell to the officer on duty on the ground floor: "Don't put anyone else through: I'm out." He went back to his desk, giving the heater a kick as he passed. The Po valley climate was getting him down. "This boat is like a stray dog," he said. "Every single port from Parpanese to San Benedetto knows about it, but its draft allows it to put in anywhere it chooses along the banks of the river. It travels with no cargo and seems not to do much fishing."

"Have you got all the moorings under surveillance?"

"How could I? I don't have enough men. I've mobilized all the stations along the river, but I can't call them all out. We've put all the moorings downstream from Pavia to Piacenza under surveillance on alternate days: Chignolo, Corte Sant'Andrea and Somaglia, as well as Mortizza, Caorso, San Nazzaro, Isola Serafini, Monticelli, Castelvetro… but these people move under cover of darkness. To have the least idea where they were, you'd have to attach a motorboat to their stern."

"Do they know they're being watched?" Soneri had decided to ignore the maresciallo's histrionics.

"I assume so. It's not that they've caught sight of uniforms, but my men have called at every boat club along the banks. And" – he added, with an eloquent gesture of one hand – "they all know each other."

"Does the boat moor for long outside Torricella?"

"No. Sometimes it stays overnight at some port or other in the district near Reggio or Mantua, but in general it goes back home."

"Is it your view that they're in the same business as Tonna?"

"Who can say one way or the other?" the maresciallo said, with some vehemence. "We're not talking big numbers, more a question of selected trips. These people are smart. They can draw alongside, embark and disembark at will. They know the river better than they know their own wives."

Soneri could not restrain a sly smile, and Aricò noticed it. All that attention in the press, a couple of appearances on the television and the praise from the magistrates had convinced the maresciallo that he had the chance of a lifetime. Perhaps he was dreaming of promotion and of going back to Sicily, to those lemon groves he could not get out of his head.

"Aricò," the commissario said, mindful of the sensitivities of his colleague, "our inquiries are proceeding in parallel, so we can give each other a hand. If you can keep the river under surveillance and keep a record of the movements of the *magano*, this will be useful both to yourself and to me."

The maresciallo thought it over. He was not an ungrateful man, and he knew that if the inquiries were to lead to his promotion, it would be down to Soneri. "I'll keep you informed," he said, "I'll send off the telex today requesting a higher level of surveillance."

*

The cold was even more intense. The thermometer outside the pharmacy registered a sub-zero temperature. There was an east wind over the plain, blowing upstream and slowing even further the river which was already sluggish with the drop in water level. Soneri walked in the direction of the port, crossing the avenue lined with cottages and heading down to the moorings. The level had dropped again, and on what must have been the riverbed he noticed the skeletons of trees dragged down after decades of flooding from the Alpine valleys to the sands of the Po. Squads of scavengers and of the merely curious had begun making their way up and down the banks in search of any strange objects emerging after long years under the water.

In the boat club, Ghezzi was listening to the radio. At Pomponesca a barge from Rovigo – apparently using old charts – had run aground, and along the Luzzara shoreline a sheet of ice had begun to form in a bend exposed to the winds from the Balkans.

"It's starting," Ghezzi said. "And tonight if the cold gets any worse..."

"Will the port freeze over as well?" Soneri asked him.

"I'm afraid so, but the boats are all ashore."

"Apart from the *magano* belonging to Dinon and Vaeven."

Ghezzi said only, "I suppose so," immediately dropping the subject as though they had trespassed on forbidden ground.

"What would happen to a craft like that if it were trapped in the ice?"

"It's pretty robust, but not sufficiently so to break through thick ice."

"So it would have to put in somewhere."

"They'll all have to put in if it goes on like this. But more than anything else, they'll be laid up afterwards."

"After what?"

"When the temperature goes back up. The river will become

impassable, a mass of ice floes that can cut like blades. It'll take days for the last of them to get to the mouth of the river."

It occurred to the commissario that if the *magano* was going to become unusable, Melegari would already have worked out some safe haven. Being a man of the river, he was bound to be aware of the consequences of the freeze. There was only one master in the whole business, and that was the river itself. It had concealed Tonna, had managed the drift of the barge and now, by withdrawing its freezing waters, it was upsetting long-established customs along its length and breadth. The men who inhabited the riverbanks were compelled to adapt to its whims as to a sovereign, so now the *magano* must be in the act of surrendering and retreating to dry land.

"The ice will be here by nightfall. The moorings at Stagno and Torricella on the right bank are exposed to the north-east," Ghezzi advised anyone who would listen.

Barigazzi came in with a worried expression. "Explain to him that I don't have the data. Someone pulled up my stake," he said, pointing to the radio and at some unspecified interlocutor. "All these folk tramping up and down the river-banks..." he added, uttering an oath as he hung his overcoat on a hook.

"If the river freezes over, they'll be walking on the waters as well," Soneri said.

"That won't happen. I've seen it covered only twice in my life, and you need a bitter cold like this every day for a fortnight."

The radio broke in with its update on the freeze. It seemed that ice was forming all along the Emilia side, where the shore was more exposed to the winds from the north-east.

"A wicked beast," Barigazzi said. "It starts off on the still water and then advances slowly on all fronts. Gradually it'll sink its grip into the riverbed. They'll need to move if they're to get all the boats on to dry land. Wood and ice don't go well together."

"There's one missing here at the port," the commissario said.

The others made no reply. Ghezzi pretended to be adjusting the radio, and Barigazzi got up to look across the river. He turned to face them and in an effort to lower the tension which had suddenly built up, he announced: "If it was up to me, I'd go at full speed. Unless they've already decided to leave the *magano* at some other port."

"Is there any way of checking?" Soneri asked Ghezzi.

Ghezzi picked up the microphone, pressed a few buttons and sent out a request for information. A few moments later, the replies began to come in. It appeared the boat had not put in at any of the ports.

"Would you keep on sailing in freezing weather like this?" Soneri said.

The old boatman shrugged. "They've still got a bit of time. There's one mooring after another and they know the river well."

Soneri turned to listen to the news on the radio. According to the bulletins, the temperature was almost ten degrees below zero everywhere.

"Like a refrigerator," Ghezzi muttered.

At Bocca d'Enzo, they had caught a silure weighing ninety kilos, and the lucky angler was now recounting the various stages involved as though he were the guest on a real radio programme.

"He'll sell it to the Chinese; they're keener on silure than on ordinary fish like chub," Soneri heard Barigazzi say as he left the club. The cold had not lifted. If the *magano* was to make it back, it would have to be that evening. He would be there waiting for them. To keep the cold at bay, he had equipped himself with supplies of parmesan shavings from *Il Sordo*.

Out in the yard, he was seized by an unfamiliar longing for company. He felt that the whole business was now coming into the final straight, like the freeze taking hold of the river bit by bit. At that very moment, the strains of "Aida" began to ring out and he saw it was Angela.

"Ah, so you haven't been sucked under by a whirlpool," she said.

"I'll never forgive myself for having disappointed you," Soneri said, feeling overwhelmed by loneliness.

"There are so many things for which you need forgiveness, but I won't go into them now because they're nearly all unpardonable."

"I know. But it makes sense to do things on a grand scale, especially with women. That way they feel sorry for you."

"Don't get carried away with yourself, and don't tell me you've forgotten what day it is today."

Soneri had indeed forgotten their anniversary. One morning many years previously, on a day every bit as cold as today with the same frost clinging to the hedgerows, Angela had appeared quite suddenly, framed by hawthorn. He had been taken by her no-nonsense but beguiling manner, which in some odd way resembled the aroma of his cigar. It had all started there...

"I'm sorry," he said, "but these inquiries..."

He heard a sigh. "What have the inquiries got to do with it? It's just that you and I are one year older, that's all there is to it."

Before he had the chance to reply, he heard the telephone cut out. Angela's tone of pain and hopelessness lingered in his ears and he called her back, but the telephone was left to ring out and he imagined her throwing herself on to the bed, in tears. He knew she was capable of that. Her tough shell disguised a vulnerable and tender heart.

With his mind occupied by this distraction, Soneri found he had walked the length of the elevated road, beyond the descent that would have taken him into the town. He only realized how far he had gone when he drew abreast of the monument to the partisans.

The frost had made the floodplain rock hard underfoot and the undergrowth bristling and sharp-edged. He made his way down the embankment and when he was in front of the small monument, he noticed that someone had tied a bouquet of roses around it. The blooms were already fading in the cold, but that spot was assuming some indecipherable significance. Three partisans and much later one old Fascist had perished there, perhaps the Fascist who had been in command at the battle and was responsible for the slaughter. The story had taken a strange turn, one not easy to comprehend.

He climbed back up to the road, wondering who the roses were for. Probably for the partisans, but who could have put them there? There would have been roses on the monument on April 25, for as long as there was some old person determined not to forget.

The commissario hurried into *Il Sordo* and ate his fill of *spalla cotta, salame* and *culatello*. He was going to need a lot of energy that night. He called Angela again, but to no avail. Back on the street, the wind cut through him as it went whistling through the colonnades. He crossed the road, leaving footprints on the frosty surface, came on to the piazza and then turned into the back lanes, passing in front of Melegari's house, where the shutters were still open. When he was in sight of the *Italia*, a form emerged from the shadows and barred his way.

"How on earth did you manage to find me?"

"All anyone has to do is hang about near an *osteria* and sooner or later you'll turn up," Angela said.

The commissario looked at her with great delight. She was looking very pretty and he was glad to see her, but this thought was followed by the realization that that night he had a great deal of work to do.

"I can't let up this evening," he said, looking at her in the hope of seeing some sign of understanding.

"What makes you think I would have anything to do with men that want to let up?" she said, coming up close to him.

A few moments later, Soneri found himself leading her along the road in the darkness which had fallen suddenly over the river. They skirted the yard before turning on to the pathway that led to the cottages. When they came to Vaeven's, he went ahead, taking great care to leave no footprints, and then ushered her up the staircase to the balcony. When they got to the doorway, he told her to wait while he made his way round the back and went in as he had done on the previous occasion. He opened the door for her and invited her in with a little bow: "Delighted to welcome you."

Angela loved surprises of this sort, and wanted to know all about the house, but halfway through his account, she pushed him into the bedroom which had the heater. Being in the cottage would be more pleasant than lying in wait on the grass slopes of the embankment, and from there the moorings were in clear view. At around eleven o'clock, the commissario began to show signs of impatience as it became clearer that the *magano* could have put in somewhere else to avoid being caught by the ice, but half an hour later he noticed a light coming steadily upstream in the direction of the riverbank. When it was no more than about ten metres from the quay, it slowed right down. Seconds later, he was aware of a thud, like a bag falling. Soneri kept his eyes on the hawsers curving in the air as they were tossed ashore and on the gangplank being set up between the deck and the landing stage.

A man came ashore and started hauling in the ends of the cables and wrapping them round the bollards. From his build, it had to be Vaeven, as was confirmed for the commissario when he saw the gangplank sag under the weight of Melegari. The two seemed to exchange a few words before setting off along the pathway. Since they were on their own, Soneri wondered where the other man was. He had prepared his plan with Angela. They would hide in the room with the plants and when the mysterious friend of Dinon and Vaeven was safely in bed and under the covers, they would come rapidly into his room and take him by surprise. However, the two men did not stop at the cottage but walked straight on towards the yard, bypassing the embankment and making their way towards the houses. They gave every impression of coming home from an ordinary trip, as relaxed as any two fishermen after a day on the river.

During the night, a light wind got up and for a few hours cleared the clouds from the sky, allowing some stars to appear, but with the dawn everything closed in again and the customary grey made its return. Soneri felt like a mole in the darkness. He left the cottage very early to accompany Angela to her car, but got back in time to see Melegari and his companion making their way down to the jetty. The ice had already taken over a strip of water stretching two metres out from the bank and almost surrounding the hull of the vessel. He heard one of the men cursing, then they both set to work to get the winch and crane into action.

The boat freed itself from the ice floe, and a ripping sound like an organ being torn from flesh could be heard as the craft emerged, dripping. Sheets of ice were clinging to the hull, whose underwater sections appeared very dark, very wide and almost flat. This was not a boat which did much fishing. Once the boat was on the land, Melegari slowly climbed the ladder he had placed against its side and walked along the short deck, closing down the hatches which led below. He stretched out a green tarpaulin which he tied down with a rope, leaving only the cabin exposed. From below, Vaeven did the rest.

Soneri had hoped that the ice might have held up the *magano* and made everything easier, but in fact it had only complicated things. Once again he had to draw on all his resources of patience and keep alert for every tiny signal. These were the virtues of fishermen and of those who lived on the river.

He decided to call Aricò for further information on the recorded movements of the boat.

"I've given up on sending telexes," the maresciallo told him. "In this weather, all sailings are suspended. Let's hope it doesn't last too long." And in this wish the commissario detected more exasperation with the cold than enthusiasm for the investigation.

"Did they report the final movements of the *magano* before the freeze set in?" he said.

"Yes, but in the most random order, with no exact chronology," Aricò replied, in an apologetic tone.

"It doesn't matter."

"Viadana, Pomponesco, Polesine, Casalmaggiore, Sacca and then Stagno," he read out. "As for the dates, the one thing certain is that the boat made one last stop at Stagno before being dragged ashore here at Torricella."

"When did it put in at Stagno?"

"Yesterday at nightfall, around six."

Soneri thought of the moorings exposed to the east wind and so perhaps at that time about to freeze over, but then he remembered Barigazzi explaining how the tributaries flowed into the stream, delaying the formation of the ice. At Stagno the Taro flowed into the Po. The place was redolent of some symbolism which, without his being able to pin it down precisely, came dimly to the commissario's mind. He remembered Stagno as being the site of great battles between man and water, of trench warfare fought with sandbags to bar the way to a slime-covered horde which had slipped through breaches in the embankments, of resistance along the unsupported line on the plain, of battles in streets and ditches, of house-to-house fighting. He even recalled a photograph published many years previously in a local paper depicting a group of bewhiskered gentlemen, the *habitués* of bars and sophisticated topers of the local wines, who demonstrated their spirit of sacrifice by stating that in order to restrain the waters of the Po they would drink every last drop. The headline above the photograph read: THE HEROES OF STAGNO.

He had a mental image of the map showing the course of the river and the towns along its banks. Stagno faced Torricella del Pizzo, and further down the valley Torricella Parmense was more or less opposite Gussola, while Sacca looked out slightly to the east of Casalmaggiore. Between Gussola and Casalmaggiore stood San Quirico – where there were no moorings – but the *magano* could have drawn into the bank at almost any point along the river. What proof did he have that things had actually gone that way? He reflected for a few moments, smoking the remains of a cigar he had found chewed and abandoned in a pocket of his duffel coat, and concluded that the only reason for thinking that something had occurred at San Quirico was the direction from which the *magano* had arrived the previous evening before it was winched ashore. If the last leg was Stagno, the boat would have taken advantage of the current from the west. In fact, it had come in the opposite direction, against the current. He had clearly heard the engine step up a gear turning into the stream and cutting diagonally across the river. It was evidently necessary to add one more stop to the records kept on board.

He switched off his mobile and walked down to the moorings. Without giving a greeting or speaking a word, he stood watching the two men working around the boat which was now resting on a wooden frame holding it about a foot above ground level. Both parties, the commissario and the two boatmen, kept their peace, the latter continuing to work, stepping in front of him without so much as turning in his direction. It seemed as though they were engaged in a competition to see whose nerves would fray first. Soneri calmly smoked, challenging even the freeze which seemed to be crawling along the river. The others kept themselves warm by working on the hull, pulling away lumps of ice.

"Made it just in time?" the commissario finally said.

The pair turned slowly, as though they had just registered a familiar voice behind them.

"It can't be any fun having to stay out on the open river when the banks are frozen."

Vaeven shrugged, conveying that the very idea was senseless. Melegari, however, said: "We're not that stupid."

"And yet, when you travel about a lot… maybe you don't always realize that in a few hours… you yourselves, for instance, when you got back, a layer of ice a finger thick was already covering the two metres just out from the jetty."

The two men stared at each other.

"It's worse here than elsewhere. There's more air," Melegari said.

"Certainly," Soneri said, "and when you're away for days on end, it's difficult to keep abreast of what is going on. The Po is a long river."

Dinon stopped his scraping and drew himself up to his full height to appear even more imposing. He managed, in spite of the obvious provocations, to appear unruffled, as did the commissario, who seemed only to be relishing his cigar as if what happened on the river was no concern of his.

"I've already told you we don't appreciate this line of questioning from policemen," Melegari replied. "It's not going to get to us. Tell us what it is you want to know and let's get it over with."

Soneri looked him up and down, openly defying him and then, after pausing a few more seconds to let the other man see how unaffected he was by Melegari's aggression, he said: "Where is he?"

"Who?"

"You know perfectly well. Stop playing the fool."

The commissario's tone was so peremptory that Melegari was momentarily caught off balance.

"We wouldn't like you to entertain any half-baked ideas about us," he said finally, lowering the tone of his voice in a way that was vaguely menacing. "You know that we're activists, don't you? Well then, you must also be aware that comrades come from all over Italy to visit, to get an understanding of our situation and to talk politics. Is there anything illegal in us giving them hospitality and taking them out for a cruise on the Po?"

"There could be if all this takes place in a town where an old Fascist officer, who was also passionate about the river and about navigating it, happens to have been murdered. But that's not certain," Soneri said, leaving his words hanging in the air.

"You people in the police," Dinon came back at him with contempt in his voice. "You always suspect us. The moment there's any mention of Reds, you have a rush of blood to the head."

The commissario waved them both away, but then, after a

longer pause, said: "One way or the other, I'm of the opinion that politics are involved with this business. From a time when politics could still cause a rush of blood to the head."

He turned away without saying good-bye, and walked towards the boat club. Halfway along the path, he rummaged in his pockets to find a light. But instead of the matches, he came out with a dirty box, the container for the hypertension pills he had found in the drawer. He had had no idea what to do with such a slender clue, but inside the box there was a receipt issued twenty days previously by a chemist in Casalmaggiore.

A mere shadow of a clue, but it was the best he had.

The chemist was an elderly man, with a large handlebar moustache and two tufts of hair above his ears. The shop was narrow and well laid out, with coloured boxes set out on the shelves in such a way as to look like a mosaic.

The man examined the box, turning it over several times before peering at the receipt. "It's a very common product," he said, as his daughter, a woman in her thirties, came over to have a look.

"I would imagine you know your usual clients. The ones with high blood pressure, I mean. Apart from them, is there anyone that stands out? A tubby, elderly man with a shuffling walk, a man who drags his feet?" the commissario said, trying to be helpful.

"It could be the man who came in without a prescription," the daughter remembered.

The chemist concentrated for a moment, then realization dawned. Soneri knew that chemists have good memories; with all those drugs with difficult names to keep them in training.

"An oldish man, yes," he said, half shutting his eyes as though to focus. "With a way of dragging his feet. He was after some product which is no longer on sale, and he didn't have a prescription."

"And you gave him this?" Soneri said, holding up the empty box.

The chemist shook his head. "We cannot sell drugs like that without a doctor's prescription."

"So what did you do?"

"He went off and came back that same afternoon with a prescription from Professor Gandolfi, who used to be a surgeon. He lives round the back," he said, indicating with his thumb some area beyond his shoulder. "He took four boxes so as not to run out."

"Was there anyone with him?"

"No, he was on his own."

"Did he have a foreign accent?"

"Anything but! He spoke in a thick dialect."

Soneri made for the door, but when he had his hand on the handle, another question occurred to him.

"Do you know Professor Gandolfi?"

"Everybody in Casalmaggiore knows the professor."

"What are his politics?"

Father and daughter exchanged glances, wondering at the point of the question, before the daughter, with an abruptness which might have been taken for scorn, said: "At the university, he was known as the Red Baron."

Her father gave her a reproachful look in which Soneri read the reluctance of the trader to voice a judgment.

Professor Gandolfi lived in a most elegant villa, which appeared to have been only recently restored. It had a definite air of local nobility. He no longer practised in a hospital, and since his retirement had limited himself to making private visits to elderly, needy patients and to some impoverished comrades sent to him by the Party.

"I work in the voluntary sector," he joked. "For people who cannot afford the fat fees demanded by my more grasping colleagues," he added, in a more serious tone.

He was of little use to Soneri, who had no way of establishing whether he was sincere or merely a gifted liar. He explained that Melegari had asked for a prescription for a drug for high blood pressure and that he had written it out without giving much thought to the matter, since he knew that Dinon suffered from hypertension.

"He eats and drinks too much," he said.

The commissario got up, taking a good look at the professor as he did so, but he could not make him out. He was well dressed and lived in a house furnished with taste. In the courtyard below, Soneri had noted a big Mercedes with a recent number plate. As he opened the gate, he thought how much he had always disliked Mercedes communists, for whom being left-wing was no more than a snobbish affectation.

Walking along with his cigar in his mouth, he became aware of a restlessness, a bothersome itch like a nettle sting all over his arm. He felt an old feeling hovering over him but he could not identify what it was. It occurred to him that he was like a hunting dog with the scent of game in his nostrils, but who has no idea which direction to take because the same smells are all around him. Perhaps that was why he set off towards San Quirico. Certain stray thoughts had taken possession of his mind. He sat at the wheel of his car with no real intention of driving off, but then, mechanically, he started the engine and turned on to a side road, more a makeshift track in the countryside, which veered away from the embankment and the river. He had not gone far before "Aida" rang out and he had to stop in a clearing where the grey curtain of the mist had lifted a little.

"Do you remember Maria of the sands?" It was Aricò, sounding unduly serious.

"Of course. Anteo Tonna's woman."

"Something odd has occurred. Last night, somebody tried to force the window on the ground floor in the hospice where she now is. Fortunately, the window bars did their job."

"Were they after her?" Soneri said. He knew the reply in advance.

"In my view, yes, but they didn't get very far. They gave up, partly because the grille was strong enough and partly because one of the night nurses looked out of the upper floor."

"Did they see anything?"

"Only a shadow. But we found footprints in the frost. A man with large feet."

In the commissario's head various ideas formed, superimposing themselves on those which were already there and reinforcing them. A lorry narrowly missed him as he was coming out of the clearing where he had stopped. For a few seconds, with no roadside verge to keep him right, he lost his bearings, and when he got back on to the road he realized it was a different one, a narrower road which cut across the plain, it too heading away from the Po embankment. In the thick fog, it took him some time to realize that, like the other, this road too led to San Quirico. Fate must have been taking him there.

He drove around a dozen or so houses sunk in the clay of the Plain, before finally making out the veranda of the old man's home. From the half-closed garden gate, he saw him behind the windows, staring into the grey emptiness ahead of him, still crouched over his walking stick. When Soneri was no more than a few feet away, the old man gave a start and began searching him out, turning his eyes this way and that, like a torch. Soneri spoke, allowing the man to locate him and to calm himself. On this occasion, he had his legs wrapped in a blanket and had a soft hat on his head.

"Is it iced over already?" he said straight off, avid for news.

"Yes, around the riverbanks."

"Tonight it will get thicker and will reach a few metres further out. They're all blocked, aren't they?"

"For normal boats, there's no way they can sail," Soneri said.

The old man looked disappointed. He would rather have been on the banks to see for himself the Po turn to ice, but even if they had taken him there, he would not have been able to see a thing.

"You've been down?"

"I have."

The man remained closed in a painful silence for a moment or two, then said: "It's been a good twenty years since it iced over."

His wife appeared at the doorway, looked over in the direction of the veranda and then, recognizing Soneri, withdrew.

"The last time it happened," he started up again, "I was still out and about with my boat."

He seemed on the point of giving way to the onset of melancholy, but then he stared keenly at the fog outside with an urgency which continued to surprise Soneri. At that point, a car could be heard passing beyond the garden, beyond the dark spot that was all that could be seen of the hedge. The old man raised a hand and pointed to some imprecise spot among the white wisps of mist floating about. Soneri remained silent until that gesture pregnant with meaning found expression in words.

"That... that noise," he repeated, like a man with a stutter. "I've never heard it before."

"I thought you were a bit hard of hearing," the commissario said, taken aback.

"I can make out certain noises very clearly and others less so. The doorbell, for example."

"But you were very sure about that one?" Soneri insisted.

"Yes, it's new. Last night and then now. I know the sound of all the cars from around here, and I can tell you that one is new."

"A foreigner?"

"There have never been any here."

"Could one of your neighbours have changed cars?"

"There are only old folk with no licence here."

"A relative..."

The old man shook his head. "Nobody comes here on weekdays. Not in this season... only the baker or door-to-door salesmen."

Something unusual about the sound had made a deep impression on the old man, and it was now beginning to intrigue the commissario as well.

"When it comes to engines, I know what I'm talking about," the old man said, in a tone that brooked no contradiction. "On the river, I could tell who was coming and going from the pitch of the outboard motor, long before they were in sight. Sometimes I would greet another craft as it passed without my even seeing the outline of its hull."

They stood in silence, broken by Soneri saying: "Have you heard other unusual noises lately?"

"No, there's never anything out of the ordinary here. I could draw up a list of all the noises you hear by day and by night. I don't sleep much. I live in darkness nowadays."

"Who could it be?" the commissario said, thinking aloud.

The old man stretched out his arms. "Sometimes people go off the road in the fog and end up in this God-forsaken place, but that never happens twice in a row. The second time, they must be coming here deliberately."

The commissario thought back to the road: a narrow, raised track running from the main road and ending at San Quirico. Someone must have known his way to one of the summer residences scattered here and there in that tangle of a village, but it could not have been, in the old man's view, someone who came regularly. Soneri walked along the path to the road on the other side of the hedge where the car had passed. On the thin white of the frost, he saw the treads left by the tyres and followed them. They led to a low villa, with chubby, plaster-cast angels in the garden. The house seemed completely shut up. The lower part of the door was even barred with a metal guard. At the side of the house, under an overhanging roof, a camper van had been parked.

Soneri made his way back, being careful to tread on patches of the roadway free of frost to avoid leaving any footprints. He was back in front of the house with the veranda when his mobile struck up with its laboured version of the triumphal march.

"Commissario, the questore asked me where you were." Juvara.

"And it was you he asked?" Soneri said, with some annoyance.

"He said he'd been trying to reach you himself, but he always found your mobile switched off."

"What does he want?"

"He's upset because he's found out that you knew about the illegal traffickers and the inquiry has ended up in the hands of the carabinieri. And he doesn't understand why you're still out on the Po instead of being at your desk. He even asked if you were away on your holidays."

"Tell him that tomorrow or the day after there will be developments on the Tonna case," Soneri cut him short. When he put his mobile back in his pocket, he was amazed at the self-possession with which he had spoken.

"Who's the owner of that low-roofed villa with the statues of the angels in the garden?" he asked the old man who had heard him return.

"The Ghiretti family. The sons and daughters live in Milan, but the older members of the family live in Cremona. They come here three times a year."

"There's a camper van under the shelter. Would that belong to the family?"

"A diesel? The car that went along the road a short while ago was a diesel."

"I think so, but it's been there a while."

"Ah then, I don't know. I don't think it belongs to the family. They must have rented the place to someone or other."

"The car, the one you heard, finished up there at the same house."

The old man stopped to think things over, but then repeated several times: "Strange, all very strange, it seems strange..."

The commissario went to stand beside him. "When exactly did you hear the car last night?"

"It was late, maybe eleven o'clock."

Soneri wrote out in large print the number of his mobile and handed it to the old man.

"Tell your wife to call me the moment she hears the car get back. It's very important."

The old man clutched the paper and nodded.

By now he should know the road, Soneri thought, but it was not easy in the fog, and perhaps he would have to return to San Quirico later that night.

It was around 8.00 when he made his way into *Il Sordo* and

he immediately felt himself enveloped by the atmosphere of warmth and beguiled by the scents from the kitchen. As he passed the open entrance to the cellar, his nostrils were filled with the mildly mildewed aroma of *salame* hanging from the beams below.

The landlord himself passed among the tables in the imperturbable silence in which he chose to wrap himself, heedless of the powerful strains of "Falstaff" echoing from the *salame*-coloured walls. When he came to Soneri, he stopped a moment to look closely at him, watching as the commissario rolled his cigar in his lips with a certain voluptuousness. He then picked up the menu, put it in his apron pocket and took out a notepad on which he had written in large letters on a lined sheet of paper: *La vecchia*.

Soneri was puzzled for a moment. *La vecchia*: the elderly woman? The old girl? The ageing female? His first thought was of Maria, Maria of the sands, but immediately he stopped himself: it was too easy to be distracted by professional concerns. His host simply wanted to let him know that he had some *vecchia al pesto*, minced horsemeat flavoured with a *peperone* sauce. Childhood memories came flooding back, and he nodded enthusiastically. The landlord kept his best dishes for those whom he considered most likely fully to appreciate them. The commissario was now of that company.

The *vecchia* lived up to every expectation and Soneri nodded gratefully to the landlord who must have cooked it especially for himself and his wife. It was like being invited to his home for dinner. Around 9.00 the *osteria* began to fill up. Barigazzi and Ghezzi came in, but when they saw the commissario, they took a table at the far side of the room. Soneri, untroubled, turned towards them, staring at them with a look which was also a challenge but at the same time keeping half an eye on the mobile which, unusually for him, he had laid on the table.

To wash down the *vecchia,* he ordered some Bonarda which bubbled like Fortanina but had more body. The bottle on offer in *Il Sordo* had so much tannin that it looked like ink. He drank it in little sips to help loosen the powerful mixture of peppers and minced horsemeat which lay heavily on his stomach. All the while he was waiting. He looked at the Christ with folded legs, at the marks of the levels reached by the floods, at the ceiling of the same colour as chopped pork and at the heads of the customers in the room, moving like the spherical blooms of onions blowing in the wind.

The jibe made by his superior, "Is he away on his holidays?", came back to him. At certain times his job did resemble a holiday, mainly in the periods of inactivity in the course of an investigation when there was nothing to do except wait for something to happen. His was the kind of work which could sometimes be indistinguishable from idleness. His father had never liked his choice of profession. As a good peasant, the man had concluded that "for the most part, you lot do nothing all day long". Furthermore, he had no taste for all that questioning, that sticking your nose into other people's affairs...

It was 10.00, and Soneri's patience was wearing thin. The unceasing hubbub in the *osteria* was making everything a blur and made him feel as though he were on the point of dropping off. Perhaps the old man had fallen asleep and not heard the car pull up? Or maybe, after all, it had not come?

The landlord reappeared and once again produced his notepad. This time he had written *polenta fritta,* "fried polenta", a fresh reminder of childhood days and one Soneri found irresistible. The man must have studied him deeply on the occasions he had eaten there and had calculated his tastes precisely. Even more, he had chosen to serve him with a deliberate slowness which seemed rather in keeping with the skills of a theatre director. Did he know that the waiting time was still likely to be lengthy? By 10.30, some diners began to rise from their tables and move to the door. The principal topic of conversation was the freeze and several of the guests seemed to be leaving the *osteria* to go down to the riverbanks and check the spread of the ice. Barigazzi, very much the centre of attention, went with them.

The deaf man then tried to communicate with the commissario, using signs the latter could not interpret. Was he referring to the food or to something else? The fried polenta was undoubtedly exceptional and Soneri replied with a sign indicative of deep gratitude, but the landlord displayed some surprise before responding with a brief shake of his head, giving the commissario the impression that there had been some misunderstanding. Shortly afterwards, the landlord came back with a liqueur glass and a large jar of cherries in alcohol. As a final course, it was somewhere between a special treat and a medicine guaranteed against all ailments, but it too brought back memories from other days.

The *osteria* was almost empty. The only ones left while the last act of "Falstaff" blared out were Soneri, whose glass was almost filled with cherry stones, and the landlord who was seated sideways at the bar, staring into the middle distance. In that pose, he resembled the old man in San Quirico, and the commissario's thoughts returned to the tedium of waiting when, quite suddenly, everything happened as in a scene in a melodrama. Verdi's music ended on a long drawn-out sharp and a *fortissimo* of brasses, sinking the *osteria* into silence and leaving Soneri and the landlord staring at each other intently. Just as "Falstaff" was replaced by "Aida", the commissario pressed the answer button, said "hello" and heard a whisper at the other end as the old woman passed the telephone to her husband.

"I've heard it," he said.

Soneri did not speak for some seconds and just as he was about to reply, the old man hung up.

As was his habit, the commissario rose immediately to his feet, and the landlord seemed to understand exactly what he was about to do. He gave a good-bye wave, and the look he received in reply seemed to convey an awareness of what was going on.

Outside the cold was as intense as ever, but the Bonarda countered it quite satisfactorily, filling him with a lucid euphoria indispensable for nights like the one ahead. In the fog, it was as ever a struggle to find the way to San Quirico. The road he had chanced on in the afternoon now seemed impassable in the wall of mist that the bonnet of his car had to plough into. After a while he found himself suspended over the countryside, and for a moment had the impression that he was motoring among the clouds. He crawled along in second gear, his fog lights incapable of picking out the verges, and every curve brought the fear that he was about to plunge down the slope.

He left the car not too far from the old man's house, thinking of him lying in his bed listening to the sound of the engine being switched off at the roadside, seeing everything in his mind's eye, as he was now obliged to follow every scene in life. The commissario wondered if the old man had heard his footsteps on the road as he passed under one of the few lampposts in San Quirico. He certainly could not have heard him when he almost bumped into the gate of the house opposite the spot where the mysterious car's tyre marks stopped.

Soneri took out his torch to examine the tracks to make sure they were fresh. The sharp definition left him in no doubt. The old man's hearing was very keen. The house was as silent as a graveyard. There were no footprints in the pathway leading to the front door, which was still barred by a metal guard to protect it from the damp. The shutters too looked as though they had been closed for some time. He inspected the camper van but there was no sign of any movement, so all that remained was to check the back of the house. It gave on to a kitchen garden with some fruit trees overgrown by creepers. And then he noticed some ten steps leading down to a cellar door.

He took out and cocked his pistol and stood for a few seconds in front of the door, the sound of his knuckles rapping on the wood announcing the beginning of a long night. No-one replied, so he went on knocking again and again until his patience ran out, at which point he took to beating on the door with his open palm, causing it to shake on its hinges.

At last, he heard the sound of footsteps dragging, and in the faint light there appeared before him a stout elderly, bearded, slightly stooped man wearing an expression of tired resignation.

Soneri stepped over the threshold, meeting no resistance from the occupant of the house, who moved to one side, just sufficiently to give the appearance of surrender. The commissario went in, stopping beside a table beneath a flickering bulb. The old man closed the door unhurriedly, as though having welcomed an expected guest, and when Soneri introduced himself, he responded with a simple nod of the head. His demeanour was grave, respectful.

In a dark corner of the room, an electric heater was blowing warm air, while on the other side a bed with a walnut headboard stood out amid the rustic poverty of the greying, rough-plaster walls of the cellar. The commissario sat down and the other did likewise. Seated at the same level, they looked into each other's eyes. The man, with his long beard and wrinkled skin, called to mind a well-seasoned *radicchio*, but what most took Soneri aback was the submissiveness he displayed towards him, a submissiveness combined with awareness.

They sat for a few minutes face to face in an unnerving silence. Now that he was able to observe him from close up, it was plain that the old man showed all the signs of hypertension: dark blotches on the cheeks, a bulbous nose the colour of *cotecchino*, the sheer mass of a body perhaps capable of explosions of rage, even if now he was sitting motionless, waiting. There was no question that waiting was the right tactic, particularly since Soneri was unable to find the words to begin.

"Was all this necessary?" he finally managed to say, realizing as soon as the words were out that they were born more of curiosity than of a line of inquiry. The inquiry was now over, but the sense of strangeness and of deviation from normal codes of behaviour remained. There were occasions, like the one he was living through at that moment, when stripping off the official uniform to assume the guise of the confidant was unavoidable. After all, the old man had no choice and was perhaps not even seeking a way out, as was clear from his state of resignation, in which Soneri perceived a sense of liberation, perhaps even of pride.

"Was it necessary?" he insisted.

The other man swallowed hard, but made no reply, not because he lacked the will to speak but because a pressure in his throat from having too much to say prevented his feelings from finding coherent expression. He had no more idea where to start than did Soneri, and so hesitated for a few seconds before coming out with an introduction dictated more by emotion than by reason. "If you had gone through what I have…"

The pronunciation of the words with a Spanish accent was confirmation enough.

"How many years have you lived in Argentina?"

"Do your own sums. From '47."

"A lifetime."

"True. I lived my life there."

"Except for your youth."

The old man wiped his forehead with his right hand and in so doing revealed a forearm with a tattoo of a hammer and sickle. "I'd have been happy to have done without that youth. I have lived two lives. I died and was reborn."

"Resuscitated," Soneri corrected him. "You have remained the same person."

"Unfortunately, a man carries his past on his back. Your blood is diseased by it forever."

He pronounced these last words more firmly, almost with finality. A rage which had remained undiminished over the decades seemed to exert a profound influence on his thinking.

"The disease still holds sway."

The old man looked at him with a mixture of amazement and irritation. "Much less now. I have done what I had to do. But if you imagine that that's enough... I have even asked myself whether it was all worthwhile, seeing that it still has me in its grip... Only time can allow hatred to subside, and my time is almost up. I have only just managed to achieve what I had promised myself for all these years."

"You should have thought of yourself as well."

The old man considered that point for a moment, then shrugged. "It was worse for others. If I got away, it was because I did think about myself. I had nothing here. I'd have had to get out whatever happened. I made up my mind after the reprisals against my family."

The allusion to the reprisals caused Soneri to run over the facts – particularly the encounter between the embankments – in his mind. He looked hard at the old man and noticed a glint in his eyes, as bright as the flash of a short circuit. "That battle on the floodplain made everything clear to me," he said. "At the beginning, I just could not formulate any hypothesis, because everything came up short against the one fact – the people who had a motive for revenge on the Tonnas were all dead, including you. But when they recounted to me how that battle in the mists had really gone, and when I found out about the disfigured bodies and the missing corpse of that Fascist… at that point I worked out how it might have gone. What I have never managed to resolve is why you, considering that you were officially dead, did not act immediately at the end of the war. After all, many on your side wasted no time in '46."

The old man raised his head proudly, but then dropped it just as suddenly with a sigh.

"Do you believe they wouldn't have found out? I was the man who had the best of all motives for making them pay, and I had the reputation of being a hothead. Some of them already had some inkling… and anyway, the Party would never have forgiven me. Don't forget that I had gone to the lengths of disfiguring the body of a comrade, and that they had previously disciplined me when I was in the Garibaldi brigade. Then you've got to bear in mind that I had absented myself from the final phases of the fighting and the Resistance. In those days, the Communist Party was highly organized and had kept intact the Gruppo di Azione Patriottica, the partisan network closest to them. I'd been lucky once not to be found out. After the Liberation, I went into hiding for nearly two years with the connivance of some of my comrades who had fallen out with the party. They were the only ones who knew anything. Do you understand now why I was not able to act after April 25? My funeral had even taken place. I went up and down the river, living in the holds of barges or in cabins belonging to people I could trust. As I relived that life in recent weeks, it seemed as though I was reliving my boyhood. Take it from me, if I were still young, if I enjoyed the health I did then, you would never have caught me. I have been on the run all my life."

"And not a single one of the partisans realized what you were up to? Or perhaps some of them just pretended not to?" asked the commissario.

"I couldn't say. I had other things on my mind. The episode of the disfigured bodies appeared sinister and ambiguous, but the Fascists got the blame. The same ones who shot my friend, the Kite, not long afterwards. Anyway, it was payback time for them, and they got what they deserved."

"It took me a long time to work out that this was the key to the whole affair. You had to do it," said the commissario. "Somebody had to take your place among the dead. So that Fascist who was recorded as missing, the savagery on the bodies of those killed in battle… it was all a set-up. You made it seem an act of hatred, you made them unrecognizable and passed off the Blackshirt as yourself." Soneri was struggling to understand.

The other man took up the story. "Yes. I had to set to work with my knife. I then picked up a huge rock and smashed it several times on the faces of each one of them until they were a mangled mess. I dressed the Fascist in my clothes before slashing and ripping his skin. I even took a photograph of my mother and put it in his jacket pocket to make the whole thing more credible. I was really sorry to lose that portrait, but I justified it with the thought that it would make it easier to avenge her for what she had been through. The Fascist was the same build as me, and it was all very convincing. Those were not days for faint hearts."

"Two lives. I can see that this was the only possible solution," the commissario said. The light flickered on and off. "The others all died before you. The members of your brigade, I mean."

"I am the last one," the old man confirmed. "And that was another reason why I felt compelled to do justice for the others … in the name of those of my comrades who were only able to live one life, and a very brief one at that."

"Has it been on your mind all these years?"

"Always. Each and every morning I went over the plan as though I were to execute it a few hours later. I made contact again with my comrades here, and twice a month they updated me on my intended victims. I lived with the fear that they might die before I had the chance to murder them. I would even have defended them if they had been under threat from anyone else. Maybe that's a kind of love, like the love you have for rabbits that you tend and look after with the sole intention of having them for dinner once they have been fattened up."

"Did the idea of forgetting the whole thing, of coming back here and starting over, never cross your mind? After all, nobody could have done anything to you after the amnesty," Soneri said, lighting another cigar.

"As far as people here were concerned, I was dead. That was true of the Party as well," the old man said with a shrug. "They would not have looked me straight in the eye, and I would have lived year after year in isolation, a stranger, so I was just as well off being a real stranger elsewhere. Until fifteen years ago, what they took to be my body was buried in the graveyard. Thirty years after my disappearance, they dug it up, but since there was no-one here to pay to have it transferred to the ossuary, all trace of it has been lost. The Party said the records in the National Association for Italian Partisans and the stone on the floodplain were monument enough, so I had no doubt that the one amnesty I would never have received was the one from the Party. As I've already said: they had no qualms, they were pitiless."

"You would have had to explain too many things and mix

personal histories with the political struggle," the commissario said.

"That's not all. I felt myself still too young to…" He stopped in mid sentence, overcome by conflicting emotions. "Now," he began again, the words tumbling over each other, "now I'm of an age when I have nothing to lose."

Soneri peered at him through the bluish smoke which acted as a lens. He was able to feel what the man wanted to express, but not to put it adequately into words. He feared that too direct a question might stem the old man's flow. The discussion ought not to be an interrogation so much as a series of prompts for a confession and so, lingering over certain details, he raised queries which aimed to strip away the mystery, layer by layer.

"Did you feel any remorse over those boys whose faces you made unrecognizable that day down by the river?"

The old man sighed. "How would *you* feel after smashing the head of someone you grew up with, someone you had shared your best years with? I knew that I was saying good-bye to all hope of happiness and consigning myself to the loneliness of an existence far from my own home. Do you think I didn't miss the Po? My dialect? All the time I was away, I always forced myself to think in dialect, but I had nothing left here. I would have been an ordinary emigrant, like so many others. I deluded myself into believing that with a new identity I could be more free, but the desire for revenge never left me."

"And your life in Argentina?"

"I did what I could to get by, enjoying all that I could enjoy. I didn't lack for anything, women, the good life, holidays… but when you live like that, you have to be careful not to put down roots, because otherwise the present covers the past and is in its turn, day after day, ground down by boredom."

"What about your family? Did you ever think of them?"

The old man gave another start, threw his arms in the air and then let them fall heavily on the table in front of him. The bulb began to sway once more and the stagnant smoke was disturbed by the ripples and currents of air.

"My family!" he said sadly, more to himself than to Soneri. "Did I ever think of them? Of course I thought of them, but I thought of them as dead or violated. Ida, the eldest, they dragged her round the back of the house… there were seven of them… the middle sister managed to escape down to the river, but was chased by the Blackshirts. She threw herself in to get away from the bastards, but the current pulled her under. My father tried to save the women in the family… he came out with an axe, but they killed him with one burst of gunfire. The only one that got away was my sister Franca, the youngest of the family. Ida was left distraught and filled with shame and she disappeared. No-one heard from her again. The sister who jumped into the Po was washed up at Boretto and was brought back home on the cart of some travelling puppeteers. My mother died of a broken heart a few months later at her sister's house, since ours had been burned down." He had laid both his hands, palms down, on the table, and the two enormous hands seemed like the paws of some wild beast ready to spring. Then he lifted them, clenching them into fists, muttering in a broken voice: "Nothing, nothing left."

Soneri went on gazing at him, an old man scarred by a deep, incurable wound. As he pondered the condition of those who, like him, had been caught up in violence and had sought in vain all their lives for some escape route, he had no difficulty in locating the kernel of genuine humanity behind a thick cover of hatred. In the wrinkled face he could still detect the trauma of the boy who, with one terrible leap into hatred, had become an adult.

All the while, the commissario felt a powerful need to put the one question that he nevertheless suppressed, afraid that it might yet be premature. He preferred to allow the discussion to drift in the hope that in the account it would slip out. He looked at the old man sunk in memories which had hardened into a fixation many years earlier, and which could not now be loosened. He knew almost everything now, specifically who had killed the Tonnas and what the motive was. In his role as commissario, he could relax and think of the case as closed, but curiosity held him in a tense grip which would give him no respite until it was satisfied.

"Ghinelli, Spartaco Ghinelli," he said softly, as though the name had been whispered from a dark corner of the cellar.

The old man looked up and peered at him intently. It was his way of offering confirmation.

"Ghinelli," Soneri repeated, "Argentina must be very beautiful... did you never think of..."

The other man understood and replied frankly. "No. One of the beautiful things about Argentina is that there's plenty of space for everyone, and you're not always treading on other people's toes. The cities are very big as well, so if you want to lose yourself in them, you can. But I was there only provisionally."

"Was there never some woman who asked you to start living again?"

"From the moment they came into my life, I removed any illusion they might have had. How could I do otherwise? Every time I thought about it my family came back to mind, and I would have been a coward if I had forgotten. The Fascists would have won. And that Tonna who carried on sailing up and down the river, while on riverbanks on the other side of the world I looked in vain for something similar to what he had... Oh, I wanted a life, that's true, but I could not erase the past."

"But they too, the Tonnas, their lives were destroyed. They were never happy," Soneri said.

"They brought it on themselves," was Ghinelli's furious answer. "It was other people's lives they chose to ruin, our hopes for a more dignified future. The Party gave us that hope, because the priests never gave it to us. With a few exceptions, they too were on the other side."

"Now the Party too is dead."

Ghinelli clenched his fists tightly while his face turned a deeper shade of scarlet, but it lasted only seconds before quite suddenly the tension evaporated. "It's a time of plenty, and people have forgotten the grim days of the past. In an age of prosperity, everybody hates everyone else because egoism springs up everywhere, and nowadays that's the only foundation of the world. Mark my words, poverty will return and people will seek unity again, but it'll have nothing to do with me. At the most, I'll have left an example, and sooner or later someone will follow it."

The commissario rolled that ambiguous remark around in his head, then asked: "Where you inspired by some example from the past?"

"I killed them with an ice-pick. Does that tell you anything?"

"Trotsky was no Fascist."

"He was a dangerous visionary. I trust those who describe him in those terms. If we had paid heed to him, they would have massacred us all, each and every one of us."

Soneri felt as though he was back at the debates he had listened to as a student. These were words he had heard declaimed thousands of times at assemblies in occupied sports halls and cinemas, and now they left him with a bitter savour of nostalgia and of passion spent amidst the glittering well-being of today. It seemed as though a century of history had gone by, but in fact all that had passed was the brief period separating youth from the present.

When he came back to himself, he saw Ghinelli looking at him intently, communicating thereby his need to retell his story. Soneri then felt entitled to put the question that he had been wanting to ask from the outset.

Before he got the words out, the old man resumed in a new flurry of words. "In what I did, I wanted there to be something symbolic, can you understand that? Something that would leave a mark on people's minds. It wasn't only the ice-pick that might make people remember me, nor the act of revenge in itself. I understood that the value of what I was doing was linked to the timing. Revenge more than fifty years later. A crime of the post-war period, left suspended but executed a half-century on." Ghinelli went on relentlessly, warding off Soneri's question. "Never mind curiosity about the incident and journalistic tittle-tattle. What matters is the coherence of my act. They'll say I was mad, but I know that some people will remember me and will hold to an idea that was mine. In times like these, all you can do is keep the flame alive. When the time is right, it will act as a detonator."

The commissario relit his cigar. "Maybe," he said dryly, "but the majority will look on it as a crime committed among pathetic old folk."

"I know," Ghinelli said sadly, "but I don't much care."

Soneri felt there was more to be said. He had an overwhelming sense that besides the politics and the desire for revenge, there was a private motive behind Ghinelli's flight, and once again the urge to ask the question became strong, but at the crucial moment, he found himself lost for words. What was lacking was the more intimate, the perhaps less noble but infinitely more human side of things. All he could do was whisper, "You have not told me everything."

The old man once more peered at him with focused menace and deep rage, and this allowed the commissario finally to utter the question, the question he should have asked first, even though he also knew that if he had, he would never have found out what he now knew.

"Why after fifty years?" he said, ignoring the replies he had already been given.

His insistence implicitly meant that he wanted to know all the rest, the factors that now seemed to him the most important of all.

He watched Ghinelli's face dissolve among its wrinkles into an expression which could produce either laughter or tears. Finally it settled into a bitter, sardonic grin, perhaps one of shame. "Because first I wanted to live," he said.

Acknowledgements

The author would like to thank Edgardo Azzi for his expert advice on the river Po, and Simona Mamano, police assistant and organizer of literary prizes dedicated to crime novels.

The translator would like to thank Nick Gray and Maggie Armstrong for commenting on the first version of the translation, and especially for their assistance with the technical boating and bargeing terms.